Witness at Hawks Nest

There are some stories that cannot stay hidden, that cannot lie forgotten in the dusty annals of the past, stories with voices that can never be silenced. They are the stories buoyed up by passion, heroics, greed, love and death. Like the tragedy of the Johnstown Flood, what happened at Hawks Nest all those many years ago is too epic to ever fall into obscurity. It demands a voice again, and it has one in Dwight Harshbarger's fine and thoroughly researched book.

— **Cathie Pelletier**, author of *The Funeral Makers* and *Running the Bulls*

I truly loved it. Why? The story is grippping; evocative, believable, sensitive and scary, horrific, especially as we know the events about the disaster to be basically true. The addenda provides convincing evidence. Harshbarger's main characters are well developed and real. With his continuous appeal to the senses, readers (at least this reader) vicariously experience the episodes as they unfold. The climax was great! Frightening.

— **Beth Sulzer-Azaroff**, Professor Emeritus, University of Massachusetts, Amherst, author of *Who Killed My Daddy?*

Witness at Hawks Nest engaged me completely. I found myself unable to put the volume down. Page after page, chapter after chapter, I wanted to know what happened next. Harshbarger spins a compelling yarn that reflects the avaricious greed that oft infects corporate policy. This volume helps us understand what is happening throughout our world today. Readers, beware.

— **Bill Reger-Nash**, Professor of Community Medicine,
West Virginia University School of Medicine

*In a world dominated by frivolous writing and me, me, me books, Dwight Harsh-barger's **Witness at Hawks Nest** is a welcome exception. It is a complex tale of one of the nation's most devastating industrial travesties told through characters whose challenges and decisions illustrate the span of human possibilities for good and evil.*

— **Yvonne Daley**, investigative journalist and director
The Green Mountain Writers Conference.

Witness at Hawks Nest

Dwight Harshbarger

Mid-Atlantic Highlands

Mid-Atlantic Highlands
Huntington, West Virginia

Cover Design: Betsy Martin and Erin Mulvaney
Interior Design: Mark S. Phillips

10 9 8 7 6 5 4 3 2

Printed in the United States of America

Second Printing

Library of Congress Control Number: 2009929432

ISBN-13: 978-0-9840757-2-0

Mid-Atlantic Highlands
An imprint of Publishers Place, Inc.
821 Fourth Avenue – Suite 201
Huntington, West Virginia 25701

www.publishersplace.org

Dedication

THIS NOVEL IS DEDICATED to the motormen, brakemen, pitboys, switchers, drillers, muckers, shovel operators, steel nippers, shovel runners, dinkey skinners, and powder monkeys who dug and drilled Hawks Nest tunnel;

To Hubert Skidmore, whose novel, *Hawk's Nest,* first told of their betrayal;

And to Martin Cherniack, whose epidemiological research documented the character and scope of the tragedy.

Acknowledgements

POET ROBERT BLY wrote, "...no one writes alone. One needs a
community." I owe much to the people of my writing community.
Posthumous thanks to Hubert Skidmore for his courageous novel
Hawk's Nest, published by Doubleday-Doran in 1941. He described the
construction of the tunnel through the lives of workers who trusted their
employer only to learn, as their lungs failed them, that they had not been
told the whole truth. Thanks to epidemiologist Martin Cherniack, whose
The Hawk's Nest Incident: America's Worst Industrial Disaster, provided
definitive documentation of the tunnel's chronology and engineering, and
the scope of its human tragedy. His book bears the scholarly imprint of a
scientific researcher.

The West Virginia Archives provided documentation of Hawks Nest
tunnel's history as well as a rich collection of regional history of the New
River gorge and Fayette County. Special thanks to former Director Fred
Armstrong for his support and to Archivists Debra Basham and Greg
Carrol for their guidance.

The staff of the *Fayette Tribune* in Oak Hill, WV, steered me through
the newspaper's microfilm records of articles on Hawks Nest tunnel and
Fayette County community life in the 1930s.

The members of my Central Massachusetts writing group supported
and sustained my work. Never more than eight active members during
the writing of this novel, their criticism and coaching made me a better
writer than I otherwise might have been. My deepest thanks to Paul
Eisenberg, Ted Grosch, Jen Kulia, Allyssa Kvenvold, the late Ann Levison,

Joyce Mannis, Richard Meibers, Carolyn Mitchell, Tayve Neese, and Alice Rennie. Special appreciation to Richard for his friendship, editorial advice and intellectual challenges, to my writing partner Carolyn for her endless support, and to Tayve and Paul for their counsel and always-fresh perspectives.

Yvonne Daley and the participants of the Green Mountain Writers Conference, Tinmouth Pond, Vermont, critiqued portions of the manuscript and encouraged its completion.

Early readers and thoughtful critics included Cindy Ashworth, Beth Sulzer-Azaroff, Tara Kasey, Mary Kay Miller, Rebekah Pavlik, and Martie Pritchard. Karen Rogers gave much valued technical support. Rebekah has been a tireless champion of the novel, ever searching for better ways to bring it into public view.

My now-adult children, Amy and Dave, encouraged me to stay with my passion and give life to this tragic story.

John Patrick Grace and the staff of Publishers Place have a special place in my community. Patrick's editorial contributions have crafted my manuscript into a published novel. I value his guidance and personal support.

This is a work of historical fiction. The chronology of events in the life of the tunnel is accurate. So too are the deaths of hundreds of tunnel workers. Large numbers of them lay in graves temporarily marked by cornstalk crosses in an abandoned field near Summersville until the rebuilding of WV Route 19 displaced them. Shirley Jones lived and died as written; his autopsy brought the first clear evidence of silicosis as the cause of tunnel workers' deaths. A shack rouster named McCloud ran a gambling and drinking shanty. O.M. Jones served as Chief Engineer in the design and construction of the tunnel. Construction methods and shipments of silica to a Union Carbide subsidiary, as well as milestone events such as the tunnel's expansion, the "hole-through" of the shafts, and the gala celebrating the tunnel's near-completion, occurred much as written. The names of industrial and political leaders at the gala are accurate. R.M. Lambie served as Director of the WV Department of Mines; C.C. Waugh worked as an underground supervisor. Dr. Leroy Harless provided medical care to local residents. C.A. Conley served as sheriff of Fayette County. John L. Lewis held office as President of the United Mine Workers from 1920 to 1960. Orville, Armen and the book's other characters are fiction.

I have made every effort to remain true to the history of Hawks Nest tunnel and the region. If I have failed, I bear responsibility for the errors.

Dwight Harshbarger
Morgantown, West Virginia
Spring 2009

There are two spellings for Hawks Nest--with or without an apostrophe. Where previous works used "Hawk's Nest" we have respected that usage. The West Virginia State Park uses "Hawks Nest" and that is a contemporary preference. This usage signifies a place where hawks gather rather than a nest hawks possess.

Prologue

EARLY MORNING ON December 3, 1984, at a Union Carbide pesticide plant in Bhopal, India, water leaked into a holding tank containing 43 tons of methyl isocyanate (MIC). The resulting chemical reaction led to overheating and the release of toxic gas. Heavier than air, the gas rolled along the surrounding streets of Bhopal. The city's transportation system collapsed. People attempting to run ahead of the gas trampled those who fell. 3,800 died that morning or shortly afterwards. 20,000 died later. 500,000 people had direct exposure to MIC. 120,000 continue to suffer from the long-term effects of the gas, including cancer, birth-defects, blindness, and breathing difficulties. Every day one person dies from the long-term effects of Bhopal MIC.

Union Carbide conducted an internal investigation and concluded that sabotage by one employee caused the incident. The company has never publicly identified the individual, nor has that person been prosecuted.

Other investigators tell a different story. Early in the 1980s the market for pesticides had declined. The factory operated at a loss. Cost-cutting initiatives led to reductions in maintenance, safety training, instrument readings and supervisory staffing. Workers used English operations manuals, even though only a few had a grasp of the language. Tank alarms had ceased to function. The flare tower and vent gas scrubber had been out of service for five months prior to the incident. The refrigeration system for the MIC tank had been left idle. Slip-blind plates that would have prevented water from leaking into the MIC tank had not been installed. The MIC tank had malfunctioned for a week prior to the incident.

Today Union Carbide Bhopal is cited as the world's worst industrial disaster.

The company's path to Bhopal began a half-century earlier at Hawks Nest.

In southern West Virginia's Fayette County, high on the rim of the ancient New River gorge, the boulders of Hawks Nest overlook command a nearly limitless view of the Appalachian Mountains. John Marshall, later chief justice of the U. S. Supreme Court, explored this section of America's oldest river in 1812 and wrote about its potential for navigation and commerce.

On March 31, 1930, a few miles from the town of Gauley Bridge, deep in the gorge below Hawks Nest, a young Union Carbide and Carbon Corporation began a major engineering project: to dam the New River and dig and drill a 32 to 46 feet-in-diameter tunnel through Gauley Mountain; the Hawks Nest tunnel. At the tunnel's western end, 162 feet below its eastern entrance, the New River would drive turbines to generate electric power for Union Carbide factories.

The tunnel would become America's worst industrial disaster

Nearly eight decades after construction, the tunnel and turbines continue to operate. But the tragic events of Hawks Nest tunnel are little known.

This is one man's story of Hawks Nest.

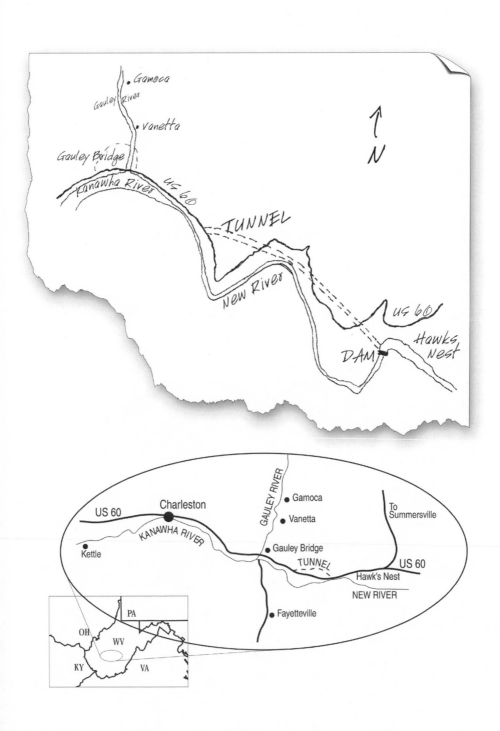

What three things can never be done?

Forget.   Keep silent.   Stand alone.

Muriel Rukeyser

U.S. 1: The Book of the Dead, Muriel Rukeyser. 1938, New York: J.J. Little & Company

1930: An Invitation from Bullhead

O N JUNE FIRST a letter addressed in a penciled scrawl to Orville Orr
arrived at the Kettle, West Virginia, Post Office. Orville read it,
pocketed the letter and ran home.

He burst into the kitchen. Bertie, her curly blonde hair wrapped in a
scarf, stood by the sink washing dishes.

"Honey, put down that plate. Listen. This letter's from a man over in
Fayette County. He was a sergeant with me in France. He says," Orville
laughed, "well first he writes about us drinking too much red wine the
night we shipped out for home. 'Orville do you remember...'"

Bertie interrupted, her voice flat, "You can skip that part."

"Then he says, well here, I'll read it to you." In a staccato monotone, his
cadence more like a student than a man of thirty-three, he read, "'I don't
know what you are doing for work these days, Orville, but I need the help
of a man like you. A man I can trust, with a steady hand and a strong arm.
The pay is five dollars a day, six days a week, plus meals and a room.'"

"Five dollars a day!" Bertie yelled, and then added in a subdued voice,
"It's a answered prayer." Her brow furrowed pulling her eyebrows into a
single line. "What's he want you to do for that kind of money?"

The letter tingled in Orville's hand. He burst into a wide grin, "You'd
be a deputy sheriff of Fayette County and report directly to yours truly
Delbert McCloud – I'm the chief deputy for Hawks Nest Tunnel, the
shack rouster they call me. More about that later. Orville, I'm knocking
niggers' heads every day. Can't do it alone. Need help. I'll furnish the
blackjack (ha, ha).'

1

He signs it, 'Your old Army buddy, Bullhead McCloud.'"

Bertie pointed to a small folded rectangle of newspaper lying on the floor. "What's that? It dropped out of Mr. McCloud's letter."

"Honey, he's not Mr. McCloud. He's Bullhead. I could tell you stories about him…why one time I saw him sneak behind a German machine gun nest, capture the four men in it, then line those killers up in front of their own gun and …"

"Stop! I don't want to hear it." She picked up the square of slightly yellowed newsprint and unfolded it. "It's a article on that tunnel, that Hawks Nest."

"Let me see." Orville took the article from her and read in silence. "Well, I'll be…this clipping is from The Fayette Tribune. It's about the groundbreaking in April for Hawks Nest tunnel. Going to take the New River straight through Gauley Mountain. Nine million dollars – half for the tunnel, half for an electric power plant. Imagine that."

"You want to share or not? I can read too, you know."

He handed her the clipping.

Bertie read aloud, her smooth voice reflecting years of reading Bible passages to Sunday school classes at the Kettle Methodist Church, "When completed, the tunnel will divert the New River through the base of Gauley Mountain and drive turbines that will send power to the Union Carbide metal alloy factory three miles away. The tunnel represents a dream come to life for Mr. O.M. Jones, the project's designer and chief engineer. At the moment when, if it had been a ship's launch a bottle of champagne would have been broken on the vessel's bow, Mr. Jones climbed to the platform of the steam shovel brought in for the occasion. Then he sent the great prongs into the earth to turn the first shovelful of dirt for the tunnel."

Orville whistled. "Think of it, honey – over a million dollars a mile."

Bertie handed the letter and news article to Orville. She stared at the paper messengers and took a step backwards, as if to assess the visitors. Then she sat down at the kitchen table, extended her long legs and sighed, "A million dollars a mile…" she sat up straight, "and we've got just enough money to buy food through Saturday." She stared hard at Orville, her face drawn. "I'm tired, Orville, tired of stretching what we got too little of. Tired of stretching me. I'm about to break."

Orville held the letter at arm's length, his face a mixture of joy and apprehension, then firm with certainty. "Where's my fountain pen? I'll tell Bullhead I'm coming."

In his next letter Bullhead wrote, "Meet me in Gauley Bridge at noon on July 1st , Bridge View Café. Gauley's not much of a town, maybe a thousand folks. It's been rough with the mines closed, but the tunnel's picking up the slack. And now outsiders are coming in to work in the tunnel. Here's directions – drive to Charleston, then follow Highway 60 about 35 miles east. The town sits at the base of the mountain where the New and the Gauley Rivers meet to form the Kanawha. The Bridge View's easy to find. Yellow brick building on Main Street just before the bridge."

Early on the morning of July first, the air humid and warm beneath an overcast sky, Orville drove thirty-three miles along Rt. 42 northeast from Kettle to Charleston, and then turned east on U.S. Highway 60 for the second half of his trip.

More than once Orville gave thanks for his good fortune. Soon he'd be a provider again, do what a man's supposed to do. Bertie could stop stretching.

THE MORNING'S GRAY SKY brought Orville memories of that day in January when life had begun to change. Orville and his boss, Ralph, had stood in the showroom and gazed at Main Street through plate glass windows bearing red letters so bright they screamed "Ralph Morrison Ford." On the nearly empty street beyond them, men shuffled past; old work clothes, eyes down as if searching for lost coins, collars turned up in the winter drizzle.

A week earlier rumors had flown through town that the Bank of Kettle would close. Already some businesses had shut down. It could happen to a bank, too. Even to Ralph Morrison Ford. Orville wondered how long he'd be inside the showroom looking out.

Ralph took a drag on his cigarette. "Damn, I wish those boys had jobs. For sure, I'd sell one a car." Mr. Five by Five, folks used to call him, joking that his girth equaled his height. His ruddy face bore a flattened nose, a mine accident some folks said. Others speculated he'd been a prize fighter. Ralph kept his hands in constant motion, first jiggling pocket change then twirling a key chain. He placed a fresh cigarette between his lips, lit it from the near-finished butt, and stared at the street as if he might will it to produce customers.

Orville, six feet two, muscular shoulders, sandy-haired, stood motionless, hands in his trouser's pockets. His gaze traveled across the street to homes, past the maples that lined the river, continued to distant hills so dark they merged with the gathering storm clouds. Dark everywhere. Weather, hills, businesses; all of a piece.

Beneath the showroom's crystal light fixtures sat two Model A Fords, a black coupe and a dark green touring sedan, its canvas top lowered to display a saddle leather interior. The polished fenders of the cars, along with Ralph's silver hair, glowed. The cars' electric headlamps, shiny brass, pointed towards the street. Like the eager eyes of the two men, the headlamps seemed ready to flash at prospective customers.

Ralph slammed a fist against the palm of his hand. His face tightened and he spoke in a voice thin and strained, not the resonant baritone that for fifteen years had commanded the dealership. "Damn, Orville, we've not had one sale since before Christmas."

Orville stared at Ralph's shirt collar. Even though buttoned to the top and a necktie pulled snug, it gapped and wrinkled around his neck.

"Folks are scared, Ralph. Jobs are disappearing. Lots of money was lost in the crash."

"You're not talking through your hat – I own five thousand shares of Blue Diamond Chemical. A few months ago I was in the money – a millionaire. Yesterday Blue Diamond listed at ten cents a share. What's worse, I figure I better take the ten cents. The overhead for this dealership is eating me alive." Ralph removed the yellow silk handkerchief that peeked from his coat's chest-pocket and wiped his forehead. "Could be worse I guess, but I don't see how." He coughed into the handkerchief, wheezed a deep breath, then put a fresh cigarette in his mouth and lit it with the one half-smoked. He dropped the butt on the terrazzo floor and stepped on it.

"Bertie and me lost money, too."

"You got anything put away for a rainy day, Orville?"

"Wouldn't take much rain to swamp my boat. Like you, we put a lot into Blue Diamond. Figured it would keep climbing. Had some Ohio River Trust stock too. Now all we got is paper. We're living pretty much hand to mouth."

Ralph's face rounded into the smile he wore after selling a Ford. "If Ohio River goes under, maybe I won't have to repay my loan." His quiet laugh turned into a cough.

"That wouldn't do either of us any good. You'd lose your business and I'd lose ten years of hard work."

ORVILLE HAD RETURNED from the war to learn of his daddy's death. Soon his mom would die from the Spanish flu. Then came his battle with the farm's untended fields and fences; the demands of crops and livestock. He'd plowed fields and mended fences until dark fell, one day after another – but the farm demanded ever more, taunting him until he came to the end of his savings. Then, though the memory tried to duck out of consciousness, in April of 1920 he'd told Bertie, "I'll have to find work in Kettle." He knew when he said it there'd be no turning back. They'd sell the farm.

The next morning, dressed in his army sergeant's uniform, brass polished, creases sharp, he'd stood inspection before Bertie. He smiled; shoulders back, chest out.

"No business will be able to say no to hiring a handsome soldier with strong arms and the sweetest grin on the face of this earth."

"Tell that to folks in town."

"Well I just might." Bertie smiled and gave him a lingering kiss.

He stroked her hair, passed his hands down her back, and rested them on the gentle curves of her hips, "Maybe I'll stay home, look for work tomorrow."

"Scoot, Orvie. Harness up Buford and get moving."

He sat erect as Buford pulled the farm-wagon to Kettle. As they neared the livery stable, odors of hay, dung and horse sweat hung in the air. Orville left Buford and the wagon at the stable and walked down Main Street. He eyed each business, assessed its prospects for a job.

A Model T's horn sounded a raspy "Ooo-gaa." At hitching posts along the street horses flinched and shuffled their hoofs, one whinnied. Orville flinched too. The Ford stopped in front of a new three-story brick building with a sign above and across the sidewalk – "Ford." The Model T drove through the wide doors of the building.

He stood beneath the sign and peered through an open door at two Model T Fords.

"Well I'll be…is this Thursday morning or what? Look who's here," Ralph Morrison yelled across the showroom, his gaze fixed on Orville. "By God it's the man who single handedly took on the German army, Sergeant Orville Orr." Ralph extended his hand. "Come on in, buddy." He beamed a bright smile.

When Orville returned home he found Bertie in the kitchen and the house filled with the aroma of a sugar-cured ham. He leaped into telling her all that happened at Ralph Morrison Ford, and then, his voice triumphant, announced, "Honey, I've been hired as a Ford salesman – I got a job!"

Bertie dropped her spoon into the green beans and rushed to hug him.

He laughed, "Well, you're more excited than Buford. I told him about it on the way home and he didn't do nothing but swish his tail."

"I can swish my tail, too," Bertie laughed and wiggled her hips.

Orville swatted her lightly on the rear. She pressed her body against him. "Come on, Orvie, supper can wait." Bertie turned off the stove, took his hand and led him up the stairs.

Over dinner Orville spoke excitedly, "And if we sell the farm soon, we'll get a decent price. We'll buy a house in Kettle and have some money left over."

"What about Buford?"

His smile disappeared. "Bertie, this is Buford's home. He belongs here. But come to think of it, in town he could live in an outbuilding behind our house." He paused then said, "But it wouldn't look right."

"What do you mean, wouldn't look right?"

"I mean me selling Fords and at the same time keeping a horse, another form of transportation. On the farm what we do is our business. But a salesman in town lives in the public eye; has to live up to his professional calling."

Bertie squared her shoulders and sat up straight. "Never thought of it that way, Orvie. You got a professional calling. An' I'm a professional's wife."

Winter to Spring, 1930

ORVILLE AND RALPH watched a Model T drive down Main Street. "Smooth. That car's running smooth, just the way it ought to." "It still seems unreal, Ralph."

"That car? What does?"

"The last two and a half months. On October 29th we had wealth. The next day we didn't. Where'd it go?"

Acey Burton, a leather ball cap over his curly salt and pepper hair, shuffled from the repair shop behind the showroom towards the two men. With his right hand he pulled from his hip pocket a rag as brown as his weathered face. He placed it between the front of his coveralls and the stump of his left arm that ended at the wrist, and wiped his hand on the rag. "I seen you boys surveying the street like you owned it. Figured I should join you. I might be an owner too. Ain't that right, Ralph?"

Ralph raised the palm of his hand towards Acey. "Hold on, Acey. Me and Orville only make money if we sell Fords. But I'm paying you by the hour – every time the clock ticks I put money in your pocket. You checked the gas line yet on that pickup?"

"Un-uhh, but I'm starting…"

"Good, Acey, starting is good." Ralph smiled and patted Acey on the shoulder. "Soon as you find the problem, tell me. Counting on you, buddy."

Acey turned and, heels dragging, walked out the showroom's rear door.

The following Monday Ralph came to work at noon, face drawn, and asked Orville to join him in his office. Orville braced himself for bad news. In France men said, "Somewhere out there there's a bullet with your name on it. Just a matter of how long it takes to find you." Business had its own version of those bullets – they killed jobs and earnings, left men flat on their backs.

The fresh-lit cigarette between his lips bounced, "Orville, I been to see Doc Simonton. Last night I had chest pains, couldn't sleep."

"You okay?"

"Doc says I had a mild heart attack. Told me to take better care of myself. Maybe I can, but if we don't get some sales, I …well, I don't know how long I can keep this dealership alive. Got a letter yesterday from Dearborn telling me to ramp up, make some sales, or risk losing my franchise."

He'd dodged the bullet. But Ralph stood in the line of fire. And if he falls…Orville didn't want to think about that.

Then on Friday, at a time when Orville and Ralph usually had coffee together, Ralph took Orville by the arm and guided him into his office. He shut the door, lit a cigarette and put his hand on Orville's shoulder. "You're more than an employee, Orville. I love you like a son. But I got to face the facts. Our sales have been at zero for six weeks. And the prospect of moving any cars looks awful slim." Ralph stared at the tan carpet then looked Orville in the eye. "I'm sorry, but I got to end your draw. If you want to, you can sell on straight commission, but I can't give you a weekly draw any more."

Smack in the gut – the bullet with his name on it.

Ralph handed Orville an envelope. "Here's a little something for you and Bertie."

He couldn't will his hand to reach for the envelope. Then as if it belonged to someone else, his hand put the envelope in his coat pocket.

Orville lurched out the door, walked to the men's room and stood in the darkness. No draw? And the prospect of sales – zero. He slammed his hand against the sink and wished he could smack the banks, the stock market, Henry Ford, Ralph.

Later – maybe five minutes, maybe an hour – he walked into Ralph's smoke-filled office. "I got to earn a living, Ralph. I'll look for work."

Ralph slumped in his chair.

Say goodbye, thanks for a great ride? Punch him out? Orville walked out of the office and across the showroom, his gaze fixed on the street. He banged open the front door. Cold air slapped his face. His stomach felt hollow; a sour taste filled his mouth, dry as sand.

Orville parked behind his home and stared at his knuckles clenched white on the steering wheel. One part of him said "It's over," and struggled to accept what had happened. Another part said, "No, it can't be." He shook his head sidewise, then again, hard, as if a jolt might cause the memory of what had happened to trickle out and disappear.

He braced himself with a deep breath then told Bertie the news. She burst into tears. His voice, at first firm, betrayed him and cracked as he said, "We got a little money saved, hon. I'll find work."

"When, Orvie? How? What'll happen to us? Maybe we could've made that farm work." Her face reddened and she yelled, "But no, you had to be Mr. Professional Ford Salesman."

He recoiled then stepped forward to put his arms around her.

She pushed him away. "Leave me alone." Bertie ran up the stairs and slammed the bedroom door. Her sobs bounced down the stairs. He imagined her lying face-down on the bed, her body heaving. He wanted to lie down beside her, comfort her. "Leave me alone," echoed in his thoughts and on his chest he still felt her angry hand prints. She could cry alone.

Orville found part-time work around Kettle. Each new job prompted Bertie and him to wonder if this one might become full-time. But a few days, sometimes a week, later, each job ended in disappointment. The first few times, Bertie cried. Then one day she stopped.

In March Orville worked a morning at Gruber's Department Store unloading produce from a railroad car. Afterwards he walked down the street to Ralph Morrison Ford.

Only one of the showroom's crystal fixtures still beamed. With neither a display-model Ford nor a customer the room seemed cavernous. Drifts of tobacco smoke gave the only signs of life. Orville's footsteps resounded across the terrazzo floor. Ralph hustled through the door of his office, even thinner than the last time Orville had seen him. He walked towards Orville at a brisk pace, a smile on his face, a cigarette in his left hand and his right hand extended once more in a greeting. Then his pace slowed, his smile weakened and disappeared; his hand dropped to his side. "Uhh…hi, Orville." The smile re-appeared and, like the mechanical movement of a child's wind-up toy, Ralph's arm rose, his hand extended in a greeting.

They chatted but Ralph seemed preoccupied. In a near-whisper he said, "I keep telling myself, tomorrow folks will start buying again. Tomorrow." He extinguished his cigarette and lit another. A moment later, as if reassuring himself more than Orville, he said, "President Hoover's an engineer. He'll turn things around."

"Guess I'd better be going. I'll go back to the shop and say 'hi' to Acey," Orville said.

"Nobody back there. Last week I had to let Acey go." Ralph turned and walked away.

On Sunday afternoon Bertie prepared a dinner of baked chicken, its aroma thinner and less pungent than the once familiar rich fragrance of turkey stuffed with dressing. About to set the table, Orville answered a knock at the door. Acey Burton stood on the front porch dressed in clean blue coveralls, hair combed, leather cap in his hand, and a red bandanna tied around his neck.

"Just walking by, Orville. Thought I'd stop and say 'hi.'"

"Come in, Acey."

"Mmmm. Something smells good." Acey smiled.

"Want to stay for dinner, Acey?" Bertie asked.

"Thank you kindly. Being alone on Sunday is painful hard on a man."

So is not working. And time alone with Bertie. "Glad you can join us."

July, 1930: Welcome to Hawks Nest

RAIN BEGAN TO FALL as Orville drove east out of Charleston. He passed, one after another, small groups of men walking along the road. Two men stood on the road's shoulder beneath a ragged umbrella, one of its struts angled skyward, their blue coveralls streaked with mud. As the Ford approached they raised their thumbs. Orville slowed and pulled off the road.

"Only going to Gauley Bridge, boys."

One of the men, heavy set with at least a two-day growth of beard, smiled and displayed a wide gap instead of two upper front teeth. "Thanks, mister," he said with a slight lisp. "That's where we're headed too." The men climbed into the back seat of the Ford, filling the car with odors of wet cotton and sweat.

"What takes you boys to Gauley?"

The smaller of the two men, balding, his otherwise smooth face etched from forehead to chin with a lattice of tiny lines, leaned forward, "They're building a tunnel, mister. There's work to be had – paying twenty-five or thirty cents an hour. I'm from over at Logan. The name's Kincaid. Harry here," he pointed towards the other man, "he's from Knoxville."

"I'm Orville Orr, from Kettle."

The men nodded.

"Knoxville, you've come a long way."

Harry's large jowls rippled, and he spoke in a slow soft drawl with an overlay of mountain twang, "It's nothing. Men are coming from all over.

13

Walked yesterday with two fellers from Cincinnati. And all them coloreds back along the road?"

"Yes."

"Some are from Huntington, some from Charlotte. Others from down in Tennessee and Georgia. Everybody's going to Gauley Bridge."

Kincaid added, "They showed me printed handbills promising jobs. Same one I got in Logan. The pay ain't great, but something is better than nothing. Specially when you're broke. I got kids to feed."

After a small sign, "Gauley Bridge," Route 60's macadam became the brick of Main Street. Orville stopped the car. The men stepped out and thanked him. "Owning a car like this, you're probably not looking for work. But if you are, check on that tunnel."

"Thanks. I just might do that."

Directly ahead along Main Street stood three blocks of brick buildings, downtown Gauley Bridge. Then a bridge, probably the town's namesake, spanned the Gauley River. Route 60 continued over the bridge and along a narrow shelf in the New River gorge, then snaked up Gauley Mountain. Behind downtown, streets angled like railroad switchbacks crawled up a steep mountainside. The fronts of many homes perched on stilts, their backsides dug into the earth.

Downstream from the bridge, the Gauley and New Rivers merged and gave birth to the Kanawha. Orville gazed upstream at the fast-moving blue-green water of the New, smooth boulders rising above its surface. "Oldest river in North America," Bullhead had written. And somewhere upstream Union Carbide would change the river's course and take it through Gauley Mountain – add a final touch to God's handiwork. Maybe he'd help add that touch.

Orville parked just beyond the only yellow brick building on Main Street. Its wide front door separated by two plate glass windows, each with large blue-bordered yellow letters, Bridge View Café. In front of the entrance stood a man nearly as tall and wide as the doorway itself, khaki shirt and trousers, a bright gold star pinned to his shirt. He grinned and waved at Orville.

Orville's skin prickled like he'd touched a live wire. A wide smile jumped across his face and his heart raced. He slammed the car door and ran to greet his old army buddy.

The two men shook hands and pounded each other on the back. They hurled old army insults and nicknames at one another, followed by bursts of laughter and backslaps. "Hey Shoeless," "You old mudbuster," "I remember you, Sergeant Bullshitter," "You still stand like a ramrod."

"Come on, Orv, let's get some grub."

Orville followed Bullhead's heavy frame through the café's front door. Dark oak booths lined the wall to their right; to their left chrome stools topped with red leather seats hugged a marble counter. Frosted mushroom-shaped globes hung in two rows along the ceiling. The aroma of brown gravy filled the café.

The back of Bullhead's neck bore his florid complexion. His voice sounded as Orville remembered it – deep and resonant, words spoken in short bursts, a few at a time, like the call of a bullfrog. In the ten years since he had last seen him, Bullhead had added weight around his middle and become bald, though a wide ring of shaggy black hair wrapped his large head. Bullhead motioned towards an empty booth and the men sat down.

They talked of France, the 80th Division, and the captain. Orville laughed as he recalled the time they captured a German trench that netted them a case of brandy.

"And Andy, Charlie too, remember the day they made PFC for the third time?" Bullhead said. They laughed.

Then they became silent. "I wonder, Bullhead, if they'd taken a step to the right or left would they still be alive?"

"No point to thinking about those sorts of things."

The men wiped gravy-soaked crusts of bread across their plates and ate the last of their meatloaf. The waitress, tall with long curly black hair, smooth olive skin and high cheekbones, refilled their mugs with steaming coffee. She replaced their dinner plates with two pieces of lemon meringue pie. Orville looked up. Her brown eyes held his gaze for a moment. He wished he could say something, not just gaze at her with his mouth open.

After she walked away Bullhead laughed, "She gotcha, Orv. Quite a piece, ain't she?"

"Who is she?"

"Armen. Never did get her last name. Dodigian, Bodigias, something like that. Lives up a holler around here. They say her daddy's a miner, maybe a tunnel worker, but I never seen him. If I did I'd arrest him just to make his daughter come talk to me."

"She's beautiful."

"Imagine cutting into that, Orv."

"I'm married, Bullhead. That kind of imagining is likely to get me in trouble."

"Don't matter. With Armen, imagining is all anybody can ever do. She keeps to herself. Disappears after quitting time. I suppose I could follow her, but that's a lot of work for a little nookey. There's plenty of women around. With money as tight as it is, I got no problem finding anything I want. Night or day." Bullhead grinned. "Eat up, Orv. Lunch is on me and Union Carbide."

Orville ate his pie.

Bullhead said, "Well, we've cov…," his eyes bulged then a cascade of air rose from his stomach and became a loud belch, "we've covered the basics." Bullhead scooped the meringue off the top of his pie and forked it into his mouth. He spoke through the rich white paste, "Hawks Nest ain't far from here, a couple a miles up the New River. Most days a deputy's work is not hard. And in these times, men working in the tunnel, both white and colored, is thankful to have a job – any job."

That deputy sheriff's star pinned to Bullhead's shirt – would he wear one?

"Right now, there's maybe four to five hundred men total on two shifts underground," Bullhead continued. "Even though we started digging just a few weeks ago, already men are quitting and new ones are being hired. Lots of men from out of town, most living in the work camps, one and two room shanties. Eight or more men to a room in the nigger shanties. Usually two to four in the white ones. Wood slat bunks, straw tick mattresses. Outhouses, eight-holers, in the back."

Orville laughed, "That's bigger than we had in France."

Bullhead said, "Some men with families lives here in Gauley. Others a couple of miles up the Gauley River at Vanetta or Gamoca, old mining towns with company houses. That is, if they're lucky enough to get a house. Gamoca was built for coloreds, but nowadays whites is thankful to be there." He paused and studied Orville's face. "The men working on the tunnel, Orv, they got to be brought into line, just like in the army."

Orville laughed. "But you've got no boot camp, right?"

"I got my own version for the new workers – with Bullhead's rule number one."

"What's that?"

"Real simple. Teach them who's boss." Bullhead pulled his blackjack from its leather holster and dropped it beside his plate.

Orville nodded. In the army Bullhead had required men to do unnecessary chores to remind them who had sergeant's stripes and who didn't. "I'd be the shack rouster?"

Bullhead looked at his empty plate and then at Orville. "Well, I'm a deputy sheriff and the shack rouster. You'd be a deputy too, and report to me." He gave a laugh that started in his belly and climbed to his mouth, "deputy shack rouster."

Orville grinned at the prospect of earning five dollars a day.

"Rinehart and Dennis, that's the contractor from Charlottesville doing the digging, they pay my wages. But Union Carbide pays R and D and calls the shots. And Carbide keeps asking me to do things that pull me away from shack rousting."

"What's the work you want me to do?"

"Well, early mornings, six days a week, you'll make the rounds of the shanties in the company work camps. There's three camps. One's just up the road, not far from the entrance to shaft one, this end of the tunnel."

Bullhead paused as Orville took a small piece of paper and pencil from his pocket and drew a small circle on the left side of the paper, labeled it "shaft 1 camp."

"A second camp is near the other end of the tunnel, shaft four, not far from Ansted, the next town over the mountain."

Orville drew a small circle on the right side of the paper, labeled it "shaft 4 camp," and connected the two circles with a line.

"If that line's the road between the camps, Orv, you better put some curves in it. Route 60 winds up and around Gauley Mountain."

Orville drew a squiggly line over the straight one.

"And up on Gauley Mountain above the midway point in the shafts," Bullhead pointed to the half-way point in Orville's drawing, "is the third camp; mostly niggers."

Orville placed a circle on the paper, just beyond the tip of Bullhead's index finger. "They dig from each end and the shafts meet in the middle of the mountain?"

Bullhead laughed. "Mr. Jones, Mr. O.M. Jones, he's the chief engineer and the man what designed the whole thing, was way ahead of us. There's an opening that drops into the mountain at about the midpoint of the tunnel."

"So the men hike down to it?"

"Yep. At the opening some turns right into shaft two. They dig towards Gauley Bridge and the men tunneling from the western end of shaft one. Other men turn left into shaft three. They dig east towards Ansted. Sooner or later they'll connect with the men in shaft four digging towards them."

Orville studied the simple map and imagined men, machines, noise.

Bullhead fingered his blackjack. "At the colored shacks I smack my partner here against the door – wake them boys up." He slammed the blackjack on the table.

Orville flinched, then laughed, "Warn me when you're about to do that."

"Sort of like reveille in our old army days, Orv. I roust 'em loud and firm."

Orville smiled. He remembered the chatter, the laughter, the quiet rustle of men rising early morning in the army barracks in Virginia, then the tents in France. He could hear the clangs of mess kits and smell the pungent aroma of fresh coffee. His smile disappeared at the thought of friends who awakened to their last morning.

"We got a drilling schedule to meet – twenty-two feet a day, over three miles straight through Gauley Mountain. Need to make sure workers are up and out – on the job by seven o'clock. The afternoon shift's got to be there by five." Bullhead grinned, "Rest of the time, I patrol the work camp, make sure no outsiders have wandered in."

"Sounds like work I can do."

Bullhead sipped his coffee, "Sure you can. But keep this in mind, Orv. Though it's a problem you'll see soon enough. Two-thirds of the men underground is darkies. At night," Bullhead chuckled, "those boys drink moonshine and shoot craps. Sometimes till all hours of the morning – then they want to sleep all day."

Orville grinned, "Breakfast in bed?"

Bullhead gave a half-smile, shook his head, "Not them beds. Smelly old ticks on pine-slat bunks sometimes stacked three-high. At some of them shacks I need to put a clothespin on my nose."

"Pretty bad, huh?"

"Well, in the colored shanties there's up to twenty men. And with two ten-hour shifts, men share bunks, one man sleeping while the other one works. In the overlap hours it's two men to a bunk. You'd think they'd want to keep the place clean but they don't. And some of those boys, colored and white, they ain't got a change of clothes."

Armen refilled Bullhead's coffee mug. He placed his large calloused hand over hers and looked up, "Thanks, darling."

Her smile vanished. She pulled her hand away, then turned and disappeared behind the swinging doors of the kitchen.

"Touchy, touchy," Bullhead said in a sing-song voice. Then in a confidential whisper, "Her skin's smooth as a baby's." He sighed. "Bet she's that way all over." He looked towards the kitchen entrance. "Now what was I saying?"

"The shanties."

"Oh yeah. Sleep in their work clothes. The white shanties are not so crowded. Also, some of the Carbide engineers and office folks stay in the white camps. Two to a shanty. Got their own rooms."

"Do the men cook? I mean, where do they eat?"

"No cooking – fire hazard. We have a mess hall, tables for niggers on one end, whites on the other. The company charges each man for meals. And a quarter a day for rent. When cold weather comes, another quarter a day for coal. The company pays darkies in script after they deduct meals, rooms, and medicine. Whites get paid in cash. A couple of company doctors take care of workers."

Orville finished his pie. "Like a mining town?"

"Pretty much. Only there's more coloreds here than in the mines. If it was all whites, I probably wouldn't need a deputy. Most of the niggers work underground – drillers and muckers – not fit for much else."

"I know what a driller is. What's a mucker?"

"Muck, drill, blast. That's the tunnel's work cycle, Orv – muck, drill, blast. The rock and dirt after a blast, that's muck. The muckers clean it up. First thing every shift. Then drill and blast at the end of the shift."

"Any white men underground?"

Bullhead's brow furrowed. "Let's see, there's foremen and supervisors. A few drillers. Some that runs the dinkeys, the trains carting muck out of the tunnel. And ..." his voice trailed off and he closed his eyes for a moment, then opened them with a smile of discovery, "oh yeah, mechanics that keeps the drills and dinkeys repaired."

"I get five dollars a day, meals, and a room? A blackjack and a deputy's badge?"

"That's the deal, buddy."

"Where do I sign on?"

"You just did." Bullhead extended his right hand across the booth. "Welcome to Hawks Nest, Deputy Orr."

Orville grasped Bullhead's hand. Arms pumping, the two men looked each other in the eye and beamed broad grins.

"Come on, I already got you a room over at Mrs. Jimison's place."

They left the café and climbed into Orville's Ford. A light rain had begun to fall.

"Drive down Main Street to the next intersection, then go up the hill."

The Model A's engine strained up the incline until, a quarter mile up the mountain, they reached a level section of street. Orville looked across the wet gray valley below. Intermittent wisps of fog blew along the rivers. "Reminds me of Le Havre," he said.

"Gauley's dark and damp enough," Bullhead croaked, then laughed, "but there's no red wine."

Spring, 1919: Chance

ORVILLE AND BULLHEAD walked in a light drizzle along the crowded gray piers of Le Havre. They nudged their way through crowds of soldiers, many shaking hands, others giving bear hugs, a few embracing young women; all saying goodbye. The day their army orders called "your departure date" had arrived.

Orville wished he could give the day a kick in the butt – knock it forward to the evening when he and Bullhead would board their troop ship. After days on the water, the Statue of Liberty, at first a small bump above the ocean's waves, would rise until she filled the horizon and became New York; became America, home. He and Bullhead would go to Camp Lee, Virginia, get their army discharges, then board a train and cross the mountains. His mom and daddy would be at the station, Bertie too. She'd wear her organdy dress, a smile pulling up the right corner of her mouth.

Bullhead yelled over his shoulder, "I want a drink – time to celebrate."

"Not till we find our ship."

Dark clouds hung low over the gunmetal gray of the harbor. Ships, former ocean liners converted to troop carriers, lined the piers. Columns of soldiers moved up gangways. On the ships soldiers stood two and three deep along tarnished brass railings, yelling and waving in choruses of excitement and joy, sadness and resignation.

The two men pushed through the crowd of young women pressed against heavy ropes along the edge of the piers, many waving red, white, and blue scarves. Some women sang, the sharp edges of English lyrics

21

rounded by French accents, "Over there, over there, say a word, sing a song, say a prayer, the Yanks are coming…" Some of the women substituted "going" for "coming" until, tears in their eyes, they fell silent.

At Pier 32 Orville yelled, "There she is," and pointed to a ship, wisps of smoke rising from its smokestacks, the ship's long gray hull streaked with rust. At the base of the ship's gangway a sign announced, "80th Division – board NLT 2000 HRS."

A half-hour later, inside the Coeur d'Or, a small bistro a block from the wharf, beneath amber lamps they sat at the bar alongside fellow soldiers and a sprinkling of Frenchmen. The room's warm air wafted layers of cigarette smoke and an aroma of garlic laced with spilled wine. The bartender, bald, heavy jowls, the long white sleeves of his shirt banded with red garters, scurried back and forth behind the bar. He had a decanter of red wine in his right hand and another of white in his left as he filled tumblers. Orville and Bullhead tapped their glasses on the bar's marred mahogany surface and gestured towards him. Soldiers filled the half-dozen square tables beyond the bar. Others stood three deep between the bar and the tables and spilled along the walnut paneled walls. A piano player banged ragtime on an upright, but his notes carried only a few yards into the bistro's din. Young women laughed as soldiers seized them by the waist and danced into others who shouted, "Encore, encore."

Orville leaned towards Bullhead, "The hills around Kettle'll soon bloom with dogwood and redbud. Me and daddy will burn brush on the tobacco beds and get ready to plant." He took a drink of his red wine, "How about you, Bullhead, what'll you do when you get back to Fayetteville?"

"I've got no family there any more. Reckon I'll head over to Gauley Bridge and rent a room. Hope my old foreman's job at the mine is still open." After a pause he slapped the bar then, face flushed, added, "You know Orv, sometimes I wish this damn war wasn't over. If I had my druthers, I'd keep shooting Germans. The bastards. Guess I ain't got it all out of me yet." He looked around the bistro, "Maybe we'll find some others from the 80th."

"Not likely. At least not the men we shipped over with." They'd lost over three-quarters of the division at Meuse-Argonne – men he drank and laughed with, men who followed his orders and walked smack into machine gun fire. Orville gulped his wine and yelled at the bartender, "Vino, encore." The bistro's lamps added color to his face, still pale and gaunt from dysentery a few weeks earlier. He swung his arms to the rhythm of the ragtime tunes, as if directing the piano player.

The bartender refilled their glasses. Bullhead leaned over the bar and doffed his cap, "Mercy bow-coop" in a deep croak.

A young woman in a long black coat moved through the crowd towards the bar, her head turning left and right as if looking for someone. A soldier's clumsy dance pushed her into Orville. He grasped her forearms and his gaze locked on her blue eyes. He admired her thin angular face and smooth skin, and tingled when her light brown hair fell across the battle ribbons on his chest. She leaned into him, lifted her chin, and closed her eyes. Orville touched his lips to hers – or did she touch her lips to his?

In a throaty whisper, soft yet strong, she said, "Je m'appelle Marie."

"I'm Orville."

A woman in his arms – she felt warm and natural. He searched her face for a clue about what to do next. She took his hand and stepped towards the front door.

Nearly three hours later Orville and Marie returned to the Coeur d'Or to find Bullhead still seated at the bar. He gestured to the corporal seated next to him as if he held a rifle and said, his voice loud, "Buddy, I sneaked in behind that German machine gun nest, got the drop on them boys and yelled 'Ach-tung! Ach-tung!' They jumped and jerked around like somebody kicked 'em in the ass."

Images of what had happened that day at Meuse-Argonne leapt at Orville. He tried to step in front of Marie before Bullhead could continue, but failed.

Bullhead laughed, glanced at Orville and Marie, then slammed his hand against the bar. "I waved my rifle, signaled for them boys to put their hands up. Then I marched 'em a few yards to the left, in front of a little knoll. Kept my finger on the trigger and stepped back, real slow-like, to their mounted machine gun, then I whipped that baby around and..." He imitated the sounds of machine gun fire then gulped his wine. "You never heard such wailing and screaming. Maybe they was yelling for mercy, I don't know – don't speak German. I let 'em scream for a few seconds then sprayed blood, guts, and brains all over that knoll – God-damn krauts. Wish I could've made 'em die slower."

That night aboard ship, lying in the dimly lit quarters two levels below the main deck, Orville relived his afternoon with Marie. Holding hands, they walked the two blocks from the bistro to her brownstone, passed through a wrought-iron gate and descended the three stone steps to her garden apartment. The squeak of the heavy oak front door, the apartment's one large room, a bed to the left, a couch to the right, beyond it a small kitchen alcove; the room's warm air carried the aroma of cooked garlic. A single oil lamp cast a golden glow. Without a word, Marie removed her coat, turned to him and unbuttoned his tunic. She placed his hands on the buttons of her bright red blouse. Soon he felt her delicate breasts against him, and after they lay down on the bed the smooth curves of her body on top of him. She guided him into her, then moved slowly and rhythmically. She whispered words he didn't understand. Her lips locked on his and their joined movement quickened. She threw her head back and gasped; moments later he gasped too. Spent, they lay in silence then dozed. Later, still silent, Marie stroked his chest and slowly moved one hand down his body. He placed his lips on her small erect nipples. She pulled him on top of her and they made love all over again, slow and gentle.

The ocean sliced and gurgled past the ship's hull. Could he, might he, have stayed in Le Havre? As quickly as he asked his question, he knew he had no choice. Things might've been different if he'd gone to officer's candidate school. The captain had said, "Get a commission. Orville, you're more than smart enough."

That evening as they boarded ship he'd told Bullhead he wished he could've stayed in Le Havre. "Maybe transferred to another unit. Bet if I was a commissioned officer I could've arranged it. Things would've been different."

"Things would've been different, all right. Most likely you'd already be home, a second lieutenant done dead and buried."

He and Marie had laughed as they took turns dressing each other. Did she come to the bistro looking for a friend? Or just anyone, working at what the captain called the world's oldest profession? Had fate led them to each other? He wanted to believe in fate, but decided she'd been at work; that a country boy like him wouldn't attract a woman as lovely as Marie. When he reached for the wallet in his hip pocket, however, Marie's hand quickly rested on his. She pushed the partially lifted wallet back into place. He hugged her.

What if, back in the bistro, she hadn't been pushed into him – had fallen against another soldier, even Bullhead? The randomness of life and death struck him again. His platoon advanced towards the German trenches. Bullets tore through men on either side of him; in the wrong place at the wrong time. Today he'd been in the right place at the right time.

He drifted into sleep – it was only a glance, just a glance.

June, 1930: On the Hawks Nest Payroll

"THAT BIG WHITE HOUSE ahead, that's Mrs. Jimison's place," Bullhead said. The men got out of the car in front of a three-story Greek-revival home with columns, slate roof and wide lawn. "You sure we're at the right place?" Orville asked. The home contrasted with smaller homes along the street. In a second look Orville noticed the house's peeling paint and a front window missing a shutter. The yard needed to be mowed.

"Come on Orv, let's go in."

The men climbed the steps to the wide front porch, its white wicker furniture arranged to capture a view of the valley and the distant hills. Bullhead opened the front door and led Orville into the high-ceilinged foyer. He picked up a small brass bell from a silver tray on a table and shook it. Clear pings filled the spice-scented air.

The door at the end of the hall opened. A woman, tall and angular, shoulder length salt and pepper hair and bright blue eyes, approached them, her hand extended.

"Mr. McCloud, it's nice to see you."

In France a soldier had played low notes on a flute – full, deep, resonant. Those notes and this woman's voice; one sounded like the other. Her accent lengthened each word into the soft patterns of the deep south, not the drawl and twang of southern Appalachian mountain people.

Bullhead shuffled his feet and looked down, his expression suggesting that one of them had misbehaved. He looked up and extended his hand. "How'd do, Mrs. Jimison? This is Orville Orr, the fellow I told you about."

27

Mrs. Jimison extended her hand to Orville.

Her face, smooth and delicate, yet resolute, bore lines that suggested a past filled with smiles, love and worry. She wore a gray skirt and maroon blouse. And her left ear had no lower lobe. He gazed at it until an inner voice said he'd stared longer than he should have. He felt his face redden as he took her hand – how could it be so soft on the surface, yet hard beneath?

"Mr. Orr, welcome. Mr. McCloud tells me you'll be working with him."

"Yes, ma'am."

"You come highly recommended," she glanced at Bullhead, "that is if I can trust your reference." She laughed. After a moment so did Bullhead.

"Come upstairs, I'll show you to your room. Mr. McCloud has made arrangements for the rent." On the wide staircase, curved and carpeted, she said over her shoulder, "Breakfast is served from five to seven o'clock. Other meals are on your own."

The room, last door on the left at the end of the hall, held a double bed, dresser, an easy chair, a straight-backed wooden chair and a night stand. Lace curtains hung over the wide double window; the blue wallpaper had small gold fleur-de-lis.

Mrs. Jimison instructed, "The bathroom is down the hall, opposite side. The three other men who live here are managers at the tunnel." She reached into a skirt pocket. "Here's a key to the front door in case you're locked out, though we leave it open most all the time." She grinned and added, "No alcohol and no women."

Orville nodded.

Mrs. Jimison left, though her sandalwood scent lingered.

Bullhead snapped his fingers, "Hey Orv, she's gone. Come on, let's bring in your suitcase. I got to get you over to the construction offices. Howard's waiting to put you on the payroll. And the sheriff's coming later to swear you in."

On the drive to the tunnel Orville asked, "Mrs. Jimison – who is she? What happened to her husband?"

Bullhead answered in perfunctory croaks, "He owned a coal mine. Died there in a rock fall. Five years ago."

"How about her – where's she from?"

"Somebody said Charlotte. Others say Richmond. Never gave it much thought."

At the tunnel site, Bullhead led Orville along a path of wide boards laid over a muddy expanse in front of a white frame house. A wide rectangular sign above the narrow front porch, black letters on white background, bore the words, Rinehart & Dennis Co. – Hawks Nest Tunnel.

A long squeak of the screen door announced the arrival of the two men. They stepped into a narrow hallway.

"In here, Bullhead," came from the room to their right. They pushed open the door and entered an office.

A skinny middle-aged man seated behind a desk in a rumpled white shirt and blue necktie took a last drag from his cigarette and extinguished it in the dome-shaped pile of butts in the large metal ashtray on a wooden stand. The air smelled of smoke and ashes. Bulletins and charts covered the walls. He extended his hand to Orville, "McComas is the name. Howard McComas." The corners of his mouth turned up as if to smile, but the rest of his narrow face, from the receding line of his light brown hair, past his thin eyebrows, grey eyes, and sunken cheeks, remained unexpressive, even wary. "Payroll, that's my job. Payroll."

"Orr, Orville Orr, Mr. McComas."

"Call me Howard." He motioned towards an oak worktable, "Take a seat, Orville, and fill this out." He handed Orville a pen and a form, Rinehart and Dennis Employee Information printed across the top. "When you're done, I'll put you on the payroll, then make sure you get your…" He turned, "What'd you offer him, Bullhead?"

"Five dollars a day."

Howard exhaled a burst of air. "Five dollars a day? A lot of money these days. I hope you're good at what you do, Orville."

"I'll do my best…"

Bullhead stepped forward and pressed his thick thighs against the desk. "I got hundreds of men to keep in line, Howard, and it ain't easy. I need help. If me and Orville wants editorial comments on our work, we can read *The Fayette Tribune*."

"No offense, Bullhead, Orville. Some days the foremen over at the tunnel add men so fast I can't keep up. They're offering twenty-five and thirty cents an hour to niggers; shiftless and good-for-nothing. Gets to me sometimes." Howard looked at the papers piled on his desktop and shook his head. "Come on, Bullhead, let's go for a smoke while Orville fills out his form."

Orville began to complete the form. Name: Orville Samuel Orr. Date of birth: October 2, 1897. Home address: 32 Maple Street, Kettle, W.Va. Next of kin: Alberta Givens Orr – wife. Education: Kettle Public Schools, 1903 – 1914. Describe your past work experience: Family farm from age 5. US Army Infantry, 1917 – 1919, France, sergeant. 1920 – January 1930 salesman, Ralph Morrison Ford, Kettle. He could've written so much the form couldn't hold it all; Fords, the life of a salesman. And before that, how the farm had made a good living for his daddy and his daddy before him. Then, while he fought in France, his daddy down after a heart attack, weeds and brush had invaded the fields. After his return he'd fought those enemies day after day, morning to dark, until he ran out of money. Would his daddy have borrowed money and kept farming? A vise pinched his stomach. Maybe he'd taken the easy way out.

The table vibrated as a locomotive roared past, less than twenty feet from Orville's chair. Behind the engine came a tender with C&O stenciled in white letters, then empty flat-bed and coal cars. Each car's wheels pounded a rhythmic clickety-clack as they passed from one rail to the next. Their metallic beats became those of the Pullman car that carried Orville and Bullhead across the mountains after they'd mustered out of the army.

Soldiers and a few civilians crammed into every seat, the aisles too. Near midnight Orville found a seat then leaned back and wondered what tomorrow would bring – mom, daddy, and Bertie at the train station, a home-cooked meal with his folks telling stories of all that'd happened since he left. Most of his stories – machine guns doing their work, gas too, bloody arms and legs orphaned in the mud – he'd keep to himself. And Marie would remain his secret.

Howard poked his head through the office door. "Take your time,

Orville. Me and Bullhead's going to the mess hall for coffee."

The now-awakened memories of his return home pulled at him, like a sore hangnail that demanded to be tended.

May, 1919: Homecoming

B ULLHEAD AND ORVILLE'S TRAIN had arrived at the C&O station in Charleston the morning after they departed Camp Lee. "I'll write if you will, Bullhead."

Bullhead grinned and said he didn't write well; doubted if he'd do it often.

"Truth is, I probably won't either." They laughed and shook hands. Orville surprised himself and grabbed Bullhead in a bear hug. They slapped each other on the back.

Bullhead waved from the passenger platform as Orville boarded his train, a local that would stop at each of the small towns between Charleston and Huntington, one of them Kettle. Each time the conductor announced a familiar town, Orville looked for streets, buildings, people he'd known, eager to connect to someone, something, that would confirm the word smack in the center of his thoughts, home. At Winfrey he glimpsed a white frame church where he and Bertie had attended a revival meeting. Afterwards they couldn't wait to be alone. As she pulled him into her, Bertie said, "Do it for the Lord."

He'd later laughed, "I wouldn't mind doing the Lord's work all the time."

The conductor yelled the words Orville had long waited to hear, "Next stop Kettle, Kettle coming up." He bounded into the aisle and before the train came to a stop leaped to the station platform, a wide smile on his face.

Orville stood alone in the bright cold morning. A brisk spring wind nudged the overhead telegraph wires, the only movement on the empty platform. He walked to the train station and stared at his pale reflection in the tall windows. The loneliness he'd known after a battle ricocheted around his gut.

An elderly man, stooped, wearing a round grey cap, C&O in metal letters above the cap's bill, stepped out of the station. The screen door slapped a lone voice of welcome.

Over the noise of the engine Orville yelled, "Hey, Mr. Johnson." The man had stood straight and tall when he'd last seen him. Orville's mom had written that Mr. Johnson's son had served in France and been killed in battle.

"Hey, son."

Removing his overseas cap, Orville ran his hand through his hair and smiled. "Remember me? Orville Orr."

"Can't say that I do." Mr. Johnson pulled Orville's duffle bag from the baggage car and lowered it to a wheeled baggage carrier. "But if you're home, welcome. Welcome home, I mean." He muttered, "I've no way of knowing if this's his home." He rolled the carrier through the station's wide center door.

Orville followed Mr. Johnson into the passenger waiting room. He inhaled the familiar odor of the oiled wood floor. The room's two long high-backed benches sat empty. Where's Bertie, mom and daddy? At age six his mom had taken him to the circus; he'd gotten lost and wandered among the tents and wagons until a clown wearing an oversized frown that mirrored Orville's feelings took him by the hand and found his mom. He wished for his clown.

He carried his duffle bag out the front door. Across the street a rectangular sign the length of the building announced Gruber's Department Store in block letters. Along the rutted street, horses and watering troughs shared space with a Model T Ford. Orville eyed the shiny black car, a door set squarely in the center of each side, a tool box bolted to the running board. Could his mustering-out pay buy him one of those?

"Orvie! Orvie!" Her blonde curls bouncing Bertie ran out the front door of Gruber's, crossed Main Street and hurled herself into his arms. Her lanky body pressed against him, her lips on his and her long arms around him. He shut his eyes, put his hands on her hips and pulled her tight. He breathed her scent, felt aroused and alive, ready for anything.

"Been too long darling," she whispered.

His mom, short and stout, her gray hair in a bun, stood beside Bertie. Her face drawn, Ruth Orr's eyes filled with tears.

Orville turned and hugged his mom. "Missed you, missed you so much." He looked around, "Where's daddy?" then laughed, "him and Buford are plowing, right?"

Ruth began to weep. She removed a handkerchief from her purse and wiped her eyes. "I'm sorry, Orvie, I got bad news for you."

After each battle the captain had said "I got bad news for you" before he read the company's casualty list and transformed buddies into memories. Over there Orville had pulled down a mental curtain and kept his feelings behind it. He reached for the curtain's imaginary cord, but had waited too long.

His voice quaked, "What happened, mom?"

"About two weeks ago, he..." she sobbed and took a deep breath.

Orville sat down on a wooden bench beside the station's front door, slumped forward, elbows on his knees, and closed his eyes. Bertie put her arm around him.

"Orvie, that evening ..." Ruth wiped her eyes, "that evening Sookey, she was mooing to be milked. Wilbur walked out to the barn. I found him a-laying in front of the barn door. Fifty-four. Just fifty-four."

Sudden death – in France men jumped out of the trenches and into it. Orville gazed at his mom, his eyes pleading for her to alter the past, "But, daddy and me... I thought when I came home we'd...he wouldn't...no, he wouldn't ..." Orville put his head in his hands. His chest heaved, as if it could throw the loss out of him. The captain's hand touched his shoulder. "It happens, sergeant, it happens."

Bertie drove the wagon home. Orville sat beside her and spoke little. His mom recited a long list of events in Kettle since he left, including friends who'd died of Spanish flu. Would it never end – over there, over here?

Approaching the farm, broken strands of barbed-wire in the fence bordering the road seemed to leap towards the wagon. Weeds and saplings had overrun the fields. The barn roof had missing shingles. Orville scanned the old two-story white farm house. It needed a new coat of paint, patches for the porch screens, too. Neglect had snuck in like Germans in the dark of night.

"Mom, what happened to the dogwood tree beside the front porch?"

"Not long before he passed away, your daddy cut it down. Don't know what got into him."

"I do," Bertie said. "He kept it in the barn."

During a dinner of fried chicken, mashed potatoes, and green beans, Ruth described Wilbur's declining health. "But son, we didn't want to worry you with all that."

"Figured those Germans gave you enough problems," Bertie added.

They could've written the bad news, not saved it to turn a homecoming into a wake.

"One morning not long after you left, your daddy complained about chest pains. Then at the breakfast table, before his first bite he fell forward. Doc Simonton said he'd had a mild heart attack. Gave him some pills, told him to take it easy."

"Wilbur took it easy, all right," Bertie said.

Ruth scowled at Bertie. "After that day it seemed like he just drew into himself. He'd plow some and then rest. When he planted crops, it was just a row or two at a time. Then he'd let plants and weeds alike, grow. I asked him to get some help, hire the Cuthbert boy from down the road, but he wouldn't hear of it."

"Daddy was stubborn, proud too." Orville had admired his daddy's strength, his willingness to take a long view of events. When life in the trenches took a dark turn, he remembered his daddy's words, "Things will turn out all right in the end. You may have to wait for the end, but it'll come."

Ruth continued, "Then your daddy caught the Spanish flu. It weakened him."

Bertie added, "The flu took eleven folks in Kettle, including Mayor Baumgartner."

Orville added the mayor to an imaginary casualty list. Who will next fall? Maybe that's what eventually gets the best of old folks – their casualty lists get longer and longer, each new name another package of grief, until finally they can't carry the weight anymore.

Bertie sputtered like a rapid burst of machine gun fire, "And there was the corn liquor out in the barn."

Ruth slapped her palm against the table, "Enough, Bertie."

"Well, it's true." Bertie's face reddened and her brow furrowed. "Orvie might as well know. Wilbur'd take a drink ever morning when he milked Sookie. Through the day too. Told me it was good for his heart."

When Orville and Bertie went to bed she yanked off her nightgown and pulled him on top of her. Her lips next to his ear, she giggled and whispered, "You still able to do your duty, Orvie?"

This moment – again and again he'd thought about it, dreamed about it, in muddy trenches, aboard ship.

"Let's find out."

She thrust herself against him and then moved with such abandon that they spent themselves in what seemed only seconds. Soon after a good night kiss Bertie lay still, her breathing gentle, steady.

"Honey?" he whispered. No answer.

When he enlisted in the army, a few months after their marriage in February of 1917, "to do my duty to my country" he had said, they'd laughed about his doing his duty as a husband. Bertie would remind him, "Do your duty," most every night. Always so fast, so intense, so soon over.

Falling asleep he again felt Marie's touch and breathed her scent.

Morning sunlight lit the bedroom window. Legs thrashing, Orville dreamed he ran through a long trench at the front. His boots churned in the trench's mud, gas floated above the trench, dropped towards him. "Noooo..." he cried and jerked upright, sweaty, his heart racing. Bertie lay beside him, still asleep. He willed the images aside and calmed himself by inhaling the aroma of fresh coffee and bacon. On summer mornings his daddy would yell, "Come on, Orvie, let's get cracking." Already he could hear the barn and fields calling him to come and put things right – plow, fix the out-buildings, care for the livestock. His daddy got a kick out of a good tobacco crop, Buford, healthy sheep and milk cows. But Orville farmed only because his daddy asked him to do it.

Bertie whispered, "What're you muttering Orvie?"

"Nothing, just thinking out loud."

"Come here." She pulled Orville against her, ran her hands over his body, and scooted beneath him. One hand on each of his cheeks, she pulled his face to her breasts.

We Struck Gold

Howard and Bullhead jostled one another and laughed as they entered the office. Howard sat down at his desk and Orville handed him the completed form. He scanned Orville's entries and nodded. "Okay, Orville Samuel Orr, everything seems to be here. You're on the payroll as of," he raised his left hand, pointed his index finger at Orville, and with a punch in his voice said, "Now!" Then with a faint trace of a grin, he added, "You're starting mid-week. Brief week, just a peek." Howard's face fell to its resting position, stern and firm, "And July fourth is coming up. It's a holiday for some folks, but not for us. The company's got a schedule to meet." Then his lips widened and their ends angled up, "Holi-day, some spend pay. Not for us, we work all day." In a tone of dismissal he added, "Come here Satur-day – you'll get your pay."

Bullhead grinned and shook his head. "You're always a pleasure, Howard."

"Guess we're done, Orv. We'll wait outside till Sheriff Conley comes to swear you in." As they approached the door Bullhead turned to Howard. "Quiet around here today."

A grin crept across Howard's face. "Not like last time you were here. A week ago last Tuesday – that was our big news day."

Bullhead laughed. "You should've heard the commotion, Orv." He pointed to a chair, "I was sitting there when all of a sudden, Lordy, upstairs men started laughing and cheering like they'd won some kind of championship."

Howard laughed, "One of the big boys upstairs, they're the ones what

39

run things, came down, stood in that doorway and yelled, 'We struck a goldmine!' The three men looked towards the empty doorway.

Bullhead shook his head. "Forty-six feet, hard to believe."

Howard's voice turned as smug as his face, "Well, Mr. Jones has got it all figured out, count on that. And our jobs don't change one whit." Then, as if to correct himself, "Not a bit. Not one whit."

Orville asked, "Goldmine – what happened?"

Howard said, "This tunnel is, or was up to then, thirty-two feet in diameter, Orville. Thirty-two feet, floor to ceiling, tall as a three-story house. Then turn that house on its side and thirty-two feet from its left to right walls."

"Pretty big hole in the ground," Orville said.

With the formality of a teacher giving a classroom lecture, Howard said, "All four shafts started out in dirt and shale, but it wasn't long before they hit solid rock. That's what we're now drilling through. Solid rock. Ten days ago the boys upstairs got a call from Union Carbide in New York. A sample of the rock we'd been drilling out of Gauley Mountain got assayed. The report said it was high grade silica, what the company uses in processing metal alloys. New York told our boys we could stop purchasing that stuff and drill our own – we'd struck a gold mine. Their words – 'gold mine.'" Howard smiled, "Then they told the engineers to increase the diameter of the tunnel to forty-six feet!"

Bullhead said, "That's more'n a four-story house."

Howard placed Orville's form on a stack of papers and said, "Then I understood why they laid rails from the site down to that factory we're building in Boncar. They'd done core drillings well before starting the tunnel. Already had plans to ship the innards of the mountain down there. Just weren't one hundred percent sure about the insides of ol' Gauley."

"Where's Boncar?" Orville asked.

Bullhead answered, "About ten miles downriver. That's where the Electro-Metallurgical Company, EMCO we call it, is constructing a big metal processing plant. EMCO is part of Union Carbide, too. I say, 'Side by side, we're all Car-bide.'"

"Boncar," Orville said, "that's an odd name. French? Indian?"

Howard and Bullhead glanced at each other then joined in a quick burst of laughter, Bullhead's a deep roar, Howard's little more than a single "Ha."

Howard said, "Union Carbide and Carbon Corporation, Orville. Carbon. Bon-car. Get it?"

"I got it."

Howard continued, certainty mixed with awe, "You got to get up pretty early to get ahead of Union Carbide."

When Sheriff Conley arrived he asked Orville to stand beside the desk. Gray hair, chiseled face, lean athletic body, his steel-blue eyes level with Orville's, the sheriff held a Bible in his right hand and raised his left hand, palm towards Orville. "Place your left hand on the Bible, son, and raise your right hand." He waited for Orville to comply. "Repeat after me. I, state your full name."

"I, Orville Samuel Orr..."

After the oath Sheriff Conley, then Bullhead and Howard, shook hands with Orville. Bullhead grinned as he handed Orville a blackjack and holster, and a gold deputy's star.

Orville thrust out his chest, pinned the star to his shirt and strapped the blackjack to his side. People would clear a path for the law.

Driving to Gauley Bridge Orville wore a broad grin. Bullhead sat beside him. Yesterday he'd been out of work and uncertain about his future. Today he'd become a deputy sheriff with a job to do. And come Saturday Howard would put money in his pocket. The day might be chilly and damp, but life had warmed up, even taken on a glow. Enlisting in the army he'd sworn loyalty to the United States. He'd risked his life to honor his oath, to do his duty. Now he'd sworn another oath, and he'd do his duty as a soldier for Union Carbide.

"Does Sheriff Conley come to the tunnel very often?"

"He lives in Gauley Bridge, but his office is in the courthouse over in Fayetteville. Spends most of his time there, or visiting around the county. He don't want a bunch of out-of-town niggers, whites too, running around Gauley and Ansted creating trouble. So he checks in oncet in a while and reminds us to keep things in order. I told him I needed to get you swore in today."

Orville's Ford approached men walking towards them. Bullhead squared his shoulders and sat erect, his gaze straight ahead, his face expressionless. Once past the men he slouched down in the seat.

"Bullhead, those men are white from head to toe. Covered with something – what is it? They all look alike, even the Negroes."

"It's dust, rock dust. They're drilling through solid rock. Think about it Orv, sort of like in the mines. At the end of a day's work, coal miners come above ground covered with coal dust, looking as black as the coal itself." Bullhead laughed, "Can't tell the niggers from the whites. Well, it's the same thing here, only reversed. Men come off work covered with dust. Instead of turning white men black like in the mines, at Hawks Nest everybody is turned white. In fact, most of those men that we just passed was darkies, but you probably couldn't tell it, could you?"

Orville pointed to a heavyset man walking alone, his khaki shirt and trousers, as well as his wide-brimmed hat, dusty white. He carried a baseball bat. "Who's that?"

Bullhead waved and the man raised his baseball bat. "Him? Ermil Dothan."

"How come he's carrying a baseball bat – got a game after work?"

Bullhead croaked a laugh, "He's carrying it for the same reason you got a blackjack. Difference is he'll use his bat oftener than you'll use your blackjack. Ermil's a foreman."

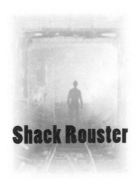

Shack Rouster

O RVILLE AWAKENED. Through the lace curtains of his room's tall window, one so unfamiliar that for a moment he thought he dreamt it, a streak of rose thrust across the horizon above hilltop silhouettes. It hovered below a band of robin's egg blue that stretched upwards until it merged into an ink-black sky, then lost itself in crystal points of light. Gauley Bridge, that's where he'd gone to bed. Gauley Bridge, not Kettle. Alone, not with Bertie pressing toes to cheeks against him. At least she used to. Now she slept on the other side of the bed. No man's land; the space between them seemed more like territory between the German and American trenches than his bed.

Down the hall someone knocked on the bathroom door. "Anybody in there?"

LATE ON A JANUARY AFTERNOON Kettle Police Chief Arthur R. Tackett had knocked on Orville's front door.

Over his khaki shirt the chief wore a blue windbreaker, unbuttoned to accommodate his ample belly. The bill of his cap rested low over his eyes. He glanced into the hallway as if he didn't want Bertie to overhear him. "It's about Ralph," he whispered, "he's got no family, and I got to identify a body. Could be him. Ralph, I mean. I remembered your army service carrying dead soldiers to Flanders. And you knew Ralph better'n anybody."

Driving along Rt. 42 to the town of Tipple, Chief Tackett said, "Yesterday I got a report of a dark blue Ford parked along the river. Sounded

43

like Ralph's car to me, and so it was. I suspected foul play. But in the back of my mind I figured it might've been foul play Ralph had done to his self. He'd had a hard time of it lately."

"Ralph's had it rough," Orville replied. "But so has everybody."

Neither man spoke again until the chief's Ford passed from Rt. 42's macadam surface to the red brick of Tipple's Main Street. The dim light of gas streetlamps fell on storefronts, some boarded shut with "For Rent" signs tacked to the wood slats.

"You know, Orville, sometimes Ralph seemed bigger than life. I never in a million years would've thought he might end up like this, that is if it's him."

Orville stared out the side window.

At the mortuary a man in a black suit led the chief and Orville down a dimly lit corridor. Each few steps brought a drop in air temperature. The three men entered the room at the end of the hallway. Two gas lamps cast pale blue light through the room. Chilled air carried the acidic odor of formaldehyde. On a table, beneath a rumpled shroud lay a body. The undertaker lowered the cloth and exposed the corpse's silver hair and the sagging white tissue of a water-logged face.

Orville's nod said, "Yes, it's Ralph."

"Well I'll be…is this Thursday morning or what? By God it's the man who single handedly took the German army." The war, men dying in the trenches. Some gassed, others shot or blown apart. Flares burst; luminous green light flickered over the face of Jimmy Campbell, only a day earlier awarded his corporal's stripes. His intestines snaked through a bloody rip in his shirt, his head resting in Orville's lap. Jimmy's eyes gazed at Orville and his lips moved but made no sound. Then the movement stopped. His eyes dulled and the opaque glass of death crept across them.

Chief Tackett put his hand on Orville's shoulder, "You okay?"

ORVILLE SAT UP, fully awake. The bright rays of a just-risen sun lit tiny dust motes above his bed's patchwork quilt. From beyond the bedroom door, murmurs of voices and footsteps in the hallway signaled the day's beginning. He inhaled the aromas of coffee, sausage, and fresh biscuits.

Work . . . soon he would go to work. Today. Then again tomorrow, and the next day. Each day he'd be five dollars richer. Bertie would feel different after he sent some money. Orville bolted from bed and pulled on his khaki trousers and shirt, the gold star pinned to its pocket.

Downstairs in the dining room two men sat with Howard McComas at a long mahogany table. An empty place setting of china awaited Orville, silverware beside it; a napkin in a silver ring lay across the plate.

Howard stood and extended his hand, "Morning, Orville. Boys, this here's Orville Samuel Orr from Kettle, West Virginia."

The man to Howard's left took a bite of scrambled eggs and stood up. His long frame towered over Orville, but his eyes, dark as coal, stared at the plate before him, as if his food couldn't be trusted if left unwatched. The man then glanced at Orville for an instant, ran one hand through his thick black hair, and muttered in a deep bass, "Lloyd Sykes is the name." He sat down and wolfed a large bite of scrambled eggs.

Across the table a short round man, bald, small deep-set eyes behind the round wire-rimmed glasses, raised his hand in a wave and said in a high-pitched voice, "High-dee." A moment later he added, "Oh, I'm Billy Webster Ribble. Some folks call me Billy, some call me Billy Webster."

Orville nodded.

"Howard used to tell folks they could call me anything they wanted, long as they didn't call me late for breakfast."

Howard and Orville joined Billy Webster in laughter. Lloyd glanced up and scowled.

"Old joke, Billy Webster," Howard said, "that's why I stopped telling it." He gestured towards Orville. "Orville here, as you might guess from his badge, is joining Bullhead McCloud as a deputy sheriff for the project."

"Another shack rouster," Lloyd said, eyes on his plate. "How many of you boys does it take to keep the niggers in line?"

A wiry Negro woman with lines etched deep into her face entered the dining room. She wore a white uniform and gold-rimmed glasses, her hair braided and pinned around her head. She glowered at Lloyd then flashed a quick smile at the other men. In one hand she carried a plate of hot biscuits and in the other a pot of steaming coffee. "Well, good morning. You must be Mr. Orr. Welcome. I'm Pansy. Here, take a couple of these biscuits – just out of the oven, some coffee, too." She filled Orville's cup and smiled at him.

Orville stared at the two gold teeth at the center of Pansy's smile. He shifted his gaze to the biscuits.

"And there's plenty more of everything." Pansy glanced towards the swinging door and lowered her voice, "Mrs. Jimison keeps a good kitchen."

"Only because of you, Pansy," Howard said.

"Well, upon my honor, Mr. McComas, you take one of these biscuits; put a little honey on it, honey." A smile lit her face as Howard took a biscuit. "I'll get you boys some more eggs and sausage. I got to get you fed for your new job, Mr. Orr."

Orville spooned scrambled eggs and sausage on his plate. "I met Howard yesterday, filled out his paperwork." He looked at Lloyd and Billy Webster, "What do you fellows do at the tunnel?"

In a tone that suggested Orville should have known the answer to his question, Lloyd said, "Timekeeper."

His voice a bright contrast to Lloyd's, Billy Webster said, "I'm one of the engineers."

Howard quickly added, "Billy Webster is the right-hand man for Mr. O.M. Jones." He grinned, "Some folks say he's the brains behind the whole project."

Billy Webster's face turned deep red. "Folks say lots of things, Howard." He looked at Orville. "I just try to do my job. Help Mr. Jones, keep the project moving. Twenty-two feet a day through solid rock."

Lloyd dropped his napkin on his plate, emitted a loud belch, and left the room.

Howard waved his hand towards the doorway, "Don't mind him, Orville. Lloyd stays pretty much to himself. He keeps time on the workers like he's paying them out of his own pocket. But I'll give him credit. Nobody has ever won a dispute with Lloyd over time on the job." Howard paused, looked at the gold chandelier above the table, and then turned to the small group, "Ten hours is the pay. The pay for the day."

Billy Webster grinned, "Hey, a good one Howard, and early in the morning too."

"Men don't punch in and out on time clocks?" Orville asked.

"Nope," Howard answered. "Not the way Rinehart and Dennis does business. Anyway, we got so many men quitting and new men signing on, if we had a time clock Lloyd would spend all day teaching them how to punch in and out. Most of the underground workers are niggers. Can't read nor write – imagine what they'd do with a punch-in time clock?"

Orville nodded and forked his last bite of sausage.

Howard continued, "Lloyd memorizes all the workers' faces. At each shaft he checks workers off his list. Them that are present get a day's pay. Then Howard imitated Lloyd's deep voice, "I learn the white men's names and I give the niggers numbers. Numbers is easier to remember than Bubbles, Banjo, Long-un, Sunburn, and what not. Don't know why them people can't have regular names like white folks." Howard shook his head sidewise and laughed. Billy Webster joined in.

AT THE ENTRANCE to the work camp on the mountain, high above the portals to shafts two and three, Orville parked next to Bullhead's dark green REO, a ton and a half pickup truck, Rinehart and Dennis Co. painted on each door in square white letters. Bullhead stood beside it. For a moment Orville gazed at the vast space of the New River gorge, the tiered rows of blue-green mountain tops on its other side topped by a cloudless blue sky.

Bullhead pulled the shiny black bill of his cap low over his eyes, raised his black jack and waved it towards Orville. "Morning buddy. Come on, let's you and me do a little shack-rousting. Tomorrow you can come here on your own."

Orville and Bullhead walked from shanty to shanty. Bullhead pushed doors open, peered inside then walked in. Orville followed him. Most of the shanties had been vacated, the men already at work, though their presence lingered in the stench of dirt and sweat in the dark unventilated rooms.

In one shanty Bullhead found a black worker asleep on a bunk's straw tick. He slammed his blackjack against the inside of the door frame and yelled "Rise and shine." When the worker didn't awaken, he walked to the bunk and with the speed of a rattler struck his blackjack against the bunk frame inches from the worker's head. "Crack!"

The worker's eyes popped open. He blinked at the form towering over him. Like a dynamite explosion, Bullhead's voice blasted the worker's face with the wake-up call he'd used in France, "Off your ass and on your feet, soldier. This ain't church camp." The worker jumped from his bunk fully dressed, shoes on, and for a moment stared at Bullhead as if to confirm that time to go to work had arrived. Then he ran out the door.

In the next shanty another worker lay on his bunk. At Bullhead's command, followed by the crack of the blackjack on the bunk, his eyes opened, their large corneas near yellow against dark brown skin. Not a muscle in his long body moved. Then his lips slowly twitched, sections clinging together until they stretched open and he whispered. "Sick, bossman. I'm sick." The man stared at Bullhead, "Can't work today. Can't."

"You lying to me, Sunburn?"

Sunburn's head rolled from side to side.

Bullhead tapped the bunk frame with his blackjack and spoke softly, "Okay. You know the options – go to work or get yourself down to the doc's office. Tonight don't drink so much."

"Okay."

Outside Bullhead put his hand on Orville's elbow and motioned for him to walk with him. Once away from the shack Bullhead looked around then said, "Orville, my rule is this. If a worker's sick, he don't have to go to the tunnel. But," he said louder, "he's gotta go down to the doc's office. Rinehart and Dennis is paying docs good money to take care of these boys. I saw Sunburn last night – too much to drink." Bullhead smiled, "Though at the time he seemed right happy about it."

"What can a doc do if a man drinks too much?"

Bullhead replied, "Dang little, I'd guess. But maybe tonight that boy'll think twicet about his liquor. Though to tell the truth, I don't much care." His tone hardened, "But always remember this, Orv, underground a sick man is a dangerous man. And there's white men down there. We already had a couple killed."

They walked towards the shanties yet to be rousted. Bullhead stopped and said, "Oh, before I forget, tonight I'll take you to the place where the darkies do their drinking. Gambling too. A special little place." He pronounced special, "spatial."

"Special?" Orville answered.

"You'll see tonight."

After they completed their rounds of the three camps, Bullhead smiled and gave Orville a pat on the back. "That's about it, Orv. You just finished your first shack roust."

"Sure beats day labor in Kettle. Even with the dirty shanties."

"Pay them no mind, buddy. Come on. Let's go down to the mess hall, that's what everybody calls it, just like in the army. Union Carbide calls it the commissary. We'll have some coffee. Then I'll show you how we do daytime security work. Not much to that either." Bullhead grinned, "And the pay is good."

Muck, Drill, Blast

ORVILLE RODE BESIDE BULLHEAD in the REO. Bright sun streamed through the truck's windshield. Across the valley waves of mountain tops undulated against a blue sky, their distant green surfaces dappled purple by fluffed clouds.

"Gonna be hot today, Orv."

Orville nodded, "Summer's like that." Each man smiled.

The truck bounced and rattled along the rutted dirt road down Gauley Mountain. When a tire dropped into a deep rut Bullhead yelled, "Got that one, Orv," then gave a belly laugh. At the base of the mountain they passed a large sign, "No Trespassing. By order of Rinehart and Dennis Construction Co." They parked next to a long white building.

Bullhead led Orville into the mess hall, its main room almost as large as the building itself. Four columns of pine tables extended the length of the room; straight-backed wooden chairs lined their sides. At the room's far end, smaller wooden tables, each with four chairs, sat near a serving counter with coffee urns. Men seated at two of the small tables drank coffee and talked in low voices. At one table men wore white shirts and neckties; at the other khaki work clothes coated with dust.

Bullhead pointed towards the urns, white porcelain mugs stacked beside them. "Come on, Orville, coffee's on me and Union Carbide."

Each man filled a mug. "Let's sit over there," Bullhead pointed to an empty table between the two groups. "The men in the white shirts are engineers. Except for Howard McComas. You remember Howard from yesterday."

"Yep. Had breakfast with him.

"See that man facing us?" Bullhead whispered. He nodded towards a middle aged man, balding, dark blue necktie and wire-rimmed glasses. "That's O.M. Jones. He designed the whole project." Bullhead's tone conveyed reverence.

Lines etched O.M. Jones's forehead. Did the tunnel produce them? Or did he have a wife like Bertie who had withdrawn to the other side of the bed? Bullhead's newspaper clipping about the groundbreaking had likened the tunnel to a dream come true for O.M. Jones. How in the world could one man dream something this large, then bring it to life? Union Carbide had the muscle to make dreams come true. And it provided jobs for men with hungry children. Now those families could eat regular.

"Here's the way the project works, Orv." Bullhead took a pencil from his shirt pocket. On a paper napkin he drew a long squiggly line in a wide arc. "This here's the New River." He nodded towards the front door, the river just beyond it. He drew a perpendicular line across the right end of the arc. "That's the dam we're building," again nodding towards the river. "When it's done, there'll be no water in the river bed below the dam," he smiled, "except when Union Carbide says it's okay. After a heavy rain or a big snow melt they'll open the gates for the overflow. Come to think of it, maybe Union Carbide'll figure out how to fix the weather, too. Take over for Mother Nature." Bullhead spoke in a whisper and glanced towards Mr. Jones. "Billy Webster says O.M. Jones is smart enough." He laughed and Orville joined him. "Billy Webster and the engineers are already calling the old riverbed 'the dries.' Once the water stops flowing, me and some of the boys want to get down there. Folks say there's gold shipments from stagecoach robberies laying on the river bottom. You can come too."

Bullhead drew a dotted line across the napkin and connected the ends of the wide arc. "This is the tunnel through Gauley Mountain. Over three miles long. She drops one hundred and sixty two feet from the entry point to the western end." He raised his eyebrows as if waiting for Orville to react.

"Pretty impressive." Orville sipped his coffee.

"You bet." At the downriver end of the dotted line, Bullhead drew a rectangle then extended straight lines, like the bristles of a brush, from it to the edge of the napkin. He placed his pencil on the rectangle. "This is the power house. These," he pointed to the bristles, "are power lines. Billy Webster told me the turbines will produce enough electricity to run the city of Charleston. But it's all going to Union Carbide. The most modern turbines in the world. And this old river," he smiled, "the New, will turn them. Lloyd says Union Carbide is thinking about changing the river's name – from the New to the Old." Bullhead laughed. "That's about as close as Lloyd can come to a joke."

Orville smiled.

Bullhead added, "And, by God, Union Carbide's powerful enough to do it."

At the next table men in khaki stood up. One said, "Let's get back. Twenty-two feet a day don't happen by itself."

Orville and Bullhead walked from the mess hall to the nearby dam construction-site. They stood on the river's shore. Bullhead pointed to the concrete buttresses extending the frame of the dam across the river. The long necks of two steam shovels stretched as their engines emitted animal-like roars. The long teeth in the shovels' box-shaped mouths took giant bites from what had been, prior to the coffer dam on the far side of the river, the river's bottom. Then they reared above the wide holes aligned with the dam's foundation and turned towards shore; their gullets opened and dropped debris of rocks and sand. "Those shovels are digging the spillway. Soon those holes will be framed with wood then filled with concrete."

Along the shoreline, tall cranes stretched long cables to lift construction materials towards the tunnel opening and the dam. Ahead of them another steam shovel dropped crushed rock into the gondolas of a train. Slams of rocks against steel blasted across the gorge and plumes of dust rose.

Bullhead pointed to scaffolds latticed around a massive opening in Gauley Mountain. "That's the tunnel's upper entrance. One of these days, where we're now standing will be under water. And ol' Gauley," Bullhead gestured towards the mountain, "she'll look down and watch the New enter her."

The din of shovels and cranes, crashes of materials dropping into place, and men yelling commands, drowned out Bullhead's next words. But Orville understood – this operation had weight, girth, and power. He glanced at his gold star, stood erect, and placed his right hand on his blackjack holster, legs apart.

Bullhead yelled, "Look out!" and pulled Orville towards the mountain. Thirty feet above them the neck of a crane swung a load of boards in a wide arc. At the midpoint of the arc a board slipped from the load. It struck the earth end first to the right of them, and inches from a worker who at the last second leaped out of its path. The board stood on end, and then smacked against the shore.

Bullhead laughed, "That feller looked like a frog jumping away from a striking snake."

"Another couple of seconds and that board would've speared him," Orville said.

"He should watch what he's doing, Orv. A crane's got a job to do."

They walked towards the tunnel opening. Bullhead smiled and shouted, "Just so you know, we're now doing security work."

"We are?"

"We're checking things out, making sure there's no interference – no troublemakers, no drinking." Bullhead grinned, "You don't see any problems, do you?"

Orville grinned and shook his head.

"We're doing a good job. Without us, this place might be in trouble."

They laughed together.

Bullhead nodded towards the tunnel entrance. "Let's take a look inside shaft two."

THEY WALKED ALONG the rails leading into the shaft and paused at the shaft's entrance; on one side of it bright sunlight, on the other, darkness. For a moment Orville straddled the band of shadow that separated the tunnel's inner and outer worlds. Inside, walls and equipment in the tunnel became visible as their eyes adjusted to the dim light. From deep in the tunnel came roars and booms that reminded him of battlefields in France.

Bullhead waved his right arm towards an arched wall of smooth concrete. "That wall is sixteen feet from us, and that one," he waved his left arm towards the opposite wall, "is another sixteen feet." Then he grinned and pointed at the smooth arched surface above them, "And thirty-two feet straight up is the ceiling."

A wiry man wearing a wide-brimmed hat and covered head to toe with white dust walked towards them carrying a baseball bat. He nodded to Bullhead.

"Ermil, this here's Orville Orr. He's working with me. Orville, this is Ermil Dothan. Ermil's one of the foremen."

As Ermil and Orville nodded to each other, the distant roar of an engine and train grew louder. Ermil turned his bat sideways and gently thrust it towards the two men, "You boys better step back, dinkey's coming." The sound quickly became a roar. Ermil yelled above it, "Let's move outside."

The roar of a dinkey's drive wheels and gasoline-powered engine burst from the tunnel entrance, followed by the dinkey, a small locomotive. Behind it trailed rail cars loaded with rock and dirt, many of the rocks the size of boulders along the New River.

The train stopped and steam shovels, poised and ready, lifted boulders from the gondolas and dropped them into the wide mouth of a massive steel machine beside the rails. Its walls rose twenty feet above the ground.

Bullhead pointed to the machine. "Rock crusher." The air vibrated with explosions and screeches of steel on stone as the hammers and pistons of the crusher crunched their offering. "That boy's hungry," he yelled above the din.

Pulverized rock and sand dropped from the bottom of the crusher and tumbled down the hillside. At the lower level of the hill, another steam shovel loaded the rock and sand into rail cars.

"That train will take the rock to Boncar," Bullhead said. He laughed, "You remember Boncar, right Orville?"

Ermil hollered, "Okay, you boys can go back in."

Bullhead and Orville walked along the rails on the tunnel floor. Ahead of them echoed the screeches of drills and the pounding of jackhammers. The natural light from the entrance receded, replaced with the bright glow of electric bulbs high on the tunnel walls. The cacophony of the drills and jackhammers increased and a light fog of dust hung in the air. Bullhead pointed to the vibrating black hoses that lay to the right and left of the rails. "They carry compressed air to the drills and jackhammers at the tunnel face."

Bullhead cupped his hands when he spoke. He nodded behind him and shouted, "Back at the opening, the tunnel went through dirt and shale. Had to reinforce the walls with concrete. Now, from here to the face, and in the other shafts too, we're in solid rock. No more shoring up. No more concrete or roof bolts. All we got to do is muck, drill, and blast." Bullhead smiled. He pointed towards the ceiling where the tunnel expanded its height and width; the smooth surface of the concrete tunnel walls became solid rock.

"Check it out, Orv – forty-six feet!"

They walked deeper into the screeches of drills and slams of jackhammers. In the air's ever thicker dust light diffused and dimmed. At the end of the dinkey's rails they stood in a thick haze. Bullhead coughed.

Orville pulled a blue bandanna from his hip pocket and tied it over his nose and mouth. Bullhead laughed, "You plan to rob a bank?"

"Workers breathe this dust all day?"

"A little dirt won't hurt 'em none; you neither"

Orville left his bandanna in place. In France, more than once he'd worn his gas mask when other men left theirs off. They'd died when shells of mustard gas exploded nearby.

Bullhead waved one arm towards the tunnel's end, a floor-to-ceiling wall of terraced rock partially obscured by the dust, one that dwarfed the men working there. "That's the face." On a high stone shelf that extended the width of the face, men stood behind drills mounted on steel tripods. Other workers helped steady the drills.

Bullhead pointed to a second shelf and below it a third. "Those are benches. Engineers call this heading and bench drilling." Like giant stair steps, the benches extended away from the face, the lowest bench only a few feet above the tunnel floor.

Orville gestured towards workers carrying long steel rods and climbing over the benches, "What're those men doing?"

"They're nippers – they take sharpened drill-shafts to the drillers and bring the old ones down. The next dinkey will carry the shafts outside to be reground."

"Pretty efficient," Orville said.

"O.M. Jones don't miss much."

Orville waved towards the face, "Looks like everybody's colored."

"Most are, though with the dust you might think they're all white." Bullhead looked around. "That driller up there," he pointed to the man operating the drill farthest to the right on the top bench, "that's Buzzy. He's white, gets thirty-five cents an hour. The colored drillers get twenty-five, thirty if they're any good. Men that operate a dinkey, foremen too, they're white. Being a foreman adds another fifteen cents an hour."

"How many men are down here?" Orville yelled.

"Same here as on the other headings – about forty-five to fifty drillers, dinkey skinners, powder monkeys, muckers, and pitboys."

Drillers leaned into their machines, the size of mounted machine guns, and inched spiraling metal into Gauley's rock core. Even though some of the drill shafts had a length of ten feet, they resembled larger versions of the drill bits on Orville's workbench in Kettle. But here, instead of pulling wood shavings from the drilled hole, they brought ground rock and dust into the tunnel.

Between and behind the drillers, workers manned jackhammers that rammed the floor of the benches. Ratta-ta-tatta-ta-tatta – dust rose as their rapid slams fractured rock and rammed the steel hammers into it.

"Near the end of the shift the drill and jackhammer holes will be filled with dynamite. Everybody'll find cover, then ker-boom!" Bullhead slammed his right fist into the open palm of his left hand. "The next shift'll come in and muck, clean up the rock, and start drilling. Like I told you, muck, drill, blast. Each shift, six days a week. And on and on it goes."

The rapid slams of the powerful hammers pummeled Orville's body and pounded his eardrums. He closed his eyes. The explosive sounds, winding around and through him, became bursts of shells. He crouched in the mud of a trench at the front and waited for the guns to stop. When silence arrived he yelled "Charge!" and led his men over the top. He ran forward firing his rifle at anything in his path. On either side of him soldiers ran toward the German trenches, rifles blazing. Many fell in mid-stride. Some lay motionless. Others screamed and writhed in the mud.

Heaviness spread from Orville's stomach to his arms and crawled to the tips of his fingers. His knees wobbled. He put a hand on Bullhead's shoulder to steady himself.

Shaft One

ORVILLE AND BULLHEAD RETURNED to the mess hall for lunch. In the cafeteria line they filled trays with bowls of white bean soup, cheese sandwiches, and glasses of sweet tea, then walked to an empty table. Across the half-filled room men in white shirts, their neckties loosened in the humid noonday heat, sat in small groups alongside men in dust-covered work clothes.

After a long gulp of tea Orville pointed towards the dust-covered men, "Are those foremen and supervisors?"

Bullhead chewed a bite of his sandwich. "Uh-huh."

"No workers here for lunch?"

"No. They can eat breakfast and supper here, but not lunch. Meals are deducted from wages. Coloreds," he waved one arm towards empty tables in the back of the room, "sit back there." A hand-lettered sign, "Colored Only," hung on the room's back wall. Above one of the two water fountains a small sign announced that it served only coloreds.

Bullhead continued, "Truth is, not a lot of workers, colored or white, eat in the mess hall. Some of them do and bitch about the cost – an hour's pay for a meal. A lot of the niggers scrounge for food." Then he snickered and spoke in a mixture of disbelief and humor, "Some of 'em live on candy bars." His tone turned serious, "And they spend their money on corn liquor." He studied his soup, then with a smile said, "Remind me to tell you how that works. Maybe tonight."

"Okay."

"Come on, Orv, finish eating. Let's go over to shaft one."

BULLHEAD DROVE EAST along the shore of the New towards Gauley Bridge, Orville beside him. The wooden side-rails of the truck bed rattled as the REO passed over the washboard surface of the dirt road. He parked near a large building under construction; its concrete foundation extended into the river. Bullhead pointed towards a large opening in the base of the mountain fifty yards behind the construction site. Like giant blacksnakes crawling into the shaft's cool darkness, thick hoses paralleled rails into the opening. "That's the entrance to shaft one. And over there," he pointed to the foundation, "will sit the powerhouse with the turbines."

"It all comes together, Bullhead – everything's connected! The dam, water into the tunnel then to the power plant; electricity sent downriver to the factory. Even the rock out of the mountain goes into metal processing. Pretty slick. Efficient, too. There's one helluva genius plan behind all this."

Bullhead grinned, "O.M. Jones." The grin disappeared, "Better look out Orville, he might have a plan for you."

Orville's smile locked like the one smile on a Halloween mask. Plans for him? Like an incoming mortar round, that possibility burst and sent hot chards of emotion through him. The captain had received plans from the commanders above him. And the commanders received plans from the officers above them. And at the top, General Black Jack Pershing, like God himself, wrote the master plan. It touched every doughboy in every trench. Thousands of them would be shot or blown to bits, others gassed. Beads of sweat trickled down each side of his body.

Bullhead laughed and slapped Orville on the shoulder, "Wake up, Orv." He wiped sweat from his brow. "It's hot out here. Come on, let's go in."

At the tunnel's entrance a short pear-shaped man met them. He wore a slouch hat that, like his denim shirt and pants, carried a layer of white dust. His face, with its wide jowls, resembled a gourd, his mouth, a narrow slit at its base; eyes beamed from sockets so deep they looked like two worm-holes.

"Hey, Bullhead," the man drawled, "what 'r' you boys up to?" The slit of his mouth seemed not to move when he spoke.

"Cletus, this's Orville. Deputy Orville Orr. He's working with me as a shack rouster. Thought I'd show him around."

"Cletus Pancake, Orville." The men shook hands. "Ain't much to see out here, boys. And the afternoon heat's a-rising. Always cool inside, compliments of Union Carbide."

The three men walked along the shaft's rails, dwarfed by the tunnel's cavernous expanse. The distant pounding of jackhammers and screeches of drills drifted from the shaft.

"Seems like we're on an incline – we walking uphill?" Orville asked.

Cletus answered, "Yep, you're right about that, Orville."

Bullhead added, "Remember the map? The opening to this shaft is a hundred and sixty-two feet below the upstream entrance, other side of the mountain." Bullhead's voice rose, "How about this, Orv – imagine a block of water forty-six feet tall and forty-six feet wide, three miles long, falling a hundred and sixty-two feet and hitting them turbines." He slammed his fist against his palm, "Wham! Now that's what I call water pressure."

They laughed, a bit nervously.

Ahead the screeches and pounding grew louder.

Cletus yelled, "Them drills sounds like a bunch of screaming banshees."

Electric lights along the tunnel walls, one about every ten feet, lit the tunnel until they disappeared into the rising slope of the tunnel floor. Orville said, "Cletus, it seems brighter here than over in shaft two. More powerful bulbs?"

"Nope, same ones. But I know what you're getting at Orville. Guess again."

Bullhead said, more to Cletus than to Orville, "Maybe they turned on the fans."

"Nope, you missed that one, Bullhead. Them exhaust fans is usually on, though they're so small it's about like me or you trying to suck up the smoke from a brush fire."

"I give up, Cletus," Orville said.

"Simple. Wet drilling. We got visitors today. They're scheduled to arrive any minute."

"Who's coming?" Bullhead asked.

"Want to guess?"

Bullhead nodded. "Mmmm. I'll bet I know."

"You want to guess, Orville?"

"I'm the new kid in class, Cletus. I'll pass."

The bleat of a dinkey's horn signaled the approach of a train. The engine's headlight cast a penumbra of light and shadow around the men. Cletus motioned for Orville and Bullhead to step aside.

The dinkey pulled a single flatcar with wooden side rails. In it stood five men wearing felt hats, suits, and neckties with canister-bearing masks strapped to their faces. The men held the car's side rails. Four of the men carried clipboards and papers.

After the dinkey passed, Cletus tapped Orville's arm. "Well, I reckon you saw him, Orville, ol' O.M. Jones, the one without a clip-board. Big as life itself. Just riding along grinning behind that mask and a-nodding at us – like he's on some sort of pleasure trip. Come to think of it, for him maybe that's what this is."

"Who are the other men? Why are they wearing gas masks?"

"You want to tell him, Mr. Shack Rouster?"

Bullhead grinned, "Not like France, Orv. No mustard gas down here. They're wearing respirators. Come to think of it, those things do look like gas masks." He paused, then said to Cletus, "I figure it's some kind of inspection team – maybe state department of mines." Then to Orville he added angrily, "Even though this is not a mine. They wear them masks because they're chicken-shit office boys from the statehouse in Charleston," his tone softened, "except for O.M. Jones. He probably put one on to humor 'em."

Like a teacher replying to a student, Cletus said, "That's right." His face reddened, "Union Carbide told the state, this here's a tunnel. A tunnel is covered by rules different than regulations that covers mines. But, wouldn't you know, the department of mines still has to poke its nose in, then stick it behind a mask." Cletus looked towards the heading, "Well, by God they'll find everything in order today. Cletus Pancake has done his job. The fans is on. And my boys has got the water flowing through them drills."

"Water in the drills?" Orville asked.

"Sure," Cletus answered, still a teacher, "each drill has two hoses attached to it. One for the air pressure that drives it, the other bringing water for the drill bit. Dampens the rock dust." Cletus nodded towards the tunnel's heading, "Today, just for you, Governor Conley, we'll slow things down. Open the petcocks on the water hoses. There'll not be a speck of dust. No sir, none!" He added a sour, "And we'll go oh-so-slow." Cletus studied his brogans for a moment, scuffed one toe in the dust and looked at Orville, "Tomorrow the big boys upstairs will kick ol' Cletus' behind for not making twenty-two feet. Well, it burns my ass." Cletus took a deep breath and then said, "That's a long-winded answer to your question, Orville, about the lights and what's different in this shaft – at least today. Come back tomorrow. I'll show you another way to operate."

"Most of the time, the water is turned off?" Orville asked.

"Sure. We're drilling through solid rock. Water mixes with the rock dust and gums up the drills." Cletus extended his hands, palms up, "How else but dry are we going to make twenty-two feet a day?"

The three men arrived at the face of shaft one, its heading and benches like those in shaft two, but without the dust.

The men on the inspection team climbed up the benches. When they talked to tunnel workers they inserted two fingers between mask and cheek and spoke through the crack. Then the mask flopped into place while they listened and wrote notes.

O.M. Jones, mask in his hand, motioned for Cletus to join him.

"See you boys later. Duty calls." Cletus walked away.

Orville turned to Bullhead, "Seems to me it's better to drill with the water on. Go a little slower so men can breathe. I couldn't take the dust over in shaft two."

Bullhead laughed and slapped Orville on the back. "Dry-drilling gets us twenty-two feet a day, Orv. That's what Union Carbide wants. And by God, that's what Union Carbide gets. Our job is to help them get it."

Dinner

After work Orville returned to Mrs. Jimison's house. After the day's heat and the dust of the shafts, he welcomed the porch's shade and its clean cool air. He sat in a wicker chair, lowered his head to the top of the chair's wide rounded back, and breathed the sharp scent of the cedars that shaded the porch.

From inside the house a woman's shrill angry voice yelled, "And you keep your hands off'n me – keep 'em to your self! Hear me?" punctuated by stomps on the floor.

The screen door burst open and slammed against the house. Pansy, her hair no longer pinned up, white uniform disheveled, stormed out. She strode to the porch's top step, stopped and pointed at Orville, "Y'all tell Lloyd Sykes if he knows what's good for him, he better lay off! Pansy P. Washington is private property."

Orville sat up and nodded.

Pansy stomped down the steps and walked at a fast pace to the street.

At breakfast Lloyd had said, "Keep the niggers in line," as Pansy came into the room. Had he forced his hands, himself, on her? Lots of white folks knew how to get colored people to do their bidding. Down in the tunnel, Ermil Dothan used a baseball bat. Maybe Lloyd Sykes used his hands.

Orville again rested his head to the back of the chair and closed his eyes. Pansy's wiry frame and lined brown face had little beauty, yet her eyes shone. The dining room seemed different, charged, when she entered it. And it lost something when she left. Maybe Lloyd needed a little of what Pansy had and he'd tried to take it. In these hard times a man might steal anything, even vitality. He drifted into a half-sleep filled with images of Bertie – the power of her touch and the magnetic force of her body during their lovemaking.

ORVILLE PARKED ON MAIN STREET. "Meet me at the Bridge View about seven o'clock for supper," Bullhead had said. "I got more to show you later this evening."

In the café, stools along the counter sat empty. Bullhead occupied the last booth, directly in the path of an electric fan. He waved to Orville, who raised his chin in acknowledgement and joined him.

"Looks like you got a jump start on me." He eyed Bullhead's tall glass of iced tea dripping condensation, a slice of lemon floating on its surface. "That looks good."

When Orville turned to find the waitress she already stood next to the booth. He looked up, first at the notepad and pencil in her long fingers, and then at her face. She had high cheekbones and deep brown eyes framed by long curly black hair. He breathed in her aroma, a mixture of spice and work sweat.

"Uh, I'd like some tea."

"Sweet or regular?" Her voice flowed like a smooth mountain stream.

"Sweet."

She walked to the kitchen.

"You remember Armen, don't you?" Bullhead asked.

"Hard to forget her."

"Well, pay no mind. You're a married man."

A married man, Bullhead had that right. But Bertie…now so distant. Like she didn't care, or maybe carried a grudge.

"Hey Orv, you there?" He nodded towards Armen standing next to the booth, pencil poised over her notepad.

A tall frosted glass of iced tea sat on the table in front of Orville.

"What'll you have?"

With enthusiasm Bullhead said, "Try the blue plate special – big ground-beef patty, mashed potatoes and gravy. Green beans," he smacked his lips, "cooked with bacon. I ordered it. They got Heinz catsup, too."

"Okay. I'll have the special."

Orville stared at Armen's trim backside as she walked through the kitchen's double doors, then took a long swallow of the tea. After a deep breath he said, "Uh, Bullhead, there's something bothering me, and I need to get it off my chest."

"Sure."

"Well…Bertie and me…things have been rough over the past six months. Some nights our bed seems as wide as the seventy miles from Gauley Bridge to Kettle."

After Armen brought their dinners, Orville continued to talk, not eat.

Bullhead punctuated the pauses in Orville's story with slow nods. Other than glancing at his plate long enough to fill his fork, he kept his eyes on Orville while he ate.

"That's about it – I don't know when we started to drift apart. Maybe when I was a hot-shot Ford salesman. Ralph and I used to celebrate with an evening out after one of us sold a car, and we sold a lot. We'd go to speakeasies, blind pigs, Ralph called 'em. Raise a little hell. Women liked him – he bragged that a woman in Charleston gave him the diamond stickpin he wore every day." Orville took a bite of mashed potatoes. "I never cheated on Bertie, but you know what nights out can do to a marriage."

"Never been married, Orv. Tried, but nobody'd have me. I'll take your word for it."

"Maybe the drift started after I lost my job, I don't know. And my being this far from home doesn't help. But that's …" Orville put his elbows on the table and covered his eyes.

"Think I'll go take at look at that lemon meringue pie." Bullhead walked to the counter and stood with Armen. He spoke in a loud whisper. "Don't mind our boy, he's going through a hard time, separated from his wife and all."

Bullhead returned carrying two plates, each filled with an oversized piece of pie, wispy white meringue rising a full two inches above the fillings, what the Bridge View menu called "mile high pie." Bullhead's cheery voice contrasted with Orville's face, "Hey buddy, this'll put some spring back in your step. Have some."

Armen made listless swipes across the counter, her gaze resting on Orville.

After finishing their pie, Bullhead grinned, "Ready to go? I got a lot more to show you."

ORVILLE DROVE BEHIND Bullhead's truck along the shore of the New. Then, after a sharp turn, the road snaked up Gauley Mountain. On the far horizon the sun resembled a bright orange ball that had taken a final bounce only to be punctured by the distant mountain ridge where it rested, its inner substance draining away, top arched to the end. The turnpike continued to Richmond; after what just happened in the restaurant, maybe he should keep driving.

Bullhead turned on a narrow dirt road, Orville followed. The warm evening air, motionless but for the stir of the two vehicles, suspended an orange cloud of dust in the fading sunlight. Orville slowed to put distance between himself and Bullhead, but the dust didn't lessen. He took shallow breaths.

Bullhead drove into camp two and parked near a path to the shanties. Orville parked beside him. A pine forest towered beyond the camp.

Bullhead jumped out of his truck, motioned to Orville and yelled, "Come on Orv. Let's get to the action." They walked at a fast pace through the camp. In some shanties a single electric bulb hung from a ceiling cord and cast flat light over bunks and men. Others had no light. In one shanty, a man played a guitar and sang to the music of the hymn, "In the Sweet Bye and Bye," but with lyrics that went,

You will eat, bye and bye,
In that glorious land above the sky;
Work and pray, live on hay,
You'll get pie in the sky when you die.

Bullhead stiffened, "He'd better be careful. Singing a song like that. Might find his guitar broke over a tree limb. Maybe him too."

When Orville glanced through the doorway of a darkened shack, Bullhead said, "Night shift boys, or maybe gone to bed." Then he smiled and added, talking more to himself than to Orville, "Or up to no good."

Bright light shone from the windows of the camp's most distant shanty. Black men in sweat-darkened and dust-crusted work clothes shambled in and out of the doorway. Voices yelled and laughed in disbelief, "He done it. He got his point again – whoo-ee!" A tall man, skinny, curly hair, large eyes, stepped out the door and yelled, "Hey Dinkey Skinner, ol' Powder Monkey rolled his point three times in a row. He the richest man in camp."

"Feeling better Sunburn?"

The man flinched and backed away, "Un-huh, Deputy McCloud." Then with a burst of enthusiasm, "And thank you, bossman, thank you. Feeling much better."

"Did you go see the doc?" Bullhead asked.

"Well I would've, yes sir, I would've, but a couple of the muckers brought me a potion. It worked like Aunt Sadie's home remedy. And here I am."

"Tomorrow morning you better be up and out the door."

"You can count on me."

Bullhead turned to Orville, "You can count on him all right. Just don't count very far." At the shanty door Bullhead pulled his blackjack from its holster. He slapped it hard against the doorframe. A piercing "Crack!" jolted the room to silence. Bullhead walked in. Standing or sitting, men became motionless. Most of them held Coca Cola bottles filled with a clear liquid. All eyes turned to Bullhead.

Orville remained in the doorway. The room reeked of sweat that had dried and, day after day, renewed itself, then fermented in men's clothes and the straw ticks, even the bunks and floor.

Bullhead glared at the men seated on a ragged and dirty army blanket. One of them held a pair of dice, his cocked arm immobile. He scanned the men standing around the blanket, then around the room. The man furthest from Bullhead, high cheek bones, light yellow skin, shifted his feet and inched one arm towards a nearby bunk.

Bullhead commanded, "You got something you want to show me, Hardware?"

"No, deputy, Just checking this bunk."

"Hand it over." Bullhead boomed, "Now!"

Men flinched.

Hardware hesitated then extended his long arm. He held a half-pint jar of clear liquid.

Bullhead snapped his blackjack in a wide arc, hit and smashed the jar. Blood flowed from glass imbedded in Hardware's hand. The jar's liquid splashed over Hardware and the men near him. The pungent smell of alcohol mixed with the odor of old sweat and blood.

"That white lightening'll sterilize your cut just fine, Hardware. Next time, you remember who sells it. Who is that, Hardware?"

Hardware looked at his feet.

"Who is it?"

He gave no reply.

In a move so fast that Orville only glimpsed it, Bullhead slammed his blackjack into Hardware's face. Hardware dropped to the floor, a long gash below his left eye. Blood streamed over his cheek.

"Anybody got questions?" Bullhead asked.

The men sat motionless. No one spoke.

"Boys, you got to get it through your thick skulls. Prohibition is the law of the land. Deputy McCloud is your supplier. Nobody else. Nobody. I got the Coke bottles, and you get them, full of hooch, for fifty cents apiece. And around here it's against the law, my law, for anything else to hold liquor. Or for anybody else to sell it. That clear?"

Heads nodded.

"Is that clear?" Bullhead said, this time louder.

A few men muttered, "Uh huh, Deputy McCloud."

"I want to hear you," Bullhead yelled. "You understand what I'm telling you?"

"Yes, bossman." "Uh-huh." "Yes sir." "Got it." "Yep."

Bullhead turned in a full circle, pointing his blackjack at each man. He attempted to look them in the eye, but as the blackjack approached men lowered their gazes or looked away. "I went easy on Hardware, just wanted to teach him a lesson. Next time I may not be so easy on him or you." Bullhead inspected his blackjack. He took a blue bandanna from his hip pocket, wiped the leather then holstered it. "A couple of you boys help Hardware get on his feet. Wash his cuts, somebody."

Two men lifted Hardware from the floor to a nearby bunk. One of them poured white lightening on a rag and dabbed Hardware's cheek and hand.

"Now then," Bullhead's voice became friendly, "who's the house boy tonight?"

An older man sitting on the blanket answered, "Me, Deputy McCloud. Name's Arthur."

"Okay Arthur. You know how things work?"

"I'm the house, using your money. After we're done, I give the money to you."

"See that you do. I'll take care of you later. Remember, everything's above board. I don't cotton to cheating. Game ends at midnight. Three more hours to have fun."

Bullhead strode out the door. Orville followed him. He didn't slow his pace until he reached his truck. "Well, Orv, that's what I got. Right now I can handle it myself, but with more workers coming, I may set up a second shanty. If you want to, you can run it."

"Thanks. Maybe." Orville did not want any part of a bootleg shanty.

"We got plenty of time, Orv. May not have a second house anyway. But I wanted you to get the full picture." Bullhead looked around as if to make sure no one would overhear him, "Oncet I figured out the coloreds is crazed about two things, hooch and gambling, I went to work. Well, maybe there is a third thing, but most of the time there's no women around." Bullhead opened the REO's door. "I brought in a few women a couple of weeks ago. They said them men stunk so bad they'd never come back. I gave up that line of business. Maybe you could figure out how to make it work."

Orville followed Bullhead down the mountain, his thoughts on the shanty; dice, Coke bottles, the snap of Bullhead's wrist and the flow of Hardware's blood. A deputy sheriff making his own law. He could do that, too. But even as he reflected on the possibility he felt his insides twist.

In Gauley Bridge Bullhead continued along Main Street. Orville's Ford climbed the hill to Mrs. Jimison's place. He parked and walked up the steps to the porch.

From the shadows, Mrs. Jimison said, "Welcome home, Orville. I've made some sweet tea. Would you like to join me?"

Sweet Tea and Memories

In the darkness of the front porch, Orville sat on the wicker divan. After returning with glasses of sweet tea, Mrs. Jimison sat to his right in the wicker chair.

"How did you happen to come to Gauley Bridge, Orville?"

He told her of the years of selling Fords for Ralph Morrison, then losing his job a few months after the market crashed; of Bullhead's letter and an invitation to be a deputy at the tunnel. Of the army experiences he'd had with Bullhead. Of his return home in the spring of nineteen-nineteen to the news of his daddy's death and a run-down farm. "I worked hard to rebuild the place, but Mother Nature had a big head start on me. Selling the farm was the hardest thing I ever did. When we moved to town I felt like I left parts of myself behind." He heaved a sigh.

Mrs. Jimison took Orville's hand.

"I felt that way when I left Richmond."

A woman's touch – her touch – felt good.

They sat in silence until Mrs. Jimison said, "I'll get us more tea." She stood and held his hand until her steps towards the door pulled her hand away. One by one Orville's fingers released themselves and drifted to the table.

Mrs. Jimison returned with fresh glasses of tea. A distant whip-poor-will called. Locusts and crickets strummed the music of a summer night.

"The night sounds are soothing," she said in a voice as low as the bass strings on a guitar. "My husband, Daniel, 'Dan' everyone called him, owned a coal mine at Vanetta, not far from here. Up the Gauley River towards

Summersville. His father started the mine. It produced a good living for us. For the miners too."

Orville glanced through a porch window at the living room's oriental rugs, polished woods, and the tall grandfather clock.

"I met Dan when I attended finishing school in Charlottesville. He'd come to visit friends at the university. I was taken with his deep brown eyes and wavy blond hair. He escorted me to a dance. We laughed about how I towered over him in heels.

"We exchanged letters then the next summer I came here to visit Dan and his family. We fell in love and in August we had a big wedding in Richmond. Then a week at the Greenbrier. My father had done well in banking, and he helped us build this home. Greek revival was popular then. Ten years later daddy retired. After only a few months my mother passed away. In the stock market crash last year, daddy lost almost everything; he didn't live to see Christmas."

"I'm sorry." Orville couldn't think of anything else to say.

"Dan was a good man. But even though he cared about me, I felt like I was his possession. It troubled me. I thought about leaving him, but didn't. I did the next best thing – I built an imaginary wall around myself. I came to live more in my own world than in the one I shared with him. I still go there when life gets hard."

Orville nodded. He wished he could say something.

"One morning five years ago Dan got a report there'd been a roof fall in the mine. He went to investigate. Shortly after he reached the site of the fall, a twenty foot section of the shaft collapsed. Dan and two other men died."

Orville gripped his glass as if it might escape.

"The state department of mines closed the operation. Then they discovered Dan had robbed Peter to pay Paul. He'd directed men to use fewer roof bolts in the shafts. That saved labor costs and sped up the expansion of the mine. The business had been getting squeezed by larger operators. Dan had pushed his men to dig faster into the coal seams; he risked having to shut down. He lost that race. I sold what was left of the business. I wanted to help families of the men who died with Dan. I gave them over half of the money. I soon found I hadn't kept enough to meet expenses for this big old place. Now I run a fancy rooming house. If it weren't for the Hawks Nest tunnel, I wonder if I'd be able to stay here. Charlottesville and my finishing school seem like a lifetime ago."

The conversation ebbed, replaced by the sounds of the night, and for a while the two sat in a near-comfortable silence.

"Well, Orville, it's late. I'd best get to bed. I have to meet Pansy at five o'clock."

"Thanks for the tea. It's been nice to talk. "

"Thank you, Orville. I haven't talked about life with Dan for a long time. Tonight helped. My feelings need to breathe. So do I."

She stood and smoothed her skirt. Orville stood too. Mrs. Jimison took Orville's glass from his hand and placed the glasses on the table. Then she put her arms around him in a gentle hug. He inhaled the lavender scent of her hair, hesitated, and then put his arms around her.

"I'm pleased you're staying in my home, Orville. Thanks for listening."

After a moment Mrs. Jimison relaxed her arms and stepped back. She picked up the glasses and whispered, "Good night."

Mrs. Jimison passed through the foyer into the dining room then the kitchen door closed behind her. He walked up the curved staircase to his bedroom. Her touch and scent remained with him.

August, 1930: A Trip Home

WORK. SIX DAYS A WEEK. Like iron rail-spikes, work held him in Gauley Bridge. "I want to come home more often," he wrote Bertie, "but by train it's all milk runs, a stop at every town then a layover in Charleston. Driving to Kettle on Saturday then back to Gauley Bridge on Sunday takes almost as long." Bullhead had given him a hard time when, after his first trip home, he overslept on Monday.

The letters Bertie had written during his first weeks at the tunnel pulled at his heart. "Darling Orvie, life is not the same without you. During the war I had your momma and daddy to comfort me, and the farm was a busy place. Now I'm all alone in a house that's too big. Maybe if we'd had a child things would be different. But I failed you. And oh yes, I got Kettle to sustain me. Sometimes I think it's a town full of people with nothing to do but gossip. On the bright side – Mary Shamsford – you remember her from church? – and me volunteered to do the alter flowers for Sunday services. It's a way to stay busy. Orvie, I want you to lay beside me and do your duty."

In the weeks after he arrived at Gauley Bridge, Orville had received a letter from Bertie every day. Then one every other day, then two a week; last week only one. His letter writing, he had to admit, mirrored hers; if he received a letter from her he wrote one back.

By mid-August, he had taken only two overnight trips home. On the first his Ford had overheated and he'd arrived late Saturday night. On the second he had a flat tire; late again. Bertie seemed flat too, not her old self. Next time he went home he'd stay longer, make it a real weekend not just an overnight.

On Monday of the third week of August, he asked Bullhead for the following Saturday off. "I don't mind getting docked for it, Bullhead. No work, no pay, I understand. But," he said, business-like, "I need to attend to some things in Kettle." Then softly, "I miss Bertie."

"I'm not sure we can keep the house," Bertie had written in a shaky scrawl, as if the words pained her. "The debt we run up when you weren't working seems like it'll never go away. And everyday upkeep on the house takes what little we have. Being alone in a town of people who'd rather look in your windows at night than read the Bible is something I don't much care for. And the nights are long, Orvie, L-O-N-G."

"Dear Bertie, things will be okay. I wrote to Gruber's store – our credit is good. Enclosed is last week's pay. I kept a little for suppers and gasoline. I'll come home soon. Things will be all right." Would they? "When I get to Kettle, you can help me do my duty. (Ha! Ha!) Love, Orville."

Bullhead scuffed the dirt with the toe of his brogan. "I'll have to clear it with the big boys upstairs, Orv. Union Carbide is leaning hard on the contractor. They're hell-bent to get this tunnel dug. They don't ask about families when they measure how many feet was drilled. I guess they figure visits home can wait until the tunnel is done." After Orville talked about how tough things had been on Bertie, Bullhead said, "I'll take care of it."

Dawn on Friday brought muggy air; the New River mirrored the gray clouds that hung low over the mountains. At the end of his morning shanty rounds sweat had turned Orville's khaki shirt dark brown. At lunch in the mess hall Bullhead gave him a sly smile. "Take it easy driving home. Save yourself for tonight. You got business to tend to."

They laughed.

Late afternoon in a light rain Orville drove the seventy miles to Kettle. The weather reminded him of the day he first drove to Gauley Bridge. So much had happened since then. He smiled and touched his wallet. Now they could pay down a little of the debt. And the next two nights he'd sleep with Bertie.

WITH A BIG SMILE, Orville walked through the front door. Bertie met him in the living room, arms at her side, face somber.

Laughing, he pulled his wallet from his pocket and held it in front of him like an admission ticket. "Will this get me in the door?"

Bertie snatched the wallet from his hands and quickly removed the bills. Then she smiled and handed him the wallet. "That'll do just fine." She gave him a quick hug, turned, and walked to the kitchen. "Come on, it's late. Supper's ready."

During a dinner of cold ham and mashed sweet potatoes, Bertie said little. Orville talked about his drive from Gauley Bridge. "How're you and Mary Shamsford coming along with the alter flowers at church?"

"Mary's been sick."

"Are you doing it alone?"

"No, her husband, Hack, is filling in till she feels better."

After dinner he helped Bertie clear the table. She washed and he dried the dishes, then they walked into the living room. A radio – where'd that come from? – sat on the table beside the couch. A Philco in a high-gloss cabinet with two small black knobs on either side of a round dial of radio frequencies. Above them gold fabric covered cathedral-window openings in front of a speaker. Bertie turned the radio on and soon music filled the room.

"Where'd you get this?"

Bertie's face reddened and she answered, almost before he finished his question, "I saved my pennies Orvie – I wanted to surprise you."

How could they still be paying off debts and afford something like this?

In bed Orville hugged Bertie. His hand lingered on her nightgown. He slowly moved it across her breasts and nuzzled his lips to her cheek. She remained motionless. "If you want me to, Bertie, I can do my duty."

She pushed his hand away, "Duty'll have to wait. Been a long day. Let's get some sleep."

He lay awake – would she reach over and touch him, say something, do something – anything? After an hour he drifted into an uneasy sleep.

Saturday morning Orville joined Bertie on a trip to Gruber's Department Store for groceries. Afterwards he mowed the lawn and cleaned the basement.

Late afternoon, stepping out of the shower he breathed the rich aroma of roast beef. Downstairs Bertie had set the table with their best dinnerware. Already he could taste green beans simmering with slices of bacon and onion. And dessert sat on the kitchen counter – chocolate cake with caramel icing. Bertie seemed like her old self.

At dinner he talked of life at the tunnel, though he left out the dust and dirt, baseball bats, drinking and gambling. Nor did he tell Bertie about his late evening talks with Mrs. Jimison.

After an hour of Rudy Vallee on the NBC Blue Network, Bertie said, "Standing over that hot stove has wore me down. My back is killing me. I'm off to bed."

When Orville joined her, Bertie lay on her back, eyes closed, her breathing deep and slow. As he slid between the sheets she lay motionless. He placed his hand on her tummy and slowly moved it over her nightgown. When his fingers touched her breasts, he placed his lips next to her ear and whispered, "You awake, honey? Think I might do my duty?"

Her eyes still closed, Bertie rolled over on her stomach and muttered sleepily, "Right now the only duty you got is to help me get some rest. After cooking that huge dinner," her voice rose, "just for you don't forget. I got a duty too – to get some sleep."

Orville sighed. "Bertie, being away and all, I miss you, our… you know, our loving, something awful." He rolled towards her; aroused, he gently thrust against her bare leg.

She remained motionless. Then just as Orville started to roll away, Bertie abruptly jerked her knees under her, raised her rump and pulled her nightgown above her bare bottom. "Okay, here. Do it."

"You mean…from…that way?" Orville asked more in amazement than a question.

Her voice flat, Bertie replied, "From behind, Orville. That's the idea. Just don't ask me to roll around like an acrobat."

Orville knelt behind her. Bertie had always insisted that he be on top. "It's in the Bible," she'd said. His thoughts leaped to Le Havre and the only other woman he had known, Marie; how she had straddled him.

Her voice impatient, nearly a command, Bertie said, "Come on, Orville, do it!"

He gripped the cheeks of her rump, entered her, and thrust in slow rhythmic movements that increased in speed and intensity. Moments later he moaned and fell forward over her back.

Bertie lowered her knees and lay on her stomach. She tried to rotate her body to the side. "You're heavy, Orville. Give me some air."

He rolled on to his back and took deep breaths.

"Okay, duty done," she said.

"Bertie, that was something."

"It was something, all right, that's what it was. Something."

Bertie soon fell asleep. But Orville lay awake. His thoughts jumped in cross-currents of emotion. What they'd done continued to arouse him. But Bertie just seemed to want to get it over with. This new way – where did it come from? He liked it, but missed her sliding under him, laughing and reminding him of his duty.

SUNDAY MORNING ORVILLE AWAKENED to the aroma of bacon frying. He walked downstairs.

"Orvie, sit yourself down and have some coffee. Eggs and bacon'll be on the table in a minute." She smiled.

He returned a wide and bright smile. Bertie's lanky body looked good in her orchid robe. "Thanks." He hesitated then added, "honey." He sat down and sipped his coffee. For a moment he relived last night's lovemaking. How many ways could they do it – how many positions could there be? Would Bertie want to find out?

Orville sipped his coffee. "Nice robe, Bertie. Is it new?"

"Mmm." She placed the spatula under each of two eggs in the skillet and lightly splashed bacon grease on them. "Sunny side up, just the way you like them." Then, staring at the eggs, she said, "This robe? Just a cheap thing. I won it at the church; Ladies Auxiliary. Maybe it's a good sign."

Bertie put the eggs on a plate alongside four strips of crisp bacon and placed it before Orville. "Maybe life's turning sunny side up, just like these eggs."

"The eggs look good, honey. Thanks. I'm grateful that I'm working and we got a roof over our heads. And each other. That's more than lot of folks have these days." He looked at Bertie's empty plate. "Aren't you having breakfast?"

She removed a biscuit from the oven, placed it on her plate and joined him at the table. "I'm not hungry. This is enough for now."

"Uh, last night in bed, Bertie…what we did was different, but I liked it. Do you think we could…"

"Could? Would? Should? Orvie, we could sit here jawing all morning. Last night is over and done. Eat." Bertie stood and walked to the window. "Looks to me like there's dark clouds down the valley. They won't put themselves on your schedule. Remember the time you had a flat tire in a thunderstorm?"

He wanted to touch Bertie, hold her again.

A knock came from the front door.

Startled, Bertie jerked around and yelled, "Who's that?" Her face paled.

"Well, we could guess, or one of us could go find out." He walked to the front door.

On the porch stood Acey Burton. "Hey, Orville." In his oil-stained coveralls, Acey looked like he'd just walked out of the shop at Ralph Morrison Ford. He smiled and extended his right hand. The stump of his left arm held his leather ball cap against his chest. They shook hands.

"Bet you're wondering what I'm up to, ain't you?"

"Now that you mention it, Acey, I am. But it's good to see you."

"Good to see you too." Acey shuffled his feet, then said, "I got something to ask you."

"Okay. Come in and say hi to Bertie. Want some coffee?"

At the kitchen table, Acey sipped a mug of coffee. "Orville, I come to ask a favor."

"I'll help if I can."

"Ain't much to it. Last week over at the post office I heard some of the boys talking about hopping a freight to that tunnel where you're working at. They asked me to go with them to…what's that place?"

"Hawks Nest. You plan to hop a freight, Acey?"

"I got a different idea. Can I hitch a ride with you?"

Bertie said, "Acey, maybe you can get him on the road before that storm hits."

Orville asked, "You sure you want to go up there, Acey? It's hard work and low wages. And that tunnel is a dirty place."

"In these times, low wages is better than no wages. And hard work never scared me," Acey raised his left arm, "I give my left hand doing it. One look at these coveralls ought to tell you dirt ain't no problem for Acey Burton. I even packed a bag. It's outside."

On the front porch Orville put his arms around Bertie. "I'll miss you, honey."

Bertie stepped back, waved at Acey in the Ford's front seat, then gave Orville a light kiss. She pointed towards the elm trees waving in the rising wind. "You all better get going, Orvie. Storm's coming."

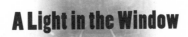

A Light in the Window

MONDAY MORNING ORVILLE MADE his rounds of the shanties. Lying in his bunk, a worker pointed at Orville's chest and muttered, "That star don't give you no right to boss me around."

"Time to go to work, buddy."

The man blinked, and then his legs stretched to the floor.

Later, outside the entrance to shaft three a foreman, his round spectacles and clothes coated with dust, yelled, "Hey Orville, got a minute?" The foreman placed an index finger against the side of his nose and snorted out white residue, then repeated the snort on the other nostril. He pointed to a short thin Negro walking away from the tunnel. Dust had turned the worker's clothes and skin white. "That's him, Orville, Frog they call him. Been working for me about a month. This morning he worked an hour then asked me for another job. There ain't no other job. I need drillers to meet my schedule. We're drilling through solid rock – if we don't make twenty-two feet there's hell to pay. I'm the guy what pays. And I got nobody to take Frog's place."

Shuffling away from the tunnel, Frog stopped each few steps to take a deep breath.

"I'll see what I can do." Orville jogged to catch up with Frog.

"Hey Frog, you're heading in the wrong direction."

"No sir. My feet is aimed right. Ain't going back in there."

Frog's deep baritone voice didn't fit his small body. His large eyes bulged as if they wanted to escape their sockets.

"You're a driller, Frog. The tunnel's got to get dug. You're part of it."

"I want a different job."

"Nowhere else to work, Frog." Orville put his hands on Frog's shoulders and gently nudged him around to face the tunnel's entrance. "You got to go back to work. Or quit."

Frog stood immobile. "Boss man, the nipper, the boy what brought drill bits to me, he was my friend, Eli." Frog's lower lip began to quiver. He pressed his upper teeth on it until the movement stopped. "Yesterday at quitting time Eli was standing next to me. We shut down the drill and he walked over to pick up his lunch poke." As if Frog had lost the air from his lungs, he gulped three deep breaths and then wheezed, "There was a boom as loud as judgment day. Eli laid flat on his back, all covered with rock 'cept for his head."

"His head was above the rock?"

"No, his head rolled over to the boots of the next driller and laid there. His eyes was open, looking up. I once heard tell a man's eyes work for a minute or so after his head's cut off." Frog took a deep breath. "You suppose Eli looked at us and wondered, 'Where'd my body go?' I stared at his head like I thought it'd get up and go find its body. A fella brought a burlap bag and put Eli's head in it. Then they laid Eli's body on a rail car and sat that bag on his belly."

"I'm sorry about Eli. Those things happen, Frog. The tunnel's a dangerous place. A man's got to be careful."

"Careful? Bossman, he was just picking up his lunch poke."

"Sorry, Frog, but you'll have to go to work or quit."

"I need the money for my mamma back home. Please, find me something else to do."

"You know what my buddy Deputy McCloud would say?" Orville put his hand on his holstered black jack, "'Me and Billy here got a job to do. Nothing personal, but Billy, he's my partner. We get the job done.'" Orville looked Frog in the eye. "That's what Deputy McCloud would say."

Frog lowered his head, "I seen Deputy McCloud's partner do his work on Hardware."

Orville walked alongside Frog as he shuffled back to the tunnel. The foreman stood in the shaft entrance, hands on his hips, red-faced, and yelled at Frog, "Boy, I'm docking your pay one hour – you just cost yourself twenty-five cents."

Eli just reached for his lunch and it cost him his life. A board fell from a crane and almost killed a man. Dry drilling – in the tunnel men breathed its dust. And every afternoon Orville blew white dust from his nose.

The week passed quickly – rounds of the shanties; coffee at the mess hall; dinners at the Bridge View. On Wednesday evening, he sat on the front porch and enjoyed a talk with Mrs. Jimison.

Orville returned from work on Saturday to find a pink envelope addressed to him in Bertie's handwriting on the silver tray in the foyer. Maybe she'd replied to the letter he'd posted on Monday. Near the end of it he'd written, "Last weekend you seemed different, like your thoughts were somewhere else. I wondered if you'd been sick. Or," and the rest of the letter concerned him, "maybe me being gone is setting wrong things in motion. One thing's for sure though, our loving on Saturday night sure surprised me. The more I think about it the more I like the new way we did it – a far cry from what you always said the Bible told us to do (joke)."

Twice he extended his hand to pick up the envelope, but stopped.

A feather duster in her hand, Pansy walked from the dining room into the foyer. "Mr. Orr, you got a letter." She picked up the envelope and handed it to him.

Upstairs in his room, Orville slit the envelope and removed two folded pink pages.

"Dear Orville..." Bertie always wrote, "Dear Orvie." His hand shook.

"Last week two boys in Kettle was struck down by polio. One of them, Harry and Myrtle Keefer's boy, died. His lungs seized up. There's a ban on public meetings, like when the Spanish flu struck. Count your blessings and stay away from Kettle." She described events at church and the alter flowers. Then she repeated her polio warning and asked him to stay in Gauley Bridge. She closed the letter, "Alberta." He read the ending again. It didn't say, "Love, Bertie." Alberta – she hadn't called herself that in years.

Possibly he read too much into her words, or the absence of them. She probably felt the way he hoped she would, just didn't write it. After all, they had made love Saturday night. And Sunday morning at breakfast she seemed happy.

Orville walked to the window. Like a trumpet, Bertie's words from long ago sounded. "Get one thing clear, Orville, I say what I mean. Always have, always will." She'd repeated those words many times over the years; sometimes in anger, sometimes to signal the strength of her convictions. His stomach knotted.

He walked downstairs, out the front door, and down the hill to the Bridge View. He went to the furthest booth and seated himself facing the café's back wall. No people or conversation, not tonight. Alone, he wanted to be alone. He muttered to himself, "That's all I want."

Armen's voice startled him. "Sorry Orville, I missed what you said you wanted." She smiled. Her white teeth sparkled against her tan face.

"Uh…I'll have the blue plate special. And sweet tea."

"Don't you want to know what the special is?"

"Doesn't matter."

Armen's smile vanished. She walked to the kitchen.

A few minutes later she served him two fried pork chops, mashed potatoes and applesauce. He left his food untouched for nearly twenty minutes.

"Not hungry, Orville? I can take it back. Maybe get you something else?"

"Mmm. No, I mean yes, I'll eat. Just thinking about a few things." With the tines of his fork he built a canal in the mashed potatoes; gravy meandered into the applesauce. The Bridge View's special couldn't replace Bertie's Saturday evening supper. But he'd gladly replace Bertie's scowls with Armen's smiles. He felt lucky to be here and have a job. But being here had a cost. Lonely nights. And dust in his eyes and teeth.

When he left the restaurant dusk had fallen. Orville sauntered along Main Street, its gas lamps lit. He paused in front of store window displays – pocket watches; shirts and pants for men, blouses for ladies; kitchen stoves; furniture and radios. Unlike Kettle, where many of the stores had closed, Gauley Bridge merchants seemed to be holding their own. The tunnel had brought people and wages to town.

His thoughts drifted to Saturday night; he and Bertie sat in the living room and listened to the radio. The radios in the store window – what does a new Philco cost? How many pennies had Bertie saved?

He walked quickly to the store with radios in its front window. Emerson, Atwater Kent, Philco. The Philco Baby Grand Cathedral, Model 20, that's the one at home. The tag read, "$49.50 plus tubes." $49.50 plus tubes? Even if Bertie got her radio a little cheaper...that's a lot of pennies. And at five dollars a day...that's a lot of work. $49.50 burrowed into him. Then inside began to kick him and laugh, and call him a fool.

In front of town hall he sat on a bench. Inner voices debated the radio – where had it come from? Some voices defended Bertie. Others attacked her; told him that anyone with half a brain could plainly see there had to be someone else, someone who could give her an expensive radio. "Hey Orville, where do you think that new way of love-making came from?" one voice said.

The clock in front of the bank struck eight. He walked slowly up the hill to Mrs. Jimison's. Undulating music of cicadas filled the warm air, always loudest where he walked. The scent of roses perfumed the air.

He climbed the porch's steps. Mrs. Jimison stood in the foyer, her silhouette outlined by the warm glow of the lamp behind her. He'd talk to her about the radio.

Then suddenly he had to see Bertie. Bertie! To hell with the tunnel. If things seemed right with her, he'd come back tomorrow. Or maybe he'd stay a day or two. He laughed, it would be like old times. He ran to his Ford, jumped in, and drove away. First Charleston, then Kettle, home – and Bertie's arms.

Shortly after midnight Orville pulled into the driveway alongside his darkened home. He shut off the engine and sat in the stillness of the night. Bertie had probably gone to bed. No, a dim light shone from the kitchen window; on its other side, movement.

He tiptoed up the back porch steps. Should he make a little noise or surprise her? His right hand gripped the banister along the steps. A step creaked; he raised his foot to the one above. He placed his hand on the knob of the back door and through the glass panes glimpsed Bertie's blonde hair and the back of her blue robe. A broad smile on his face, he thrust the door open. "Surprise, Bertie!"

She gasped.

As if the robe possessed a magic power, a man appeared on its other side. He removed his hands from beneath the robe and jerked a step backwards, his shirt unbuttoned, his face flushed.

No, this couldn't…Bertie… his guts wrenched.

Bertie cinched her robe. "Orville – what're you…" She smoothed her hair. "We were just talking…" Her face paled. She clutched the neck of the robe, her knuckles white.

Orville's lips moved, but he had neither breath nor voice.

The man, muscular, dark hair, looked familiar. He grabbed his coat from the countertop, "I'd best be going," and moved quickly towards the door.

That voice – Hack Shamsford – Orville lunged at him and, off balance, swung his fist. "Damn you!" His fist glanced off the man's shoulder.

Shamsford ran out the door and disappeared into the darkness.

Bertie cried, "No, stop!"

Orville took a step backwards and leaned against the doorframe. The room bent like an amusement park's house of mirrors.

Her face now red, eyes wide and mouth strained, Bertie yelled, "What's the idea of barging in here in the middle of the night? I got my rights."

"Your rights?"

She shouted, "You come to snoop on me?"

"He…what's…what the hell's going on?"

Her voice as cold as January, Bertie asked, "You staying or leaving, Orville?"

Orville whispered, "The radio," and then yelled, "He's where you got the radio!"

"You're talking crazy."

"He bought you that radio. God damn…and I listened to it." His voice rose, "And in bed – you put your rump up for him, Bertie?"

"What's got into you, Orville?" Bertie stomped and yelled, "I told you, I bought that radio. Don't call me a liar!" Then more quietly, "Hack's a friend come to talk."

Orville picked up the tumbler on the counter top and sniffed it. "There's liquor in this glass. Did he drink out of it?"

"What of it?"

Orville threw the glass like a baseball. It hit the distant wall and shattered.

Bertie screamed, "Out of here, Orville! Out of here or I'm going to the police!" She placed both hands against his chest and pushed him. "Out!" she yelled, then again.

He knocked her hands away, "Damn you!" Suddenly he needed air; space, he wanted space. He turned and rushed out the back door. Then no, he wanted to unload his loneliness and his hurt, give back the pain she'd delivered. He whirled and grasped the doorknob as the deadbolt clicked.

He pounded on the door, "Open up, Bertie!"

Silence inside.

"Why'd you do it, Bertie, why?"

Orville stood on the back porch's top step and took deep breaths. He negotiated the stairs as if the slightest misstep might drop him into an abyss. After starting the Ford's engine he sat immobile, his hands tight around the steering wheel. The light in the kitchen window went out, and then, like a bird flown to a higher branch, reappeared in the window of the upstairs bedroom, his bedroom. Did that room and that bed now belong to Hack?

He drove along Maple Street. "If I don't know where I'm going, one direction is as good as another." In the center of Kettle a deserted Main Street yawned at him, each storefront's plate glass window dark as a cave. Then he drove along Rt. 42 towards Charleston.

The return trip to Gauley Bridge seemed to be seven hundred, not seventy, miles. In his headlights' glow first Bertie, then Hack Shamsford, appeared, disappeared, and reappeared as if on a motion picture screen.

"Damn you!" Orville yelled. Twice he caught himself swerving to strike the images.

After leaving Charleston his eyes burned; his eyelids stuck to their rims. When the right front wheel dropped off the road he bolted upright, then stopped. In the darkness close by a dog barked.

At 4 AM Orville's Ford rolled into Gauley Bridge. He parked in front of Mrs. Jimison's house. The foyer's gas lamp cast a cold blue glow.

In his bedroom his gaze fell on the laundry bag of dirty clothes he'd planned to take home. He stared at the bag as if he'd met an old friend who needed help then and there. Who'll wash and iron these clothes? That's what he had to figure out, who would do it? The laundry bag suddenly loomed, large. The Chinese laundry beside the Bridge View had done his clothes a few times, he could take them there. Or, could he find a place where he could wash the clothes? The river?

He shed his shirt, pants and shoes, and fell into bed. But his thoughts remained on the laundry bag, as if life had soiled itself, crawled into that bag and now begged for help. Forty-five minutes later he lay awake, near a decision – the Chinese laundry, he would take his clothes there. But what if the laundry couldn't remove all of the stains? Bertie'd had that problem when he'd last taken laundry home.

Bertie!

Her name dropped into his consciousness like a rock thrown into a quiet pond. Ker-plunk, splash! Waves of her scent spread over him. His gut wrenched as he again saw the blue robe with Hack's arms inside it. Could he will the image away?

The soft comfort of his bed at home, Bertie's long body next to him, her breasts folded into his chest. He stroked the smooth skin of her back. She placed her hand against his cheek. Bertie's hand gently moved the length of his body, touched and stroked him in her special way. Then his hand moved as if Bertie, not he, controlled it. And he gasped.

Dog Days

ONDAY MORNING – muggy air and a pink dawn; the bed sheet
wrapped sweat around him. Soon after he'd gotten dressed, sweat
glued Orville's shirt to his back. August. Dog days.

He joined Billy Webster, Howard, and Lloyd in the dining room.
They exchanged greetings, except for Lloyd who stared at his bacon and
eggs. Her forehead beaded with sweat, Pansy carried a plate of hot biscuits
into the dining room. When she leaned over to place it on the table her
hip brushed Lloyd's shoulder. Lloyd put his hand on the back of her leg
and moved it over the smooth curve of her butt.

Pansy gasped and bolted erect. She glared at Lloyd and tipped the
plate's rim, dropping the hot biscuits into his lap. The biscuits rolled on
the floor.

Lloyd spoke through a mouth full of scrambled eggs, "I hear Pansy's
man works day shift at the tunnel. Maybe if he got transferred to nights
she'd have a little free time. I mean, I got money, it wouldn't have to be
free time."

Eyes wide, Pansy blurted, "You, you…" She tossed the plate on the
table and rushed out of the room.

Howard, Billy Webster and Orville sat erect. Orville's fork slipped
from his hand, its clatter on his plate the only sound in the room.

In a firm tone Howard said, "Your hand was in the wrong place,
Lloyd."

"Pansy had better be careful. I got ways."

"Howard's right, Lloyd," Orville said.

Billy Webster, seated beside Lloyd, his high-pitched voice a contrast to the others, smiled uneasily, "Easy, fellows. It's a hot morning. Quarrelsome kind of day." He picked up the still-hot biscuits from the floor and placed them on the serving plate. He brushed and blew on one, then slathered butter on it and took a bite.

Howard said, "A little dirt, that won't hurt."

Billy Webster smiled, "You're in good form, Howard, even early in the morning."

Orville ate his eggs, glanced at Lloyd, and wondered what went on in the man's head.

Lloyd gazed at the dining room wall. As if speaking to it, he said, "Maybe them that's so interested in Pansy's welfare ought to tell her I'm the timekeeper. Men get paid what I say is owed." His lips spread into a thin grin, "Pansy should be a little nicer to me."

ORVILLE STOOD OUTSIDE the last shack on his rounds. He wiped sweat from his brow, tapped his black jack against the door and entered. He recoiled at the stench of sweat and unwashed bodies. Images of the war, hot tents, dead bodies, and decay leaped into his thoughts. He stepped out the door, took a deep breath, and re-entered.

Four stacks of bunks, each three layers high, lined the walls, empty but for one. In the center bunk of the stack to his right, a small lump of a man lay under a blanket, his breathing labored. When the man spoke his words slid on top of wheezes. "I'm sick," he paused and inhaled, "boss man."

"That you, Frog?"

"Uh-huh."

Frog's body had little more bulk than a few stones beneath the blanket. Like everything in the shanty, the blanket wore a patina of white dust. Frog's large eyes, red-rimmed, had sunk into his skull. Arms over his chest, Frog's fingers gripped his ribs.

"You have to go to work, Frog."

"Huh-uh. Can't."

"Eli's dead and gone, Frog. Time to go to work."

"Nothing to do with Eli – it's something in me, bossman." He pointed to his ribs, "In here, it hurts when I breathe. Bad." He gulped air and winced. "Can't get my breath."

"You been to the doctor?"

"Yes sir. Told me I had tunnelitis. Give me them little black pills, same ones he hands out to everybody. They tastes like candy. Don't help me none, though; don't help nobody."

"I'm under orders to clear the shanty, Frog. You're not allowed to lie here all day."

"I can't move."

"Okay, Frog. Rest awhile. Then go see the doctor."

He walked to his car. He'd done what they paid him to do. Behind him a door slammed and, unsteadily, Frog left the shanty. If Frog didn't go to the doctor, or didn't go to work, Orville didn't want to know.

AT THE END of the day shift, Orville drove past the entrance to shaft one. A large group of workers, mostly colored, stood below a wide flat boulder. He stopped and stepped out of his car. On top of the boulder Hardware Washington strode back and forth. He waved his arms and yelled, "Workers're sick. Some've died. We need good doctors. And coloreds do the same work as whites – what about us getting paid the same?" Then he sang the song he and Bullhead had heard that night on their way to the craps game,

> You will eat, bye and bye,
> In that glorious land above the sky;
> Work and pray, live on hay,
> You'll get pie in the sky when you die.

Lloyd Sykes glanced from face to face and wrote in a small notebook.

Hardware Washington, the man Bullhead had hit with his blackjack at the craps game. Same last name as Pansy – her man?

Bullhead ran through the crowd to the boulder and scrambled up its back side. "Shut up, Hardware! Get your ass off this rock!" He swung his blackjack as Hardware leaped from the boulder. He ran into the woods.

Bullhead roared, "You men want to keep your jobs? Get the hell out of here. Now! Before I start taking names." Muttering, the men dispersed.

Orville approached Bullhead. "What was that all about?"

"I knew they'd be here sooner or later. Damn! I knew it."

"Who?"

"United Mine Workers, but I couldn't prove it. Thought we taught the UMW a lesson at Blair Mountain. I reckon Hardware's working for 'em. I guess we got to teach those boys another lesson."

MORE AUGUST DAYS of heat and little rain; days filled with dust and sweat. Each evening when Orville returned from work his gaze fell on the silver tray in the foyer. If an envelope lay in the tray, his heart raced. But they bore other men's names.

Three weeks passed. Then on a Saturday afternoon, hope again rising, he checked the tray. Empty. For the first time he allowed the possibility that he'd not permitted himself to think about – there would be no letter. Not now, not ever. Like a cobra, a final thought sprung at him. Hack Shamsford would take over Bertie and his bed, too.

He walked to his room, lay down and thought of Bertie; their years together, lives now split apart. The void he'd felt after his daddy's, then his mom's, deaths spread through him. He got up. Out, he had to go out. He muttered, "Do something, anything." He walked down the hill to the Bridge View.

A tall fan near the kitchen moved the aroma of brown gravy through the café. White script on the long mirror behind the counter announced the special, "ground beef patty, squash and mashed potatoes, apple pie."

When Armen asked what he'd have, Orville pointed to the mirror and nodded. A few minutes later she returned with his meal. Later she served him a slice of apple pie and smiled. "Orville, it's Saturday night in Gauley Bridge. Got any plans?"

He shrugged. Plans? "No. But thanks for asking." Do something. Anything. "Bulldog Drummond is playing at the movie house." Without enthusiasm he added, "Could go see it, I suppose. Billy Webster went last night, liked it. Ronald Coleman plays *Bulldog Drummond*."

Armen grinned, "Bet you I could fall in love with Ronald Coleman."

"Loving somebody is nice." He gave a weak smile, "Don't know if

Ronald Coleman would fall in love with you, Armen. But I'll wager he'd love that dime you'd pay to see his movie."

Armen playfully put her hand on his shoulder. "Maybe he'd love me more than that dime, Orville." They laughed.

After she walked into the kitchen, Orville realized that he had laughed. He couldn't remember the last time. It felt good. He finished his apple pie.

When Armen removed his plate, Orville took a deep breath and then said, "I'm going to go see that Ronald Coleman movie. Want to come along? My treat." Then, so rapidly his words tripped over each other, "I'll wait. We could catch the second show."

"Thank you, Orville." Armen gave a bright smile and her dark eyes flashed. The smile ended. "Truth is I have to get home. My daddy isn't doing so well. A month ago the doctor at the tunnel told him he had tunnelitis. Gave him some black pills. Daddy doesn't want to take them. I have to make sure he does."

"I understand. I'll go by myself, which is what I would've done anyway. I hope your daddy feels better. He's lucky to have you to take care of him."

"Thanks."

Walking home Orville relived the movie. Bulldog Drummond, a rich former British army officer, wanted a cause to fight for. Not for the fighting itself, but for opportunities to help people, to do battle for them. And that good-looking girl, her father trapped against his will in a nursing home, gave him that opportunity.

For him Hawks Nest had become a cause, a war to fight. Drilling a tunnel through solid rock, that's a battle for sure; Union Carbide against Gauley Mountain. He walked past a store window and glanced at his tall sandy-haired image. He smiled at the foolishness of imagining himself as Bulldog Drummond. But sometimes he helped people. An inner voice asked, "What about Frog, did you help him?"

Orville meandered along the dark street then up the hill. In the distance a woman walked towards him. Soon he recognized her: Mrs. Jimison.

"This is a surprise, Orville, a nice end to a long walk. It's been a couple of weeks...no it's been longer than that, since I've seen you."

"Good to see you too, Mrs. Jimison. I've been keeping pretty much to myself."

"And I've been visiting friends in Charleston. Well, doing a little business, too."

"I hit a rough patch in the road. For a while I figured I wouldn't be very good company for anybody."

Mrs. Jimison gave a sympathetic laugh. "Orville, you may feel that way, but you're always good company. Let's sit on the porch. I'll get us some sweet tea."

She returned with two tall frosty glasses, handed one to him then sat opposite him at the other end of the wicker davenport. They sipped their tea.

Mrs. Jimison placed her glass on the table in front of them. Her voice floated in the warm night air, "A few weeks ago, Orville, I saw you return home on Saturday evening. Then you ran to your car and drove away. If that was part of the rough patch you spoke about, I hope nothing terrible happened." She paused then added, "I'm not asking you to tell me about it. Just trying to say," she laughed, "and not doing that very well, that I hope whatever it was ...that now you're all right."

If her words could fill a pillow he'd rest his head on it. "Well, I wouldn't say it's all right, Mrs. Jimison. But things are settled. And I'm all right, more or less."

"Settled is usually better than unsettled, even when I don't care for the way things turn out. At least I know where I stand."

"True for me too, I guess. The rough patch had to do with my learning that I'm alone. That my wife Bertie is gone."

"I'm sorry."

"But I've got a nice place to live. And a job. Lots of folks don't."

"Alone? Are you really alone, Orville?"

Until today he had avoided that question. Had he known the answer all along and not wanted to face it, not with Mrs. Jimison, not with anyone? Since the night he drove to Kettle and back, nothing had come from Bertie. Nothing.

"That Saturday night, I knew I had to see Bertie. To find out the truth about me and her." Then his words came with the speed of the New River after a heavy rain. He told Mrs. Jimison about Bertie's letter, how she had signed it, about his trip home. The robe and the radio, and Bertie's keeping distance between them, even in bed.

He leaned back and took a long drink of sweet tea. "When I got to Kettle I wanted to surprise her. But I discovered that she wasn't alone." His hands shook. He clasped them together and told Mrs. Jimison about what had happened in the kitchen. "Each day when I've come back from work I've looked for a letter. That tray in the entryway has pulled my eyes like a magnet. But there's been none." He took a deep breath. "I'm thankful the magnet is starting to lose its power."

They sat quietly. Then Mrs. Jimison said, "I know that feeling. After Dan died my days became dark. Life had been unfair, I told myself. Sleep was all I wanted. Sometimes I stayed in bed all day. At night my memories would light the darkness and sleep wouldn't come." She paused and sipped her tea. "Eventually I accepted what had happened. Life rolled on. I had to make a decision to roll with it, or get rolled over by it. After I converted this place into a rooming house, my life changed for the better."

Glasses empty, they stood. Orville handed Mrs. Jimison his glass. She rested her hand on his and gazed at him.

She had once hugged him. He wanted her to do it again. She took his glass and released his hand. "Good night, Orville." She walked into the foyer, Orville a few steps behind her.

Then she abruptly turned and wrapped her arms around him. "Thank you, Orville, thank you for listening," she whispered.

He breathed her scent.

She ended the hug with a squeeze and said a soft "Good night." She walked through the dining room to the kitchen.

In bed Orville relived the evening. Armen, the movie, his conversation with Mrs. Jimison. He closed his eyes and sleep drifted over him.

Squeaks of the bedroom door's hinges awakened him. He bolted upright. In the darkness a tall form approached. He'd left his blackjack on the dresser. He braced to defend himself.

"It's me, Orville," Mrs. Jimison whispered.

She removed her robe, lifted the sheet, lay down, and extended her naked body alongside him.

In a halting voice he whispered, "I don't know what to ...you feel..."

She placed a finger on his lips. "Shhh." She kissed him. "A gift, Orville, a one-time gift." Her hands moved slowly over his body. "Not a word. Not now, not ever." Her tongue played lightly across his lips then her lips opened into a passionate connection.

Later they lay in silence and drifted into sleep.

Orville awakened. When he began to speak Mrs. Jimison's finger tips again touched his lips. "Shhh." She whispered, "A gift for you...and for me."

The hinges on the bedroom door signaled her departure.

A Cold Wind

SEPTEMBER BROUGHT BRIGHT, warm, and ever shorter days. Some mornings after his rounds of the shanties high on Gauley Mountain, Orville paused at the Hawks Nest overlook. Far below wisps of mist rose above the river like ghosts, apparitions that would disappear as the sun's rays lit the gorge. The first brilliant orange and red leaves colored the mountains. In the waning days of summer the leaves seemed determined to prolong the season, clinging to their branches like children afraid to leave home.

A week after his late-night visit from Mrs. Jimison, Orville returned from work to find her waiting in the foyer, face drawn and wearing a long black dress.

"Orville, I'm glad to see you."

"Thanks. Nice to see you too."

In a matter-of-fact voice she said, "I'll be leaving, Orville. I'm taking a train to Richmond. Tonight."

"I hope you'll be back soon."

"I doubt that I will. There's family business I must take care of."

"I see…I mean, I'll miss you."

"No, Orville, don't miss me. Just get on with your life." She turned to a vase on the foyer table and straightened the stems of its yellow and crimson zinnias. "Pansy will take care of things while I'm gone. I'm confident she'll do well." She turned to him and extended her hand.

Her touch transported him to the night of her visit to his room.

She patted his hand, then turned and walked briskly through the dining room.

He walked to the front porch and dropped on to the davenport where they'd sat the night she came to his bed. What happened to the woman he knew that night? How far away it seemed. And Bertie? A lifetime ago. He imagined himself a passenger in a hot air balloon rising ever higher into a dark sky.

THE DAYS OF AUTUMN dragged along, each morning another roust of workers then coffee with Bullhead. Indian summer's mix of bright days and soft autumn light continued into early November. Orville smiled at Mother Nature's deception – pretending she might allow summer to stay for the winter. But each day she pushed shadows at ever sharper angles up the mountains.

At noon the second Wednesday in November, a lead-gray line of clouds spread across the distant horizon, skirted the tops of mountains, and rushed towards Hawks Nest. The line became a tufted black blanket and soon covered the sky. Then a wet frigid wind blasted through the mountains, flushing away the warm air. Orville shivered. He wished he'd brought a jacket to work.

Late that afternoon Orville and Bullhead met for coffee at the mess hall. Bullhead extended his hands over the cast iron stove and rubbed them together. "Seventy-five degrees this morning, Orv. Now it feels like somebody threw a switch and sent us a trainload of winter. Must be near freezing."

Men in the work camps substituted layers of shirts for winter coats they didn't own and scurried into the forest for firewood. The small cast-iron stoves in the shanties had been designed for coal. "Twenty-five cents a bucket – that's an hour's pay," a worker said to Orville. Ten hour work days lengthened as the men chopped wood until darkness then chopped again in the early morning. But the plank walls of the shanties leaked heat. Within a few days an outbreak of flu spread through the camps. Bullhead said six men had died, "But," he laughed, "this wasn't nothing like the Spanish Flu."

A week later, Bullhead met Orville at the completion of his morning rounds. "Orville, can you take a little walk with me? I need to ask you something."

They walked to the crest of a knoll. A few steps beyond them it sloped into a steep decline then dropped sharply. Before them spread the expanse of the gorge. Behind them the tin roofs of the shanties matched the gray clouds that touched the tops of distant mountains. To their right, a foot trail led from the shanties to the edge of the gorge and became a path that descended along the switchbacks of an old logging trail. Workers walked the path to the tunnel and ten hours later tread it up the mountain.

The two men gazed at tiny men and machines in motion far below them. Orville said, "A snake's mouth poking out of Gauley Mountain, that's what the opening down there looks like. So hungry it swallows railroad tracks, men, dinkeys, even steam shovels."

"Uh-huh." Bullhead grunted a half-laugh and cleared his throat. He looked towards the path and when he spoke he kept his eyes on it. "There's something that needs to be done, Orv. If you can see your way clear to do it, there's a little money in it. For you."

"I'm all for earning money." Orville gave a half-smile, "What do I have to do?"

Bullhead turned to Orville. "A man over yonder in that pine grove," he pointed to the trees beyond the shanties, "he needs a ride to Summersville."

"I know how to get to Summersville."

"He needs to go to Mr. E.T. Sprigg's place of business. I'm wondering if you might carry him there after work. I'll give you the address."

"Sounds all right to me. I've got a Ford and time on my hands. You say there's money for my carrying him over there?"

Bullhead shuffled his right foot and looked away. "Mmmm, uh-huh."

"Sounds good. What's the pay?"

"Uh," Bullhead shifted his weight from one foot to the other. In a rising voice that asked more than it answered Orville's question, he replied, "Five dollars."

"Five dollars – that's a day's pay! I thought you said I was carrying a man to Summersville. Sounds like I'm hauling valuables. Who's Mr. Sprigg?"

"Valuables?" Bullhead laughed and the crimson of his face deepened. He gazed across the valley. "What we're facing here, Orv, is kind of similar to the army. Remember over in France, the Germans shot at us? Shot to kill. And how we done the same thing?"

"Nobody forgets that."

"And men died."

Orville nodded.

"Well, that's sort of what we got here. Men are battling against Gauley Mountain. Drilling and blasting a tunnel through her. And ol' Gauley fights back. In the fight, men die. Remember those two colored boys last week in that dynamite blast?"

"I remember."

"And now a man has died from what Doc Henderson says is tunnelitis."

"Tunnelitis? Armen said her daddy has it. What is it?"

"Doc says it's a lung problem. Caused by a man being too long in the underground dark and damp. Then not taking care of his self. Maybe drinking too much and not getting enough sleep. Doc says it resembles a combination of the flu and TB. Gets down in the lungs. Clogs the passages."

Orville said, "I've seen lots of men with trouble breathing." But Armen's daddy didn't drink too much or go to Bullhead's gambling shanty. Neither did a lot of other men sick with tunnelitis.

Bullhead spoke like an army sergeant giving a briefing. "Here's the situation, Orv. A colored worker got sick, tunnelitis, and disappeared in the night. Early this morning a couple of men found him laying over there in the pines. Dead. Could've been a heart attack, could've been tunnelitis. Hard to say. They wrapped him in a tarpaulin – he's still there. I'm asking if you'll take his body to Mr. Sprigg over in Summersville. He's the undertaker hired by the company. Five dollars for the trip."

"Anybody I know?"

"I doubt it. Not sure of his name myself. One nigger looks like another. Most aren't from around here. Far as we know, most has got no families. Course, the company wants to do the right thing for a death in the line of duty. We'll give him a dignified burial." Bullhead raised his voice and jabbed his index finger at Orville, "And the company will do the same for any man that dies, colored or white. You can hold me to that."

"You remember the duty the captain assigned me in France?"

"Sure. And I told the big boys upstairs what you done over there. That's why we're talking right now. They was impressed – asked me to ask you about doing it again. Authorized me to offer you money." Bullhead looked down the gorge and then turned to Orville. "The way I figure it, Orv, this is sort of like the army. Only difference is, instead of transporting bodies to Flanders you'll drive 'em to Summersville." Bullhead pointed his index finger at Orville, "And the company pays a damn sight better than the army."

He'd sworn to do his duty – first to the army, then to Sheriff Conley – and he'd do it.

Driving to lunch Orville stopped at the entrance to shaft one. A large crowd of workers and foremen, as well as Billy Webster Riddle and Lloyd Sykes, had gathered near the rock crusher. In silence men moved aimlessly and stared at the big machine, as if waiting for it to say or do something

Orville walked to the front of the crowd.

Baseball bat by his side and a scowl on his face, Ermil Dothan said, "Orville – about time the authorities showed up. Though there ain't a damn thing you can do now."

"What happened?"

"Parts of a man come out of the rock crusher. He must've fell into a gondola down in the tunnel and got hauled out in a load of rocks. When the load went into the crusher he went in with them."

Orville winced.

"One feller said he thought he heard a man scream when the shovel lifted the load to the crusher. Could have been him."

"Good Lord!"

"Look yonder." Ermil pointed his bat towards the mound of crushed rocks and sand daubed with traces of red beneath the crusher. "I think that there's his hand. The rest of him, if there's anything left, may still be in there. We've shut down the machine. One of the colored boys will climb in and take a look." Ermil stared at the towering machine, then turned towards a departing train, its gondolas loaded with crushed rock. He pointed his bat at the train, "Could be he's already on his way to Boncar."

Billy Webster approached Orville and Ermil. His voice trembled. "Who was it? Let's make sure he gets a decent burial."

"Billy Webster, you want to have a funeral to bury a hand?" Ermil asked sarcastically. "Somebody told me his name was Hardware – Hardware Washington."

"Isn't he the man Bullhead ran off the rock, an organizer for the UMW?" Billy Webster asked.

Orville recalled the craps game that first night. Hardware, the man Bullhead taught a lesson with his blackjack. Pansy's man?

Lloyd Sykes, standing behind Billy Webster, said, "UMW." He smiled. "Wonder if they'll send another one to take his place. Hope so."

In France Orville had fought and killed the enemy – German soldiers. Men came to Hawks Nest to make a living, not become enemies. He wondered how far Lloyd would go to do the company's bidding, or his own.

THAT EVENING ORVILLE AND BULLHEAD lay the canvas wrapped body from the woods in the rear seat of Orville's Ford. The corpse carried the rot of death. Once he began the trip to Summersville, the night air carried away some of death's odor. The corpse's legs sloped off the seat to the floor, shoulders and back flat on the seat. The road's first few miles followed the course of the Gauley River, its rapids alternating with quiet pools of water. Then it made a sharp turn and followed switchbacks up the mountain to a high plateau. In the middle of a sharp turn, the corpse shifted its position as if to become more comfortable. He imagined the man among soldiers lying lifeless on a battlefield.

The captain looked him in the eye, "This man, these men, will be buried in a military cemetery in Flanders, Sergeant Orr. Your job is to get them there." He saluted the captain, walked to the truck, and slid into the driver's seat.

Six soldiers, their bodies wrapped for burial, lay in the truck's bed, above them olive-drab canvas. All morning the sun had shone directly on the canvas. The space beneath it filled with the putrid odor of death. The training sergeant called it, them, gassy organic compounds – alcohols, degraded proteins, methane, sulfur and more he couldn't remember – all rolled into one sad sickening odor. Like a coiled snake of body tissue, urine, blood and feces, it waited inside every man for the moment to strike, to become the putrid smell of death.

When the truck hit potholes Orville muttered, "Sorry, boys." One of the soldiers, Jimmy Campbell, might not be taking this ride if Orville had spoken up when the captain ordered the eighteen year-old soldier on that mission. He knew that whoever did it would not come back. But he remained silent and obeyed orders. Jimmy died with his head in Orville's lap and his guts spilling out of him.

Now Orville drove on a mission in a different kind of war. Like Bulldog Drummond, he could help. That fellow stretched out on the seat behind him had died in the line of duty. He'd take him to a decent burial.

In Summersville Orville parked in front of a two-story white frame building. The gilded letters on the large black sign above the front door announced E.T. Sprigg and Sons Funeral Home. He knocked on the door.

A tall man in a black suit opened the door. He had graying brown hair with a small wave in the front. His lined and elongated face seemed to struggle with itself; the corners of his mouth and pale blue eyes pulled down and his eyebrows arched as if to lift his expression up. When he extended his hand to Orville, his mouth curved into a tired smile and his eyebrows flattened, as though their energy had been sucked away by the mouth's effort.

"I'm Orville Orr, from Hawks Nest tunnel."

"Hello. I'm Elam T. Sprigg." His hand, as cold as the passenger in the back seat of the Ford, gripped Orville's hand in a quick squeeze. "I've been expecting you, Mr. Orr. Please deliver the deceased to the rear entrance."

The following week Bullhead twice asked Orville to make a delivery to Mr. Sprigg. Each trip became a drive to Flanders. A week later Bullhead asked twice more. At Flanders Orville had brought along a flask of brandy. He drank it on his return trip. The second week of his deliveries to Mr. Sprigg he brought along a pint of Bullhead's corn liquor and sipped it on his trip back to Gauley Bridge. He began to bring a pint for each delivery's return trip. Half-way to Gauley Bridge he'd feel a glow. Five dollars for the day's work, another five for the delivery; not a bad life for hard times.

One night on Gauley Mountain he missed a turn before a narrow bridge. The Ford crashed through saplings into a near-dry creek bed. Orville's head hit the door frame and a knot rose on his forehead.

After shanty rounds the next morning he met Bullhead at the mess hall for coffee and his delivery pay. When Bullhead saw the bruise on Orville's forehead he laughed. "Orv, you should put in for combat pay."

At noon the next day Bullhead met Orville at the mess hall. At the end of lunch he asked, "After work, can you meet me on the Gauley Bridge side of Gamoca?"

"What's going on?"

"A little business. Got another pick-up for you." Bullhead winked and gave a small laugh. "Feller needs a ride over to Mr. Sprigg's place."

After work Orville stopped at the café for a sandwich and then drove to Gamoca, about two miles up Gauley River. Bullhead had already arrived and parked on the shoulder of the road. Orville parked behind him. Bullhead got out of his truck, stepped on to the Ford's running board and pointed towards a road into the forest, now overgrown with weeds. "Drive over there, Orv, that's where our boy is. On his way to work this morning, one of the workers, a white man, found him."

Orville parked and followed Bullhead through tall weeds. They stood beside the corpse of a tall Negro. The body had been bundled in a tattered army blanket and then wrapped with so much tape that, except for its unwrapped feet, it resembled a mummy. The big toe of the man's right foot protruded through a hole in his socks. Bullhead and Orville carried the corpse, now stiff, to the Ford. They slid him across the back seat. His feet extended through the rear door.

"Reckon I'll have to bend him a little." Bullhead grunted as he turned the body face down. He placed one hand behind the man's knees, the other on his ankles, and applied pressure to fold his legs. They didn't bend. "Don't rightly know how long he'd been laying there. So far off the road he wasn't easy to see." Bullhead studied the corpse for a moment. He placed one hand on the body's left foot, his other behind the knee above it. "Okay,

Orv, you take the other leg. One hand behind his knee, one on his foot. Push."

The legs folded to a near right-angle.

"That oughta do it. He can travel face down as easy as face up. Either way, it's money in your pocket."

Orville parked at the rear entrance to Sprigg's Funeral Home. After two raps, Mr. Sprigg opened the door. "Orville, if it's all the same to you, this time let's leave the deceased in your car. You can follow me to the burial ground. After we finish our work I'm going to my mother's place for dinner."

Surprised, Orville stared at Mr. Sprigg.

Mr. Sprigg chuckled, though neither his eyes nor mouth gave evidence of a smile, "Two cars – we'll have us a little funeral procession. I know it'll take more of your time. There's another dollar in it for you."

"Shouldn't I bring the body in so you can embalm it, or treat it in some way?"

"I usually do that. But this week I've been busy. Had to streamline things."

"Not even wash him? Put on a clean shirt and pants?"

His voice stern, Mr. Sprigg answered, "Orville, we're working under orders here, company orders. This man, these men, haven't any families," he emphasized his words, "and we're doing them a service. A service! Our job is to respectfully inter them." He glared at Orville for a moment, and then his voice softened. "And Mother is expecting me for dinner. She gets upset if I'm late."

Orville turned and walked towards his Ford. His mother expects him for dinner. And, oh yes, by the way, a man is dead.

Orville's Model A followed Mr. Sprigg's dark blue Chrysler first along a gravel road then a muddy road with deep wheel-ruts. Mr. Sprigg honked a warning at a woman in a tattered black coat and gray head scarf walking in the center of the road.

At the edge of a field bordered by a three-strand barbed-wire fence and makeshift gate, Mr. Sprigg stopped. He opened the gate, drove fifty yards into the field and parked.

Mr. Sprigg pointed to a freshly dug grave. "We'll carry the deceased there for burial."

At the gravesite, Mr. Sprigg placed two wide leather straps under the body, one beneath its shoulders and one beneath its still-bent knees. "Good idea, bending the knees. Have to remember that – the knees will nicely grip the straps when we lower him. Should make it easier for us." He laughed, "I'd wager that if his legs were straight, he'd extend beyond the length of this grave. Tall as he is, we'd have to bury him at an angle; could present a problem if coons or foxes got a whiff of him."

Grasping a leather strap in each hand, his legs spread, Mr. Sprigg grunted, "Okay Orville, grab your straps and let's position him over the grave."

Orville tightened and raised his ends of the straps. Then he dropped them. "No prayer or anything like that?"

Mr. Sprigg closed his eyes and sighed. He dropped his straps, stood erect, and clasped his hands in a prayerful pose. "Let us pray." In a sonorous voice, he said, "Lord, we ask your blessings on our humble service, and your mercy on the deceased. Amen."

"Amen."

With a firm grasp on the straps, the two men lifted the body until the straps suspended it above the earth's open mouth. They slowly loosened their grips. The long flat bands of leather drifted through their hands and lowered the body to the grave's bottom.

Orville let go of his straps, Mr. Sprigg pulled on his, and the straps passed under the body; like giant brown worms they climbed to the grave's upper edge. Mr. Sprigg removed a small towel from his coat pocket, wiped the straps, and then coiled them. "Now, Orville, if you'd please take that shovel, let's finish our work."

The first shovelful of earth landed on the blanketed corpse with a muffled thump. Thump, thump, thump until the body had a cover of fresh soil. Then the sound changed to earth falling on earth. No different than filling a hole in a garden. Orville smoothed and rounded the grave's mound.

Mr. Sprigg walked to his car and returned with two thin pieces of unpainted wood joined with twine to form a cross about three feet tall. At the head of the grave he pressed the longer section of the cross into the ground, then pounded it with his shovel until it stood firm.

Orville planted the blade of his shovel in the ground. Across the open field, vines of crown vetch, browned by frost, stood nearly shin-high. Rows of grave-sized mounds, many still raw earth, stretched to the distant fence-line. Each grave had a small cross; some made of thin strips of wood, others with pieces of corn stalks, joined with twine. He pointed to the open field, "You own all this land, Mr. Sprigg?"

"No. Mother does. She leases me a few acres. I may have to ask for more."

"Those graves, are they men from the tunnel?"

"Yep."

"Tunnelitis?"

"Most of them. A few cave-ins," Mr. Sprigg replied. "One colored fellow, buried right there," he waved his hand towards a nearby grave, "lost his head in a roof-fall." He added in a respectful voice, "I taped it to his neck before we buried him." He pulled a dollar bill from his pocket and handed it to Orville. "Before I forget, here's your money."

"That's okay. You don't owe me any extra."

"Orville, work is work. You earned it." He thrust the bill into Orville's hand.

His voice more resembling a student than an undertaker, Mr. Sprigg said, "I've heard that when a man's head is severed, there's enough fresh blood in his brain that he can see and hear for a minute or so." He gestured towards the nearby grave, "I wonder what that fellow saw."

"Maybe the roof of the tunnel. Maybe Frog looking down at him."

"Frog?"

"Fellow he worked with."

"Mmm." Business-like, Mr. Sprigg said, "Well, I must get over to Mother's. I'll probably see you later in the week. Bullhead says workers are dropping like flies," he laughed, "and he's shooing them out of town." He imitated Bullhead, "'They can go and die somewhere's else,' he says." Mr. Sprigg again laughed, "I told him, 'Hey Bullhead, don't ruin my business.'"

"From what I see here, it's a pretty good business. If you don't mind my asking, what's your fee for a burial?"

"My fee has little to do with it. The company pays fifty-five dollars. But that's a lot better than the twenty-five Fayette County pays for indigent burials."

"You just made fifty-five dollars?"

"No. I gave you one, and two dollars each to a couple of grave-diggers."

Behind the men, a colored woman walked at a fast pace across the field. Her shape resembled a miniature haystack. When she reached them she yelled in a shrill voice, "Where's my Joe?"

"Wh-What?" Mr. Sprigg said.

Orville recognized her – the woman walking along the road.

Her voice strained and tears in her eyes, she asked, "My husband, Joe Craddock, where is he? A man at the tunnel said Joe died and you brung him here."

Rising to his full height, Mr. Sprigg said, "Maam, you can be thankful that your husband received a respectful burial. We did what was right."

"I packed his lunch two mornings ago – he went to work and never come home. Now he's underground. It ain't right." She sobbed, "What'd you do, bury him in his work clothes? Is this here his grave?" She sat down on the fresh mound, covered her face with her hands and wept. "Ain't right. You done defiled the dead. And for what – a few pieces of silver? Uh-huh, you men and Judas, do what's right?"

"Mother's waiting. I'd best be going. You can deal with this as you please, Orville. Here, take this." Mr. Sprigg thrust another dollar bill into Orville's hand, walked to his Chrysler, and drove away.

"Can I give you a ride home?" Orville asked Mrs. Craddock.

"I hitch-hiked here. Reckon I can go home the same way."

"It's getting late. There's no traffic out here."

"Keep your ride to yourself. I don't want nothing to do with you and your kind."

Orville got in his car and started the engine.

"Wait." Mrs. Craddock opened the passenger door and got in. "Joe wouldn't want me to walk home."

On the drive to Gauley Bridge, Orville learned from her that five months ago she and Joe had come from Charlotte to Hawks Nest. They rented a coal company house in Gamoca. "Joe kept telling me how lucky we was to have a house and for him to have work. Some luck." She said no more during the trip, other than to give Orville directions to her home.

When she got out of the car, Orville said, "Here, take this. He handed her the two dollars Mr. Sprigg had paid him, and added a five dollar bill.

"I don't want your money." She pushed his hand away. "It's tainted."

"Please, take it."

She stared at the bills. "I don't have any money. Maybe it's a gift from Joe."

Still awake an hour after going to bed, Orville got up and poured himself a half-glass of corn liquor. The liquid burned a path down his throat. He waited for warmth to tingle through his body, and for memories of the burial and Mrs. Craddock's wails to fade.

A Tunnel?

THE FRIDAY BEFORE THANKSGIVING, Orville sat in a booth at the Bridge View. As Armen placed a tall glass of sweet tea in front of him, the glass slipped from her hand, bounced once, and then teetered as if debating whether to lurch into a spill. She reached for the glass and tipped it over. "Ohhh!"

Orville tossed his napkin on the table and spread it over the tea. Armen pulled a small towel from the pocket of her apron and wiped the spill.

Her face crimson, Armen said, "I'm sorry, Orville. So sorry."

"I'll bet there's more sweet tea in the kitchen. Things happen."

"Things have been happening to me. All day. All week." Her voice fell, "All month."

"What's wrong?" He held her gaze.

She spoke hesitantly, as if each word had to be tested. "It's daddy, Orville. He's been sick since the weather snapped cold. And he hasn't gone to work for a week. Most days he won't get out of bed."

"Is he taking meals?"

"Not often. Before I came to work I tried to get him to eat some breakfast, but he wouldn't. He lay in bed, his eyes so sad. And the past few days his breathing has turned shallow. Last night it had a hard sound to it. I don't think he slept."

"I'm sorry, Armen. Maybe he should go see Doc Henderson. The company pays him to look after all of us, including your daddy."

"Right now daddy can hardly walk to the front porch. I've got no way to get him to Doc Henderson."

115

"I could carry him to Doc's office in my Ford. That is if you want me to."

"I could use some help." Armen idly wiped the tabletop. "What are Doc Henderson's office hours?"

"He's there each morning from eight 'til noon. I don't know about afternoons."

"How about tomorrow morning around ten o'clock? We could get daddy to Doc Henderson then back home. And I could be at work by my starting time, two o'clock."

"Should be okay. That's when I usually meet Bullhead for coffee." He grinned, "He can drink coffee by himself. If we can solve one problem, I'll come to your house."

"Problem?"

"I don't know where you live."

Armen smiled. She tore a page from her order pad and sketched a map on it "About a mile up Gauley River to Gamoca, then turn on Burnt Cross road." She placed an X in a small square. "Second house on the left. White frame."

That night, drifting into sleep Orville thought about Armen; the lilt of her voice, the sparkle in her eyes. He imagined holding her close.

The following morning Orville arrived on time at Armen's home. A light dusting of snow had fallen during the night.

Armen met him at the front door. "Thanks for coming."

He glanced around the small living room; maroon linoleum floor, worn blue couch, matching easy chair and a coffee table. Armen led him through the hallway into her daddy's bedroom. A bed and dresser filled the room. Armen's daddy, wearing a white t-shirt and bibbed overalls, lay on top of the covers, his breathing labored. Deep lines etched his weathered face. Red rims circled his dark brown eyes.

"Daddy, this is the man I told you about, Orville Orr. He's going to give us a ride to Doc Henderson's office."

Her daddy slowly raised his hand. "Albert Bodigian," he whispered.

Orville gently shook his hand. "Pleased to meet you, Mr. Bodigian."

"Al," he wheezed, "call me Al." His arm fell to the bed.

After Armen helped her daddy put on a mackinaw, Orville placed one arm under Al's knees, the other behind his back, and carried him to the car. Armen held the Ford's rear door open and Orville sat Al in the back seat. Armen tucked a quilt around his legs.

Orville parked next to Doc Henderson's office, a small addition to the mess hall. Al insisted on walking to the office. Armen held one arm. He shuffled slowly; by the time they entered the office his breathing had become deep wheezes.

In the waiting room straight-backed chairs lined the walls. A short thin woman in a white uniform, a nurse's cap pinned to the back of her head, sat at a small desk. "Hello Mr. Bodigian. You folks set down. Won't be long."

To their right sat a white man with a bandaged arm and beyond him two Negroes who wheezed like Al. The white fellow worked as a dinkey skinner in shaft one, and the Negroes as muckers in shaft two, Al's shaft. The men nodded; he and Al returned their nods. These men wheezed but they didn't carouse late at night at Bullhead's gambling shanty. The pieces in the puzzle didn't fit.

A half-hour later the nurse said, "Mr. Bodigian, the doctor will see you now."

Al rose from his chair. Armen took his arm but he shook off her hand. He walked into the office with Armen a step behind him, her arms extended like a trapeze artist.

A few minutes later they returned. Al clutched a glass bottle of black pills.

Orville stood. Armen whispered, "Tunnelitis, the doctor said." Her eyes filled with tears. "Then he said the same thing he told daddy the last time, 'Get some rest, take these pills.' The same thing." She slowly shook her head. "Daddy asked Doc Henderson, 'When can I go back to work?' But he got no answer."

The nurse smiled and said, "You take your pills, Mr. Bodigian."

Al nodded and walked to the door.

Orville said, "Maybe doc's right. With some rest, he'll get better."

Armen stared at Orville, her face long and somber. Then she gazed at the floor and shook her head.

They returned home. Orville carried Al into the house and laid him on the bed. Armen removed her daddy's shoes and placed the quilt over him. Al raised his hand towards Orville, "Thanks, son."

"You're welcome. Glad to help."

At the front door Orville asked, "See you at the café this evening?"

She gave a wistful smile. "I'll stay with daddy until this afternoon. Then I'll come to work." She paused. "At least my body will. My spirit will be here."

He wished he could comfort her. Al could hardly walk or breathe. Not much good to say about that. The black pills hadn't helped him in the past, no reason to think they would now.

Armen surprised Orville with a gentle hug. She whispered, "Thanks, Orville."

He returned her hug. "I'll see you this evening."

Her smile lingered, "Good."

Driving back to the tunnel he heard her say, "Good," again and again. And he had a date this evening. Well, sort of a date.

At six o'clock Orville entered the café. To his right, empty booths. At the counter Armen served a steaming plate of food to a middle-aged man who sat alone. "Hey, Orville."

"How's your daddy?"

"He ate a little. Took his pills. Promised me he'd sleep."

Orville sat at the counter, an empty stool between him and the customer.

"Having the special?" Orville asked.

The man's bright blue eyes beamed. "Yep, always good."

"I'll have the special too, Armen."

Extending his hand, the man said, "My name's Holbert, Holbert Yancy."

"Orville Orr." They shook hands. Orville's gaze lingered on Holbert's white shirt, blue necktie, and dark blue windbreaker. In the mirror on the wall behind the counter he glanced at his denim jacket and rumpled khaki shirt and wondered if he should dress like Holbert. He could afford it.

"All set for Thanksgiving?"

"All set," Orville lied. He hadn't thought about how to celebrate Thanksgiving away from home – no, he didn't have a home – or how to talk about all the things that make Thanksgiving, well, make it Thanksgiving.

"This time of year I envy people like you," Holbert said, "people with families. I'm alone; spend life on the road; go from one town to another. Thanksgiving in Gauley Bridge will be about like Thanksgiving last year in…where was it?" He stared at his coffee as if it contained the answer. "May have been Charleston. I try to land in a nice town on a holiday. This year it's Gauley Bridge."

Armen served Orville the special, pork chops and mashed potatoes smothered in gravy. "We got something in common, Holbert. I'm away from home this year." Probably away from home next year too, and years to come. He missed his home and he missed Thanksgiving dinner.

The men ate and talked about the weather, then Gauley Bridge. Their conversation drifted to the tunnel. Orville described his duties as deputy sheriff and shack rouster.

Holbert shook his head sidewise like a tethered balloon in a light breeze then spoke softly. "Orville, I'm just a salesman from Roanoke, but I could've helped the men in that tunnel."

"How's that?"

Holbert reached into the pocket of his windbreaker. On the counter he placed a six-inch square of white cloth with single long strands of fabric attached to each of its four corners. He flattened and smoothed the square. "I had what I thought was a bright idea. I got a batch of these masks sewn in Charleston. Figured I could sell them to men working in the tunnel." He handed the mask to Orville. "Early this morning I parked near the entrance to shaft one and set up a little table behind my car. Offered masks to men on their way to work – only a quarter apiece."

Orville inspected the mask. "A quarter? That's an hour's wage to most men."

"Good investment," Holbert broke a biscuit, spooned jam on it and nibbled at the biscuit's edge. "Even though there's not much to them. Just a square of heavy cloth. But if that cloth is tied so it sits in front of a fellow's nose and mouth, it becomes a breathing mask. It'll keep lots of dust out of a man's lungs. Wash it at night then use it again the next day. One mask will last a long time." Holbert sipped his coffee.

"Makes sense. Did you sell many?"

Holbert's brow furrowed. "You kidding? Right after I set up my table, a big red-faced man wearing a star," he pointed at Orville's chest, "like yours, yelled, 'Get the hell away.' A deep croaky voice. When I didn't move fast enough, he waved a pistol at me."

"That must've been Bullhead McCloud. He's the chief deputy."

"Well, whoever he is, he prevented those men from getting some relief."

"Bullhead's trying to do what's right. The company told him, me too, they don't want outsiders hanging around ." Orville took a bite of mashed potatoes then asked, "What's a salesman from Roanoke doing up this way? What sort of products do you sell?"

"Supplies for funeral homes."

"Never thought about that as a line of work. I guess funeral homes get their goods from somewhere, just like any other business. Do you sell caskets?"

"No," Holbert chuckled. "My best-moving product is embalming fluid. I sell some cosmetics, special thread too. The flesh of a deceased person requires careful treatment."

Corpses in the back of an army truck in France; corpses in the back seat of a Ford at Hawks Nest – careful treatment?

They ate in silence.

Orville pushed his plate, still half-full, towards the far side of the counter. "Not long ago I met a fellow in your business, an undertaker over in Summersville. Mr. E.T. Sprigg."

Holbert grinned. "One of my best customers. He's had a run of business over the past four or five months. Don't know what's going on in Summersville. Reminds me of when the Spanish flu hit town."

"Spanish flu, I never thought about it being good for somebody's business."

Holbert smiled. "I'm not proud of it, but the truth is I made a lot of sales during the Spanish flu. They say it's an ill wind that blows no good."

Orville took care to sound as though he wondered about, but didn't know about, what he would next say. "I suppose pneumonia or tunnelitis, whatever sickness is taking its toll on men in the tunnel, could be driving up Mr. Sprigg's business."

"I don't see how. Sprigg's Funeral Home is twenty miles from here. Somebody would have to cart a lot of bodies across the mountain. You think that's what's happening?"

Orville sat up straight and raised his hands, "No, no, not at all." A second later, as if someone had placed a heavy rock on each shoulder, he leaned forward and put his elbows on the counter. Working in the dark of night, keeping secrets he could share only with Bullhead and Mr. Sprigg. He wanted to yell, to Holbert, to Armen, to the couple in the booth, "Me, I'm the one. Orville Orr traffics in dead bodies!"

Holbert looked around as if to make sure he wouldn't be overheard, and then spoke in hushed tones, "I've talked to men in the tunnel and some of the foremen. And I've spent most of my life around mines and underground operations of one kind or another. There's trouble brewing at Hawks Nest tunnel."

"Trouble? What kind of trouble?"

"Well, I know this much. Ninety percent of the time there's no water coming through those drills. I got to admit, dry drilling is faster than wet drilling; water gums up the drills. But dry drilling puts a powerful amount of dust in the air. And the ventilation's bad in those shafts. Small fans. Half the time they don't work. Some days workers can't see more than ten feet ahead of them." Holbert stopped speaking as Armen took their plates. After she walked to the kitchen he said, "Men are going to die, Orville. That tunnel dust will kill them. May already be happening."

"I wonder …well, maybe they are turning on the water in the drills. Fans too."

"One driller told me they do – but only when the state inspectors come around. And that's not very often."

Orville recalled the afternoon of his first day on the job when he and Bullhead had visited shaft one; the state inspectors and O.M. Jones. Cletus had been riled because of the wet drilling; they wouldn't make their twenty-two feet. The morning of that same day during their visit to shaft two, its air had been full of dust. Like night and day.

Holbert gave a wan smile. "You know, don't you, they expanded the tunnel."

"Yes, forty-six feet."

"If they allowed wet drilling they'd never make the twenty-two feet a day. But I think they're going to pay one hell of a price. Well, the company won't. The men will."

Orville stared at Holbert.

"A foreman told me there's pure silica in the center of Gauley Mountain, Orville. They're extracting and shipping it to the new Union Carbide plant in Boncar to make metal alloys. I heard they're even going to change the name of the town to Alloy." Holbert scanned the restaurant, then leaned across the empty counter stool, his face only a few inches from Orville and said in a firm whisper, "It's not a tunnel anymore, Orville, *it's a silica mine.*"

The Impinger

ARMEN CARRIED A POT of fresh coffee to Holbert and Orville, refilled their cups, and then walked to the kitchen. "I know it's dusty in those shafts. Hard to breathe," Orville said. "But if it was dangerous in there, Holbert, don't you think O.M. Jones and the Carbide engineers would take steps to make it safer?"

"You'd think they would. But I'm not so sure."

"What do you mean?"

"I don't have any fancy theory, Orville, but think about it. The company wants to get that tunnel dug. The sooner they finish it, the better. The less interference, the better. Everybody needs to keep their eye on the ball – twenty-two feet a day."

"Right. But dirt's one thing. Danger is another."

Eyebrows raised expectantly, Holbert asked, "Ever hear of an impinger, Orville?"

"No. What's that?"

"It's a device that measures the quantity particles in the air of a confined space."

"How does it work?"

"It's a metal box. When the device is opened the wet plate inside is exposed for a fixed time. Airborne particles stick to the plate; the amount of particles on the plate gives a measure of contamination in the air."

"How'd you come to know about impingers?"

"From a mining engineer over in Grundy, Virginia. Airborne particles are important in lots of places. Mines, quarries, tunnels, sandblasting, ceramics and cement production, too." Holbert grinned wistfully, "Workplaces that produce customers for my business."

Orville toyed with his coffee cup and then asked, "Are you saying the company should use impingers in the shafts?"

"It's possible they're already using them. If not, they could bring in impingers and take some measures, find out if the air is safe."

"You've seen lots of different kinds of work. You think it's safe in there?"

"Don't know. But I'm doubtful."

"What if it's not?"

Holbert shook his head. "Well, they could make it safer. For example, more exhaust fans, or they could order the men to turn on the water in the drills."

"And gum up the works, slow things down."

"Yep. There goes twenty-two feet a day." Holbert looked out the window, then turned to Orville. "Or, men could wear masks, maybe like the one I had made. Even better, get masks that are built to do the job."

"My first day on the job, Mr. Jones and the Carbide engineers came into shaft one wearing masks, respirators they called them. Looked like the gas masks we wore in the trenches in France."

Holbert nodded. "Respirators are hot and awkward. I'm told men don't like to wear them. But if their lives depended on it, I'll bet they would."

"Don't be too sure." A sad smile crossed Orville's face. "In the war, even when we knew a gas attack was coming, lots of men waited till the last minute, the last second, to put on their gas masks. Sometimes they waited too long."

With his fountain pen, Holbert wrote "22" on a napkin. "That's the target, Orville. If respirators prevent reaching it, there'll be no respirators." He underlined the number. "If wet drilling prevents reaching it, there'll be no wet drilling."

Armen approached the men. "It's nine o'clock, fellows. Time for me to close. Can I bring you anything else?"

Holbert paid for his meal then turned to Orville. "Nice to talk with you. I'll be around for a few days. Maybe we'll have a chance to talk some more."

"Hope so. And I'll ask a fellow at my rooming house about impingers.

He's an engineer at the tunnel. I'll bet you a cup of coffee, they're already using them." Even as he spoke he remembered the dust and Al's illness. But no, O.M. Jones wouldn't let dust go unchecked. Holbert had to be wrong.

"You're on. And I hope I lose the bet."

Armen wiped the long counter top. "Hard to keep my mind on work tonight."

"Can I give you a ride?"

Armen smiled. "That would be nice, thanks."

They walked along Main Street to his car. The glow of the gas street lamps softened the street and buildings. Armen took Orville's arm. Her touch tingled through his body. He glanced at her and smiled.

He parked in front of Armen's home.

"Thank you for the ride, Orville." She leaned over and gave him a kiss on the cheek. Her lips remained next to his cheek as she whispered, "And thanks for taking daddy to Doc Henderson this morning."

He leaned forward slightly and their lips met.

After a moment, Armen gently pulled away. "Whoops," then she laughed. "Sorry Orville, I didn't mean for that to happen."

"My fault. I'm sorry."

"But it felt, well, you felt, nice."

"Thanks. You too."

Orville ran his fingertips over her hand; its texture told of work; counters wiped, dishes washed, dinners served; a strong, good, hand.

"I have to go check on daddy."

"Want me to come with you?"

"Thanks, but no. I'll do it."

"Are you sure?"

"If he's okay, I'll wave to you from the front door."

She squeezed his hand. "Good night, Orville."

"Before you go, uh," he paused, searched for the right words and asked, "can I see you again. I mean, see you away from work?"

"You mean a date?" she laughed.

He grinned, "Yes." He hoped the darkness would conceal the blush he felt spreading across his face.

"That'd be nice, Orville. But with daddy's illness I don't have a lot of free time."

His voice fell as far as it had risen. "I understand. Just thought I'd ask."

"And, well I don't like to say this, but you should know. Serving dinner one night to you and Bullhead I heard you talking about your wife, and the problems you were going through. I'd like to be your friend, but dating a married man isn't, well, it isn't right."

He hadn't expected this conversation, but better to have it now than later. "Bertie left me. Months ago, she took up with another man. It hurt something awful...but I've learned to live with it." He didn't tell of nights without sleep, or how sleep came only after enough liquor to float his troubles away.

"I understand that kind of loss. I was married too, though only for a few months. He died in a mine explosion."

"Sorry."

"It wasn't easy to tell you I knew about your marriage, Orville. But I'm glad I did. It clears the air."

"The truth is I have no marriage – and I don't feel married." His voice wavered and his words came slowly, as if each one needed a burst of energy. "Bertie has someone else. Life with her is part of my history, not my future. I have to make my way."

She smiled, "I'm honored you want to go out with me. And sad I can't accept." With her index finger Armen traced an "O" on the foggy windshield, stared at it for a moment then wiped it away. "And there's something else, Orville."

"What?"

"My momma died ten years ago of lock jaw, tetanus." Armen's voice became a near whisper. "Momma's momma was Negro and her daddy was Cherokee. Eight years ago when my husband's family found that out they threatened to disinherit him if he didn't come home. He worked one more day before he was to leave me and go home. He never came out of the mine." She took a deep breath, "Orville, I'm Negro, Indian, too. My daddy's love for Momma meant nothing to folks who wanted to keep Negroes and Indians in their place."

"So what if your skin is a little more tan than most folks."

"I've easily passed for white. But I know the truth. So does my former husband's family. And for all I know they may walk in the Bridge View tomorrow."

Orville shook his head. "Still, I don't think…"

Armen interrupted him. "And don't forget, there are Ku Klux Klan meetings around here. No one has a problem with me, or Pansy at your rooming house, waiting tables." Armen gave a small laugh, "But if they knew about a Negro woman dating a white man?" Her voice rose, "A married white man?"

"You're you – Armen." He gazed at her long black hair, dark eyes and high cheekbones. "A lovely woman." And more – her shadow merged with his; her voice touched his heart.

"And you're a good man. I would like to be your friend." She gave his hand a light squeeze. "Now I got to go check on daddy."

"Thanks for your honesty, I guess."

"It's the only way, Orville. Good night." Armen opened the door and walked into the house. A minute later she waved from the front door.

Orville drove to town. The night seemed like life itself – dark and cold. He shivered.

Thanksgiving

A<small>T BREAKFAST ON</small> M<small>ONDAY MORNING</small> Billy Webster asked, "Howard, do you plan to leave work early on Wednesday and go home for Thanksgiving?"

"Like to, but I'm not sure the trip is worth the effort. Arrive home late Wednesday night then on Thanksgiving evening come back. The C&O will be on a holiday schedule. It'll take forever to get anywhere. Think I'll just have Thanksgiving in Gauley Bridge." He looked around the table, grinned, and then added, "Might as well stay, rest for a day."

The men smiled, all except Lloyd.

"How about you, Lloyd?" Howard asked. "I remember from your employment form, you're from Matewan. You going there for Thanksgiving?"

Lloyd stared at Howard, raised his fork above his plate and dropped it. The fork clattered on the china. "Memory can play tricks on you, Howard. Where I'm from is between me and the company. No business of yourn." He glanced around the table then took a large bite of biscuit. "Anyway," he spoke through a half-filled mouth, "home's where I hang my hat. Right now I hang it here."

After a long silence Billy Webster asked, "How about you, Orville? Will you go home to Kettle?"

"I've no reason to go to Kettle. Reckon I'll do the same as Howard. Stay, rest a day." Memories of last year's Thanksgiving, the roast chicken dinner he and Bertie shared, contrasted with memories of his years of plenty. Every Thanksgiving Ralph had given each employee a fifteen pound turkey. Even now Orville could close his eyes and breathe the aroma of Bertie's Thanksgiving Day dinner.

MID-AFTERNOON ON THANKSGIVING DAY, Orville, Howard, and Billy Webster climbed into Orville's Ford and drove to the Bridge View.

As they entered the café Holbert Yancy stood in front of the cash register paying his bill. "Hey there, Orville. The turkey dinner is good. Cranberry sauce is homemade. Good as Thanksgiving dinner at home. Maybe better," he grinned at Armen, "cause we got this lady to take care of us."

Armen's face reddened. She smiled and left to serve customers.

"Enjoy your dinner, boys. Time for me to go take a nap."

The men seated themselves in a booth.

Carrying dinners to customers, Armen flashed a smile at Orville and his friends. "No menus today, fellows. Thanksgiving dinner – turkey with all the trimmings."

"Great," Billy Webster said, "that's what we came for."

Howard added, "Thanksgiving dinner. Bridge View's a winner."

Orville thought about his conversation with Holbert yesterday evening. Dust, the impinger, and measurement. He should have asked Billy Webster about it over breakfast.

Armen served plates bearing thick slices of roast turkey, dressing, a generous helping of mashed potatoes and gravy; green beans and cranberry sauce.

The men talked of life at the tunnel. Howard said, "Past couple of months, seems like men quit as fast I fill out paperwork. A month or two on the job and they're gone. Shiftless niggers, Lloyd calls them. Says that's about what to expect. Most of the time I think he's right."

After they finished dinner, Armen stood next to the booth. "You get a choice of dessert – pumpkin or mincemeat pie." She smiled, "And if you want, I'll put a scoop of vanilla ice cream on it."

All three men grinned like schoolboys; mincemeat pie for Billy Webster, pumpkin for Howard and Orville; ice cream all around.

"We're over six months past the ground-breaking," Billy Webster said.

"Mr. Jones estimates we'll finish the digging in the summer of thirty-one. Almost a year to go."

"That's a year of work. In these times that means a lot," Howard said. "Never shirk when there's work. There's hard times across the country. Thanks to Union Carbide, we got jobs. I say, abide with Carbide."

Orville and Billy Webster groaned then smiled.

Armen brought their slices of pie, each with a large scoop of vanilla ice cream on top, and mugs of coffee. The men grinned at her and took large first bites.

"Good pie, Armen," Orville said.

"Mmm-hmmm," Howard and Billy Webster confirmed through full mouths.

After dessert, Armen returned with more coffee; its aroma hovered over the table.

Billy Webster said, "Yesterday I looked over the specifications for the turbines. Mr. Jones says they're world class – best there is." He gave a proud smile. "And they're right here at Hawks Nest." His high-pitched voice reached a near-squeak, "Those turbines'll produce enough power to light the city of Charleston."

"Can't wait to see the gates open, send the river into the tunnel," Orville said.

Billy Webster added, "The biggest engineering feat in the history of the state!"

"Bullhead tells me there's valuables from stage coach robberies on the bottom of the New." Howard glanced around the table and grinned, "After the river is diverted we'll walk along that river bottom, pick it all up, and walk out rich men." He burst into laughter, "Work no more, never be poor."

Orville and Billy Webster chuckled.

Orville said, "The other day I talked with a fellow who said he worried about levels of dust in the tunnel. Thought it could be producing illness among the workers."

Billy Webster replied, "Trust me, Orville, the tunnel's air is not dangerous. I have it from Mr. Jones, there's 7,000 cubic feet of air per minute pumped to the face of each shaft. A twenty-four inch pipe brings it from the entrance. Coal mine regulations require only 5,000 cubic feet a minute." He gave a knowing smile, "We're way beyond that."

Armen removed the empty pie plates and wiped the table.

Howard craned his neck around her and said, "There's a lot of tunnelitis going around. The men, mostly the coloreds, bring it on themselves. Smoking, drinking, gambling till all hours. And our friend Bullhead don't help none with his late night shanty."

Armen stopped wiping the table and gazed expectantly at Orville.

He glanced at her then turned to Howard. "You may be right some of the time, Howard. But what about men that don't carouse like that and still get tunnelitis?"

"How should I know – ask Doc Henderson. For all I know, tunnelitis is contagious."

Armen's lower lip trembled. She walked to the kitchen.

Orville waited until she passed through the kitchen door then said to Billy Webster, "The fellow I mentioned told me about a device that measures dust in confined space. An impinger. I didn't know about it. You ever hear of an impinger, Billy Webster?"

Billy Webster's face became flat, expressionless. "Yes, I've heard of an impinger."

"Are we using them in the shafts?"

His voice matter-of-fact, Billy Webster described the device and how airborne particles stick to the wet plate, just as Holbert had described it last Saturday.

"Well, Billy Webster, we understand what it is. The question is, are we using those things?" Howard grinned, "What's the news? What do we use?"

Billy Webster scooted his coffee mug over a wet spot on the booth's table, then raised and lowered the cup. Each time it left a moist ring. He stared at the rings, then spoke softly toward them. "Mr. Jones says on each tunnel face we're well above minimum standards for cubic feet of air per man."

"No impingers?" Orville asked.

"No need for the expense, the big boys upstairs tell me. Plenty of air in there." The men stared at the rings on the table top as if they held more answers.

Howard said, "Well, whatever that tunnel is or isn't, new workers and a stack of papers will be waiting on me tomorrow morning. You boys about ready to go home?"

Orville stretched. "Count me in. I got rounds to make in the morning."

Billy Webster remained silent.

The men paid Armen and stepped out the door. A cold wind blew along Main Street.

Six months ago Orville didn't know these men. This afternoon they'd shared Thanksgiving dinner, a meal he'd always shared with his family. And before they broke bread he had forgotten, well Howard and Billy Webster had forgotten too, to give thanks. During dinner it seemed like the dust of the shafts settled over the table. With it came Frog and Al, their breathing labored, too sick to work; bottles of little black pills; corpses delivered to Mr. Sprigg; cornstalk crosses on graves. And no impingers. He owed Holbert Yancy a cup of coffee.

Christmas

In early December the weather warmed. Orville often gave men rides to the doctor's office and an arm of support into the examining room. There Dr. Henderson, heavyset and imposing in his white medical coat, placed his stethoscope on men's backs and chests. Going into his office men often told Orville the doctor's next words, "Sounds like tunnelitis." And then he did the other thing they'd said he would, handed each man a bottle of small black pills. "Take two of these at mealtime."

Leaving the office, men on first visits sometimes gave Orville a small smile and showed him their bottles of pills. Men on return visits, their breathing labored, kept their eyes down, as if the floor might trick them into a slip and fall.

During his shanty rounds Orville found increasing numbers of men in their bunks, too sick to work. A day or two later many would have gone away.

Bullhead commented, "You'd think in these times they'd want to work. Niggers, hard to understand 'em."

They just want to stay alive. Armen's daddy should've quit early on.

As newly hired workers occupied vacated bunks, Orville wondered where the old workers had gone. Could've hopped a freight train and headed home. Though a man who couldn't breathe well would have a hard time hopping even a slow-moving train. He had seen some of them on the streets of Gauley Bridge.

He tried but failed to shut down a small inner voice, "Maybe they went looking for a place to die." Since mid-November, two, sometimes three times a week he and Bullhead had retrieved a worker's corpse from a shanty or nearby woods. Orville had carted each body to Mr. Sprigg. Armen's daddy, would he die too?

The third week of December an all-day storm dropped six inches of wet snow. A day later, the snow had melted, but for many nights afterwards, treacherous patches of ice stretched across the roads. One night as he drove to Summersville, in the middle of a hairpin turn the Ford skidded. Orville pounded the brake and jerked the steering wheel first left then right. The car continued its path towards the precipice and stopped a few feet before the road's shoulder dropped into the gorge. After a moment of relief, a wave of anger rose from Orville's gut. He yelled, "It's not worth the money, Bullhead!"

He sat with his fingers tight around the steering wheel. He waved towards the gorge then turned towards the corpse in the back seat, "Me and you, buddy, we could've been buried together down there."

Orville resumed the drive to Summersville and sipped from his pint bottle. The calendar soon would roll over to 1931. And Mr. Jones had said, well Billy Webster had said he said, the shafts would be completed during the year and the underground workers released. Without workers to be rousted his job would end. Then what? Bullhead had it right, Union Carbide paid better than the army. Tomorrow's sun would melt the ice. The next trip would be safer.

The number of deliveries to Mr. Sprigg, and Orville's earnings, increased. But he often lay awake, sleep settling on him only for short periods, punctuated by twitches of an arm or leg that seemed to have a life of its own. It helped if he drank a shot or two of corn liquor before going to bed. Even then, a couple of hours later an arm or a leg would awaken him. Often he'd not sleep again unless he drank more.

Next Thursday would be Christmas. A year ago he'd had Christmas at home. The gifts he and Bertie had exchanged – a pin for her, a work shirt for him – had been as simple as their dinner. He missed Bertie and the cozy warmth of Christmas. He hated the thought of her and Hack Shamsford spending Christmas together.

The Tuesday before Christmas Bullhead met Orville after work.

"I got good news for you, Orv," though his face, like his voice, bore no expression.

"What's up?"

"Well, you know we got two days off coming up, Christmas and the day after. Tomorrow, the twenty-fourth, is our last work day 'til Saturday, the 27th."

Orville clinched his hands tight in his pockets. He didn't worry that the tunnel's management would take away one of the days off – he feared they'd give a Christmas gift of one more.

"Can't forget two days off," he said, trying to sound positive. He didn't tell Bullhead about his loneliness; about how rousting shanties and night-time trips to Summersville put order and purpose into his life. He didn't want the company to take that away, not even for a day. He searched Bullhead's face for a hint of the news. Under the folds of his slack expression, he found only eyes as spent as burnt cinders, the face Bullhead had worn into battle.

The cinders suddenly glowed and Bullhead burst into a smile. "A Christmas gift, Orv – they're giving us Saturday off!"

"No," Orville gasped, then remembered to smile.

Bullhead laughed and slapped Orville on the back. "Yep, at the end of work on Wednesday you got a four-day pass! Don't have to report for duty 'til Monday morning."

Orville forced a grin and extended his hand. "Thanks."

On Wednesday morning Orville awakened an hour early. His heart sank – after today, time off. At the shanties he tapped each front door with his blackjack and yelled a half-hearted "Merry Christmas." From inside came coughs and the shuffling of feet. That night he had dinner at the Bridge View, hoping to talk with Armen. But she had the night off. He returned to his room and drank corn liquor until he drifted into sleep.

The next morning he awakened to bright sunlight, threw off his quilt and leaped out of bed. His heart raced – he'd overslept, he'd be late for work. But no footsteps padded down the hall. Silence replaced the familiar sounds of doors opening and closing. Like an unwanted gift, the day sat before him. Christmas morning had dawned.

He lay down and stared at the pattern the lace curtains threaded across the morning's cold blue sky. Then he closed his eyes and pulled the covers against his body.

The metallic tick-tock of the alarm clock on the bedside table filled the room as its third hand, like a tiny grasshopper, jumped from second to second. Seven o'clock. He wished he could will it to move faster – get to Monday. Five hours until noon. He could go to the Bridge View and wish Armen a Merry Christmas. Five more hours until dinner. Take a long nap – then to the Bridge View again? Then Friday, all day. How many times will the clock's second hand jump before that day ends – can a man make time run like a racehorse?

The hours would pour over him like a slow amber stream of warm molasses. If he didn't take action they'd glue him to his bed.

Downstairs, plates and glasses clattered. He dressed and sauntered down the staircase.

He sat opposite Lloyd at the large table. Howard and Billy Webster had gone home and wouldn't return until Sunday. Pansy served pancakes, scrambled eggs and bacon. "Merry Christmas," she said to Orville. She glowered at Lloyd, who didn't look up.

After comments about the pancakes, the two men ate in silence. When Orville finished his eggs, he said, "Merry Christmas, Lloyd," and extended his hand across the table.

Lloyd looked up and took Orville's hand. "You too," he muttered, and then returned to his eggs.

The empty days ahead loomed as large as Gauley Mountain. He had to dig a tunnel through time. The routines of work waited at the other end, he just had to get there.

Late each evening, alone in his room, Orville drank the white lightening he bought from Bullhead. He wondered how Bertie spent Christmas; if she thought of him. He counseled himself, tongue in cheek, that with a full pint bottle he still hurt when he thought about her. But by the time the bottle emptied, the pain disappeared. In time, he hoped, the pain would be gone without the bottle.

Saturday night Orville went to a movie – *Little Caesar* – starring Edward

G. Robinson. Back in his room he poured himself a half-tumbler of white lightening and thought about Robinson's character, Enrico Bandello. Rough, tough. A killer. Bullhead could be Bandello. Or, better yet, if they made a movie about Hawks Nest, Edward G. Robinson could play Bullhead. He refilled his tumbler with the clear liquor, then imagined black men white with dust shuffling out of the tunnel. One of them opened the rear door of Orville's Ford, stretched out on the back seat, and died.

Orville refilled his tumbler. He missed Howard and Billy Webster; he wished he had someone to talk to, laugh with. Even Lloyd would do. Yes, even Lloyd. He looked at the empty tumbler in his hand. Hadn't he just refilled it? He'd heard Lloyd come in a while ago. Maybe he hadn't yet gone to bed; he might like some company. Sure, why hadn't he thought about that before? Orville laughed aloud as he imagined Lloyd's surprise, even gratitude, that he'd knocked on his door. Yep, this little visit would break the ice that had frozen their connection for too long.

Two glass tumblers and a pint of white lightening in his hands, Orville walked down the hall. He grinned as he knocked on Lloyd's door.

Lloyd cracked the door and peered out. His hair disheveled, he wore only the bottom half of long underwear. He stared at Orville.

Orville held the glasses and pint bottle before him. "A little Christmas cheer, Lloyd. Thought we might have a drink together."

From behind Lloyd a woman's voice whispered, "Shut the door."

"Go away, Orville." Lloyd slammed the door.

Orville gazed at the door then walked to his room. Fool! Why hadn't he left well enough alone? And when – how – did Lloyd get a woman in here?

Orville had another drink, stretched out on his bed and fell into a deep asleep.

Hours later he awakened with a start. Lloyd's room – the woman's voice – Pansy!

January, 1931: Measurement

A BITTER COLD WINTER settled into the New River gorge. Each snowfall, usually a three-day event – a day of snow, a day to linger, a day to melt – lasted a week, sometimes longer. Men walked across the New River. Coal smoke rose from furnaces then cooled into a blanket of gray fog that spread over towns; the acrid smell lingered and seeped into homes. Black dust painted the snow.

Orville bought a new pair of knee-high lace-up leather boots. Their thick soles kept him dry as he trudged through slush. Workers' worn-out brogans offered them little protection. He gave thanks for his good fortune.

At breakfast in late January Pansy brought in a plate of hot biscuits. "Y'all should know that Mrs. Jimison is coming home. She'll be here in a couple of days."

Howard laughed, "Pansy, no more shirking. Mrs. J'll have you working."

Billy Webster said, "It'll be nice to see her again."

"Good to have her back," Orville said, more to himself than to the others. Though after her abrupt, even cold, departure, he wondered about their nighttime tryst.

Lloyd glanced at Pansy. She gave him a firm and abrupt nod, her lips thin. Controlled gestures Orville read as clear as a Western Union telegram. "Now leave me alone. Stop. Hear me? Stop." She whirled around and walked to the kitchen.

Two days later Mrs. Jimison came to breakfast. A tall man about thirty-five accompanied her. Orville felt a twinge of jealousy. Then he noticed that the shape of the man's face, along with his dark hair and eyes, resembled a male version of Mrs. Jimison. The four boarders put down their forks and gazed first at Mrs. Jimison then at her companion.

Her rich voice filled the room. "Good morning, fellows. Nice to be back and see you again." She gestured towards the man beside her, "I'd like you to meet my baby brother, Roy Junior." She laughed and added, "Though in our family he's forever stuck with the nickname, Bubby. Bubby, this is…" she nodded towards each man seated at the table as she introduced him. Each man extended his hand to Roy Junior who, when he shook hands, looked down.

Billy Webster asked, "I reckon you're from Richmond, Roy Junior. What brings you to Gauley?"

"I'll be," Roy Junior paused and closed his eyes, then opened them and in a voice too loud spit out the word, "working," followed more quietly by "at the tunnel." He paused then added, "Assistant to Mr. Jones."

Billy Webster's face reddened; he raised his voice, articulating each word, "Well, it'll be nice to work with you, Roy Junior."

"Bubby received his engineering degree from the polytechnic institute in Blacksburg. We're proud of him." She smiled at her brother. "I've fixed him a downstairs bedroom. I'm sure you'll enjoy getting acquainted."

"Sis makes too much of my degree. I just like to use numbers to make things…" he again closed his eyes and pursed his lips until, like a student released at the end of a long school day, "work" burst out.

Lots had changed since Orville had last seen Mrs. Jimison. Men dying. The impinger. Armen's daddy. And Armen. His thoughts lingered on her even as he remembered Mrs. Jimison's one-time gift.

THE PACE OF ORVILLE'S SHANTY ROUSTS had slowed in recent weeks. Increasing numbers of men coughed and wheezed; many refused to go to work. Often, after he insisted that a worker go to Doc Henderson's office, the man would extend a bottle of black pills towards Orville as if to show evidence that he'd already done his part.

The afternoon of the first day of February, Orville agreed to transport two bodies to Summersville. After work Bullhead helped him place the corpses across the back seat, one on top of the other. Later, driving up the mountain, as Orville rounded a sharp turn the body on top rolled to the floor. When the road straightened alongside a ravine, he parked and tried to tug the body back onto the seat. After repeated attempts, he grabbed the corpse's feet, pulled it from the car, and laid it on the forest's thick bed of snow-covered pine needles. He then pushed the other body, stiff with rigor mortis, into a board-like upright position behind the passenger seat.

Orville turned to lift the corpse from the ground – but it had disappeared. Startled, he peered into the darkness of the ravine, then made his way down the steep snowy hillside in short sideways steps, on each step driving a heel into the snow.

At the bottom lay the corpse. He took a deep breath then locked his arms around its chest. Orville clamped his right heel into the snow then brought his left leg and the body a few inches up the hillside; again and again. Twenty minutes later, sweaty and tired, he placed the corpse upright in the back seat beside its companion.

What sort of life had this man lived? And what had his own life become – carrying dead workers to Summersville? He wiped sweat from his face. He felt angry at Bullhead, angry at Union Carbide, and angry at himself.

The next evening he again delivered two bodies to Mr. Sprigg. Later in the week, two more. Had he missed another roof fall or dynamite accident? He reached under the seat for his corn liquor and wondered how long his trips could go on.

The next morning over coffee Bullhead handed him a crisp five dollar bill. "Thanks, Orville. The company appreciates what you're doing."

Orville handed the bill back to him. "We have a problem, Bullhead."

Bullhead's eyes widened.

"You need to tell me what's going on." Orville looked expectantly across the table. "Men are falling like soldiers walking into German machine gun fire. And I'm the grave corps. Except there's no Germans and no machine guns."

Bullhead laughed. "It ain't nothing you and me don't already know, Orv. Work in the tunnel is rough and dirty. And those niggers – drinking all night, shooting craps, getting all liquored up in the cold and damp. Doc

Henderson says, 'Coloreds are people of the sun, constitutionally unsuited to work underground.'"

Orville gulped his coffee then slammed his mug on the table. Bullhead flinched.

His voice low and intense, Orville said, "Remember what happened in France? So many trips, so many bodies. I had to drink myself to sleep. Same thing's happening here. If it wasn't for corn liquor, I wouldn't sleep at all."

"Well, Orv, maybe you need a couple of days…"

"The first time you acted like some kind of a rare accident had happened – a man without a family had been found dead. You said Union Carbide would be proud if I'd help out and take the body over to Mr. Sprigg. Then there were a few more. Now it's two at a time. Three times this week." Orville's voice became louder. "That's not what I agreed to, Bullhead. I don't know how much longer I can go on…"

"Quit," a voice said, "now's the time." Orville silenced it and continued, "The price's going up. Five dollars a body. Period." He hoped Bullhead would fire him. End his body carting duties.

Bullhead held up his hands. "Whoa, soldier. One body or two, same distance, same gas, same amount of time," he grumbled. "Don't see why anything should change."

Orville described last night's trip to Summersville. "You ever drag a corpse up an icy embankment a few inches at a time?" His voice rose. "And another thing. That constable in Summersville keeps his eye on me. Maybe one night he'll look in the back seat and say, 'Interesting traveling companions you got there Deputy Orr. They seem kind of stiff in their ways. And they have an odd way of dressing.'" He paused. "Just what do you think I ought to tell him, Bullhead?"

"Well, uhmmmm…"

"I could say 'Constable, those men are from over at Gauley. They're friends of Chief Deputy Delbert Bullhead McCloud. He works for Union Carbide at Hawks Nest.'"

Bullhead jerked his wallet from his hip pocket and dropped two five-dollar bills on the table. He pushed aside his coffee mug and stood. "See you tomorrow."

The bills lay before Orville. He stared at them and thought of the money he'd passed on to Joe Craddock's widow that night in the cornfield.

When they met for coffee the next morning, Bullhead acted as if yesterday's dispute had never happened. A day later he again asked Orville to carry two bodies to Mr. Sprigg, "Under our new arrangement."

That evening they met near the shanties to load the bodies in the Ford. Bullhead brought two wide-brimmed black felt hats. "These are for our travelers. Be sure to bring 'em back. Most likely they'll get more use."

Orville reflected on his shanty rounds, men coughing in their bunks that morning, and wondered who among them might next wear one of these hats.

Bullhead helped Orville seat the corpses as backseat passengers. Then he placed a hat on each man, stepped back and examined them as if inspecting soldiers in his platoon. He leaned into the car and adjusted the hat brims low over the canvas-covered faces. Orville gave his army buddy a thumbs up, and then drove to Summersville.

AFTER WORK THE NEXT DAY, as Orville entered the Bridge View a familiar voice said, "Hello, Orville. Good to see you." At the counter sat Holbert Yancy, a plate dinner in front of him and a wide smile across his face. He put aside his newspaper and extended his hand.

Orville shook his hand and sat next to him.

"Want the special?" Armen asked.

"Thanks, you're way ahead of me," he said with a smile.

"Good to see you, too, Holbert. Here on a sales trip?" He gestured towards the window; outside the lights of the café shone on the street's grey slush. He laughed, "Or did you come for the scenic views?"

"I've seen them all, Orville. This trip's business."

The two men talked about the weather and roads. Armen served Orville a crisp-fried chicken breast, green beans, mashed potatoes and gravy, and coffee.

Orville sipped his coffee. "Holbert, I figured you'd show up to collect on our bet."

"I guess that means you checked with that engineer at your boarding house."

"I did. Billy Webster said Mr. Jones told him they didn't need impingers.

That they're providing more fresh air to the tunnel than is required in a coal mine."

Orville waved at Armen, stacking dishes near the kitchen. "Please bring Holbert a cup of coffee. Put it on my check."

"Thanks. But winning that bet is not good news. I'd rather have lost it." He picked up the newspaper. "Have you seen today's *Fayette Journal?*"

"No. What's going on?"

"February 18th – take a look." Holbert handed Orville his newspaper and pointed to an article. "That story talks about the large number of deaths of colored laborers in the tunnel. Thirty-seven, it says, in the past two weeks."

"Thirty-seven?" Orville did a quick calculation. In just over two weeks he had carried about half that number to Summersville. How did the *Journal* come up with thirty-seven? If they're right, what about the rest, where had the company put them? Maybe Mr. Sprigg had leased more acreage from his mother.

"Hard to believe. Even worse," Holbert lowered his voice, "that may be just the tip of the iceberg."

"Why do you say that?"

"This afternoon I talked to a couple of old friends who work in the tunnel offices. I showed them the newspaper article and asked what's going on." Holbert toyed with his silverware.

"And?"

"They said they can't talk. Carbide and the contractor just put out the word. Anybody – from managers at the top to muckers at the bottom – who talks to outsiders about work in the tunnel will be fired on the spot. No questions asked."

"That's news to me. Guess I could be fired for having this conversation with you." Orville glanced around the café. He made a mental note to be careful at Mrs. Jimison's house. Roy Junior worked for O.M. Jones. Billy Webster and Howard worked in the headquarters. And he didn't want to test Lloyd's trustworthiness.

In a near-whisper, Holbert asked, "You realize what it means to have no impingers?"

"Well, it could mean that Mr. Jones is right. There's plenty of air being pumped in. Though that doesn't fit with all the illness. It's possible that Bullhead and the Union Carbide managers are right – the Negroes are bringing illness on themselves by drinking and carousing. But that doesn't fit with illness in men like Armen's daddy." Orville shook his head. "No, I guess I don't know what it means."

"It means that without measurement no one knows the facts. You say the air is clean, I say it's dirty. I say it's clean, you say it's dirty. Who knows? Dust could be thick enough to suffocate a man – but without measurement, it's just a matter of opinion."

He hadn't thought this through. No measurement meant protection for the company.

Holbert continued, "And then there's the logic of the thing."

"What do you mean?"

"Consider this, Orville. If machinery is set up to pump 7,000 cubic feet of air per minute to the face of each shaft, and if the engineers and textbooks say that's enough, then assuming everything works properly, the job is done. Right?"

Orville nodded his agreement.

"But if everything doesn't work properly, who would know?"

Holbert took a sip of coffee and reached for his check. "Case closed."

Revelations

B Y EARLY APRIL young leaves of maple and oak trees painted the mountains with buds of yellow, green, and maroon. And men talked of the shafts "holing through," becoming a single tunnel, by late summer. Howard set up an office pool, "Pick the date of the first hole-through, ten cents." Orville chose July 15th. Conversations about machinery breakdowns or delays in dynamite shipments or, most often, the need for new workers, always included an assessment of that factor on the date of the hole-through. Men speculated, sometimes laughed, about whose bets might be helped or hurt by events.

By May 1st the green of spring stretched from the base of the gorge to the shanty camp high on Gauley Mountain. Spring had always buoyed Orville's spirits, but this year it brought more death. He could only guess at how many men had died. He hauled corpses to Summersville nearly every night. Did Bullhead or the big boys upstairs decide which bodies went to Mr. Sprigg and which ones went…well, where did they go? Death hovered like a dark silent presence over conversations in the mess hall and tunnel offices, among foremen in the shafts, even over the breakfast table.

Like drops of water seeping through hairline cracks in a dam, hushed conversations about tunnelitis and death began. At the Bridge View friends quietly shared rumors; in the mess hall supervisors and office clerks leaned forward over tables and spoke in low voices. If a manager walked nearby they talked about the date of the hole-through. Two foremen at the entrance to shaft one stopped talking as Orville walked towards them, but not before one of them said, "Two more died last night."

Mrs. Jimison met Orville in the foyer; the grandfather clock chimed six. Her amber aroma of sandalwood drifted through the house. "Orville, could you join me for a few minutes?" A light smile drifted over her face and she motioned towards the living room.

They seated themselves on each end of the wide divan. On the low table before them a vase of red tulips sat between two glasses of sweet tea. Mrs. Jimison lifted one of the glasses, tilted it towards Orville as if to say cheers, then sipped her tea.

He raised his glass and thought of when she came to his bed.

"I need to ask you something, Orville. I'll understand if you can't talk about it."

He had forgotten the warmth of her voice; how it reached inside him.

"I've heard rumors about the tunnel, Orville. I'd like to ask you about them."

He nodded.

"This isn't easy." She looked towards the foyer, as if her question stood there waiting to be introduced. "I've heard that workers, lots of workers, are sick and dying. And their illnesses are associated with the work underground. Maybe it's something in the tunnel. Maybe something else, I don't know. I even heard that in the shanty camp up on the mountain there's an epidemic of tuberculosis. I heard that bodies are being carted away to a secret cemetery. Can you tell me what's going on?"

"I hadn't heard that, I mean, about the epidemic of tuberculosis."

"Rumors can be crazy." She took a drink of her tea. "You're there every day, Orville. You talk with the managers and visit the camps. And you're often gone in the evening," she gestured a dismissal of her comment, "though how you spend your evenings is none of my business. I just want to find out about the rumors. Are men dying?"

The grandfather clock ticked, no, pounded slivers of time, each one nudging him to speak, to say something. How much did she know? Could she be trusted?

Orville leaned forward and picked up his tea. He took a long swallow and returned the glass to the table. He stared at Mrs. Jimison, admired her long dark hair and the rounded curves of her silk blouse. Part of him wanted to tell everything about the tunnel and the deaths. Another part of him, its voice louder, urged diversion and escape. He found his route. "Can I ask you a question?"

"Of course. I know it's awkward, maybe even unfair of me to pry this way. Certainly you have a right to know why I'm asking about all this."

"How did you come to be missing one of your earlobes?"

Mrs. Jimison fell back against the couch. "What?"

"Your ear, how did it come to be the way it is?"

"And just what does that have to do with…" She stared wide-eyed at Orville. "I guess I deserved that question." She gave a wry grin. "If I say it's none of your business, then you can say the same thing about my questions. Am I right?"

"I hadn't thought that far ahead. It's just something I wondered about."

"As a four-year old child in Richmond, I ran into the street to catch a pigeon. I didn't see the horse and wagon coming towards me. The driver yanked the reins and pulled the horse off course, but the front corner of the wagon struck me. A piece of metal sliced my ear and neck. I used to have a scar on my neck but over the years it has mostly disappeared. If you look closely you can still see a thin line." She leaned toward him.

"I'm sorry. Must have been painful."

"Mmm, it was. But the real pain came later. Until age nine I believed that if I prayed long enough and hard enough, and if I attended special services for healing, the lobe would grow back." She rested her hand on his. Her voice softened. "You can see the outcome of those prayers. I thought God had abandoned me. I still wonder about that."

"Wish I'd known that little girl. I've missed you."

"And I've missed you."

Mrs. Jimison sipped her tea. "Bubby refuses to talk to me about the tunnel, even though there's lots of talk around town. If you'd rather not talk about it, I'll not press you to answer my question."

"You said you understood that I'd wonder why you asked your question. Other than natural curiosity, is there some reason you asked it?"

"Yes." She paused as if to collect her thoughts. "During the winter in

Richmond I disentangled some legal affairs of my daddy's. Bubby and I are the last of our family, and he's not good at that sort of thing. Going through daddy's papers, I found stock certificates, holdings in companies that failed after the market crashed. Except for one. If daddy had had his wits about him, he might have recognized the value of that stock. But he'd slipped into a dark depression. At times he didn't even recognize me."

"I'm sorry."

"The stock certificate represented an investment in Union Carbide. Today those shares have considerable value. Word of the shares, and who now owns them, has reached Union Carbide. Between you and me, I think that's why Mr. Jones hired Bubby to work for him. Bubby has never been able to hold a job for long. Last week Mr. Jones told me he'd talked to a few people about the possibility of Bubby serving on the board of directors." She shook her head. "That's the last thing Bubby needs."

Mrs. Jimison and Roy Junior – major shareholders in Union Carbide. And him on the board. Her words pierced his thoughts like a powerful dye.

Orville remained silent. Bring her in or keep her out? He'd missed the intimacy of their conversations. Some nights he longed for her to tiptoe through his door. If he withheld the truth and she later learned it, and she probably would, what then?

He spoke cautiously, as if his words had to cross a narrow footbridge over a dark ravine. "I can tell you a few things. For many months, men working underground have been coming down with a lung illness. Tunnelitis, Doc Henderson calls it. Says it bears a resemblance to tuberculosis, pneumonia too, and comes from the underground wet and damp. In the shanty camps, men have been found dead in their bunks. Others in the woods around the camps. Some I suppose haven't been found at all. The company arranged for burials by Mr. Sprigg, an undertaker over in Summersville." Enough! He'd told her enough. Everything in him said "Stop."

Another part of him said, "No, tell the whole truth." Then, as if the tea had unleashed his voice, words streamed out. He told of being paid to transport bodies to Summersville. "At first just once in a while, then most every evening. One body at a time, then by twos, two and three times a week." He waved his hands as he described lowering canvas-wrapped corpses into freshly dug graves in the cornfield; of nameless markers on graves; of Mrs. Craddock's arrival after her husband had been put in the ground.

Mrs. Jimison covered her face with her hands. "My God. It's worse than I imagined." She lowered her hands and stared at Orville, "And you've been...been...driving a makeshift hearse to Sprigg's Funeral Home?"

"I thought I was doing my duty. In the army, I drove a Red Cross truck and carried soldiers' bodies to the cemeteries in Flanders. I finally had to stop – couldn't sleep. It's happening again. Corn liquor helps. But maybe it's time to stop." He leaned back and felt a wave of relief.

"No maybe about it, Orville. It's time to stop." She touched his cheek. "What's happening is wrong. And you've become part of it."

"I tell myself, just one more trip. When I told Bullhead I didn't think I could go on, he reminded me of my duty."

"No one has that kind of duty."

"You're right. But if I stop, Bullhead, the company too, may give me a hard time. I'd value your support."

She placed both her hands on his. "I'll help. And I'll do something I should've done after I heard the first rumor about tunnel deaths. For that I may need your help."

"Okay." Then his left hand stroked her cheek and he ran his fingers through her hair.

She closed her eyes, "Mmm, that's nice, Orville, but we shouldn't..."

Their lips met and their arms wrapped around each other, her body warm against him.

The front door opened. "Nice to see you folks enjoying one another." A wide grin across his face, Lloyd Sykes stood in the doorway.

Announcements

FOR THE NEXT THREE DAYS Orville arrived early for breakfast, then after work he sat in the living room. "What's happening is wrong, Orville. And you've become part of it," lingered as if chiseled into his thoughts. But he didn't see her.

He'd told Bullhead he didn't know if he could keep carrying bodies to Summersville. He wanted to say, "It's over." If he did, then what would Bullhead and the company do? On that boulder, Hardware Washington had preached about standing up to the company. He came out the bottom of a rock crusher like hamburger out of a meat grinder,.

After his shanty rounds the next morning, Orville drove to the mess hall. Inside he found a meeting in progress, nearly every seat occupied. Men from the office sat among foremen in dust-covered work clothes, their full attention on the speaker at the front of the room.

Odd, he hadn't been told about the meeting. A shiver ran through him – possibly Mrs. Jimison already talked with someone at Union Carbide about the deaths and mentioned her source. "Orville Orr" had been penciled on the same list that once carried the name of Hardware Washington. His body felt as tight as a just-wound clock. Orville spotted an empty chair beside the colored water cooler and sat down.

Bullhead sat at a table to the right of the speaker, a heavy-set man Orville didn't recognize. He wore a blue suit and yellow necktie. A precise part split his slicked-down black hair from forehead to crown. The man's deep voice boomed, "And that's exactly what we'll do. Extend every courtesy. Open every door. Cooperate. There's nothing to hide. Hawks

155

Nest is a model of tunnel construction. And don't forget, we got a drilling schedule to meet.

"One more thing. This project brings sorely needed jobs to Fayette County. The tunnel puts food on family dinner tables. Before long it will produce electric power. And with that power will come more jobs. Union Carbide's going to get Fayette County and this country on its feet again. You understand me?"

The man's gaze moved from table to table. His eyes, bright beams of black light beneath fleshy folds, passed across men's faces as if to confirm that, yes, each of them understood. Some men looked away, others nodded. Some coughed.

"Tomorrow will be an important day. Now let's go make twenty-two feet." The man fastened the center button on his suit coat and walked at a brisk pace to the door.

Men sat motionless until the slam of the screen door shouted the man's exit. Then the legs of a hundred wooden chairs scooted across the floor followed by murmurs of men talking as they filed out the door.

A few minutes later, the room nearly empty, Orville walked to the coffee pot, where Bullhead talked with Ermil Dothan. Ermil stood with a mug of coffee in one hand and his baseball bat in the other. He gulped the remainder of his coffee, raised the small end of his bat towards Orville then walked away.

"I got here late. Didn't know about a meeting. What's going on?"

"No problem, Orv. It don't concern us directly. Leastways, not yet. More for the foremen and supervisors. Office people too."

"Who was that man? And what's happening tomorrow?"

Bullhead walked to the coffee pot and filled his mug. "You want coffee?"

Orville nodded.

Bullhead filled a mug and handed it to Orville. He motioned towards a nearby table.

"He's some big-shot from Carbide. The important thing is we got visitors coming tomorrow, Orv. Big time visitors."

"Who?"

"Just for openers, from the statehouse down in Charleston we got the director of the department of mines." Bullhead sneered, "Mr. Lambie. And some of his men. From the courthouse over in Fayetteville, we got Sheriff Conley. Prosecuting attorney, too."

"Why?"

"You probably saw the paper. Rumors been running like crazy up and down the gorge. Even down the river to Charleston." Bullhead looked out the nearby window, beyond it the New River. He spoke towards the window. "People are saying there's men dying, Orv. From sickness at the tunnel." His voice trailed away. "Lots of men."

They sat in near-silence, the river's low roar the only sound. Would Mrs. Jimison – could she – do something to stop the dying? Sheriff Conley had sworn him in. A soldier for Union Carbide. Now, that loyalty seemed misplaced, but at the same time it clung to him. A duty he should honor.

Bullhead jerked his blackjack from its holster and slammed it against the table. "God damn it! Why can't they leave well enough alone. Men are doing honest work. Some caught tunnelitis. Nobody's fault, except maybe their own. You and me – we're obeying orders, respectful-like. But oh-no-siree-Bob, that don't matter." He pointed his blackjack at Orville. "Maybe that prosecuting attorney will come after us."

Orville stared at the blackjack as if it had the power to make arrests.

"Maybe the boys upstairs will figure they got to nail something on somebody. They could say we're accomplices in the deaths of those men."

"Us – accomplices?"

"Sure. Accomplices to…let's see…depending on whose ox is being gored, could be lots of things. Accomplices to manslaughter?" Bullhead tapped his blackjack against the palm of his hand. "You ready for this Orv, how about accomplices to murder?"

Orville recoiled. If somebody's going to be charged with a crime, start with the big boys upstairs.

After work he returned home to find a familiar Ford sedan parked in front of the house. Orville walked to the front porch. Kettle Police Chief Arthur R. Tackett placed his glass of iced tea on the wicker table, stood and extended his hand. Patches of dampness darkened the chief's khaki shirt.

They shook hands. Had Sheriff Conley asked the chief to arrest him – accomplice to criminal acts associated with tunnel deaths? No, the sheriff could do that himself.

The chief drawled, "Good to see you, Orville." He passed his hand over his bald head; his jowls canted upwards in a slight smile. "Nice day for a drive, though it's a long one. Thelma said I shouldn't come, but I told her I had to. Couldn't do this by telegram."

Do what?

"And the hills are nice this time of year." The smile disappeared; the chief spoke in a voice as drawn as his face. "But everything considered, I'd just as soon've stayed home."

"What's going on?"

The chief hitched the holster around his belly, "This morning I got a telegram from Richmond. They first sent it to you in Kettle. Then to me." He took a deep breath. "I don't know any way to tell you except straight out. There's been a bad accident."

"Bertie? Something happen to Bertie?"

"That's right, son." The chief put his hand on Orville's shoulder. "I got the sad duty to tell you it looks like Bertie died in that accident."

Orville dropped into a wicker chair. All these months without Bertie. Now she had returned. No, she had surfaced. Only to exit. Sweat trickled down his ribs. "What happened? You said, 'Looks like Bertie died.'"

"After I got the telegram I called the Richmond police. They told me they'd had a recent stretch of heavy rain. A couple of days ago in the middle of a storm, a car they believe Bertie was riding in smashed into a truck. Then it rolled into the James River. The rain had swolled the river. Yesterday the waters receded some and they hauled the car out. In the front seat they found a purse with identification in it – Bertie's."

Orville stared at the chief. Then, as if the chief's chair rolled backwards on tracks, the chief became smaller and smaller. Tiny spangles of light danced between them; his voice echoed as if coming from a cave.

"Understand that officially she is still missing. But the officer told me most likely Bertie'd be declared dead. Deceased was his word." The chief gazed at the cedar branches that enclosed the porch. "Deceased, now there's a respectful word to tell the sad truth about a death." He sipped his tea. "And the driver, well, his body, was still in the car. They said he was pretty bunged up. Though when I think about it, once you're deceased, I suppose however much you're bunged up don't matter. At least not to you. I'm sorry, but the body in the car was Hack Shamsford."

Orville walked unsteadily to the porch rail and gripped it tight.

"Son, you all right?"

"Just a little woozy. I've seen men die – some of them by my hand on the battlefield. Others here at Hawks Nest. Momma and friends back home from the Spanish flu." He shook his head. "But Bertie…way down deep, I thought she'd come back, say she still loved me." He returned to his chair and slouched deep in it.

The chief put his hand on Orville's shoulder. "Maybe you should lie down."

As they climbed the stairs Orville stumbled. The chief caught him. Then he put Orville's left arm over his shoulder, and his arm around Orville's waist, half-lifting and guiding him up the stairs.

Stretched out on his bed, Orville asked the chief to pull the window shade. In the room's dim light he felt sleep tugging him towards a quieter and safer place.

He awakened. Mrs. Jimison held a cool damp cloth on his forehead. Behind her stood the chief and Pansy.

"Son, getting you up them steps was a chore. I believe you put on some weight since you come to Gauley Bridge." He smiled at Pansy. "Must be them breakfasts." Pansy looked at the floor. The chief gave a small laugh.

"How long did I sleep?"

Mrs. Jimison's "Shhh," stopped further talk. She dipped the cloth in a pan of water, wrung it out and replaced it on Orville's forehead. "Lie still, rest."

"I'll be heading back to Kettle. I'll let you know if I learn more. And I'm awful sorry about what happened. Bertie got on a wrong path and couldn't get off it. Could happen to any of us, Thelma tells me." The chief put his hand on Orville's shoulder. "Do like this lady says. Rest. There's no rush to do anything…" The chief walked towards the door. He stopped, turned to Orville and beamed a small smile, "...except live your life." A moment later his heavy footsteps crunched down the stairs.

Pansy said, "I'll go make some chicken soup," and tiptoed out of the room.

Mrs. Jimison removed the damp cloth from Orville's forehead. "Get some sleep." She gave him a light kiss on the forehead, then left the room.

He shut his eyes. Spring of 1919 – return from the war. Bertie in his arms; the scent of her hair. The years with her; the death of his momma and sale of the farm; selling Fords in Kettle; October of '29. Image tumbled upon image until one arrived he tried to block and couldn't – that night in the kitchen with Bertie and Hack Shamsford. In slow motion Hack withdrew his arms from beneath Bertie's robe. "I must be going."

Orville opened his eyes to erase the scene, end the pain. His little trick stopped the images. The faded light of dusk cast a dim glow through his bedroom. But when he again closed his eyes Bertie and Hack reappeared. He wanted to smash Hack's face; he again swung at him as Hack ran out the kitchen door. Bertie screamed. Then he and Bertie spoke harsh words, their last words. He drove to Gauley Bridge and fell into this bed.

Orville's breath came in spasms punctuated by gasps. He gulped air like a thirsty man slaking a parched throat. In time he breathed a little easier then dozed.

He awakened to light taps on his door. Pansy entered with a tray of chicken soup and hot rolls. He ate then fell into a deep sleep.

Visitors

THE PINK LIGHT OF DAWN awakened Orville. Memories of yesterday invaded his thoughts like a swarm of locusts – the meeting in the mess hall then the chief's hard news.

Downstairs Orville joined Lloyd, Billy Webster, and Howard at the table. "You boys are up early," he said.

Billy Webster and Howard started to reply then remained silent. Billy Webster stood, his shoulders slumped, and extended his hand. "Sorry about your bad news, Orville." He opened and shut his mouth, as if waiting for the correct words to assemble inside. "We're all, well…we're sorry, Orville. If you need anything, let me know."

"Me too," Howard added. He stood and shook Orville's hand, followed by Lloyd, who shook hands in silence.

"Thanks. Last night…I…I slept. That helped. Bertie's been gone for a long time. Now it's final. Doesn't make it easy, just final. Mom used to say God doesn't give us more than we can handle."

Pansy brought a plate of freshly scrambled eggs. "Sorry for your loss, Mr. Orr."

The men ate in silence punctuated by silver forks against china plates.

Billy Webster said, "Big day today, Orville. You know about the visitors?"

"I came late to the meeting yesterday. Bullhead filled me in."

Howard leaned across the table, "When the state steps in, go to the coal bin."

Orville had his first smile since…since…he couldn't remember when.

After his shanty rounds, Orville drove to the mess hall. At a rear table men from the tunnel offices huddled over mugs of coffee and spoke in hushed tones. Bullhead stood beside the coffee pot. He filled a mug and handed it to Orville.

Bullhead pointed towards the men. "They're getting ready. The bigshots will be here about ten o'clock." He gazed at the men for a moment, then turned to Orville. "I heard about Ber...about your bad news, Orv. I'm awful sorry."

"Thanks."

"Things like that're hard on a man." Bullhead studied his mug of coffee. "Fellow I know over in Fayetteville went to pieces after he lost his wife. Can you imagine this? She killed herself drinking battery acid. Don't understand how anybody could do somethin' that awful. They took her to the hospital over in Montgomery." He leaned towards Orville and spoke as if sharing a secret, "Wasn't much the docs could do. Her insides was all ate out."

Orville slammed his mug on the table. "I don't need to hear that."

"Sorry, Orv. It's just that he lost his wife, you lost your wife, well, sort of your wife...seemed like one loss kindly connected with the other." Bullhead looked away. "You're right. I should've kept my mouth...well, sorry, Orv."

"It's okay."

They drank coffee in silence until Orville said, "We should talk about our visitors. What do we have to do today? What's the plan?"

"The visitors don't concern you and me directly. But like I said yesterday, what happens afterwards might come down around our necks. During the war I never got in trouble planning for the worst. Guess I'm still doing it. Want some more coffee?"

Orville nodded. Bullhead re-filled their mugs.

"I got orders from the big boys upstairs. We're to keep the area secure – no troublemakers. That includes the newspapers. Reporters from the county papers will follow the sheriff and prosecuting attorney like a bunch of hungry dogs chasing a garbage truck. Most likely newshounds from the Charleston papers will trot along behind Lambie and his men. Sheriff

Conley may've swore us in, but Union Carbide pays our wages. Don't forget that. Conley and the prosecuting attorney, Lambie too, they're politicians – they can see as far ahead as the next election."

BULLHEAD AND ORVILLE, the bills of their caps just above their eyes, stood like sentries on either side of the dirt road along the New River. Beyond them the road wound around the base of the mountain to the white frame house that served as tunnel headquarters, not far from the entrance to shaft one. Between the road and the river dappled sunlight fell through the branches of tall oak trees and lit waves of pink blossoms on rhododendron bushes.

Three slow-moving cars stopped at Bullhead's signal. He spoke with the driver of the lead car, a black four-door Chrysler, and waved him on. Then he motioned the drivers of two dusty Chevrolets to pass.

Bullhead and Orville stepped into the middle of the road. They raised their hands and signaled the first of two dusty Model T Fords to stop. The driver leaned his bald head out the window. Folds of flesh hung over his open collar and a cigarette dangled from the corner of his mouth. "Hey, Bullhead."

"Hey, Uggie."

"We need to go to the tunnel headquarters."

Bullhead spoke towards the cars, his voice conciliatory, "Sorry boys, Uggie. Closed today. No visitors, not even Uggie Blessington."

"I'm no visitor, Bullhead. I live here. Remember?"

"Sorry Uggie. Under orders."

A dark green Packard coupe approached raising a ball of dust. It stopped behind the second car. Dust rolled over the cars and men. A tall man in a rumpled grey suit jumped out, yanked the brim of a straw hat low over his forehead and strode to Uggie's Model T. Uggie stepped out.

The man put his hand on Uggie's shoulder and spoke in a low voice, nodding towards Bullhead and Orville. Uggie's face remained expressionless; his cheeks turned crimson.

The men returned to their cars and the Packard sped away.

His voice strained, Uggie said, "Reckon I'm heading back to town. That was the editor of *The Fayette Tribune*. Hard to understand."

"What is?"

"Getting pulled off this story. What're they up to? Everybody said this was a tunnel then word passed around town that Union Carbide was extracting silica. Shipping it down to Boncar for metal processing. I'm told that made the tunnel a mine, subject to state mining laws. But nobody, repeat, nobody, budged till rumors spread about men dying. Now the big man from Charleston, R. M. Lambie, is here. And we got the sheriff and prosecuting attorney, too. What the hell they going to do, arrest O.M. Jones? I suppose they wouldn't want a reporter watching that." Uggie lit a cigarette and shook his head. He blew two smoke rings. "They're sending me back to Fayetteville. Kitchen in the Baptist church caught fire." Another smoke ring. "For all we know, some dishes got smashed. I have to write the story for tomorrow's paper. Can you believe it?"

Uggie drove away.

Holbert Yancy had called it – Hawks Nest had become a silica mine. Now after a year of mining, and who knows how many deaths, state officials had arrived. A good sign; things would change.

For the next hour no cars arrived. Bullhead wiped his brow. "Orville, let's mosey on up to shaft one. That statehouse Lambie was in the backseat of the Chrysler. Probably at the face of the shaft by now. Telling our boys how to do things." Bullhead laughed, "Or, come to think of it, maybe Mr. Jones is telling him a thing or two." He laughed again, "That is if Sheriff Conley hasn't arrested him for killing a passel of niggers."

At the entrance to shaft one Orville and Bullhead talked with a dinky skinner and then climbed on a small flat car behind the engine. During the ride to the face, the staccato pounding of the jackhammers and the whine of the drills rose. The tunnel's light diffused in the dust-filled air. By the time the dinkey stopped, not far from the rock benches that stepped forty-six feet, a roar reverberated off the walls; visibility became limited.

Orville tied a blue bandanna over his nose and mouth. Bullhead pointed at him and laughed, "You still trying to rob a bank?"

The visiting officials huddled in a group at the base of the rock benches. They talked and gestured. Four of them wore respirators; they pushed their masks aside, yelled to one another and pointed around the tunnel.

Ermil Dothan stood with a small group of foremen near the lowest bench, a few yards from the officials. He waved at Bullhead and Orville, and motioned for them to join him. "Don't know what them boys is so excited about." Ermil coughed, cleared his throat, and then spit a white residue. "Nothing new here."

Bullhead leaned close to Ermil and yelled, "Lots of dust today. Thought you might cut down on it on account of the visitors."

"They first wanted us to do wet drilling. Impress them officials, I guess. Then the big boys in the front office reminded us in no uncertain terms we had to make twenty-two feet." Ermil grinned and glanced at the group of visitors, "The supervisor, ol' C.C. Waugh – you know C.C. don't you, Bullhead? – said okay, y'all want twenty-two feet y'all'll get twenty-two feet." He laughed. "Now I reckon Lambie and them boys are all pissed off about the dust. Can you beat that?"

Ermil motioned with his bat for Orville and Bullhead to step back, "Steel nipper coming through." A young Negro, white with dust, walked past them. He carried a long steel drill bit. Even in the diffused light, its freshly honed tip gleamed.

One of the officials walked to a man in dusty brown coveralls and a wide-brimmed hat standing alone and commenced to shout and gesture at him.

Ermil said to Orville and Bullhead, "That's R. M. Lambie on the left, talking to C.C. He'll have his hands full." Ermil tapped his baseball bat against the palm of his hand. "The niggers say I'm tough. But I ain't nothing compared to C.C. Waugh."

C.C. listened, then put his hands on his hips and thrust his face towards R. M. Lambie. His face reddened and he poked his index finger towards Lambie's chest.

The foremen, along with Ermil, Bullhead, and Orville watched the exchanges until Bullhead yelled, "We got no dog in this fight, Orv. Come on, let's go."

Bullhead and Orville climbed on the small flatcar. The dinkey jerked forward then stopped. The dinkey skinner re-started the engine and it again died; then once more through the cycle. He jumped from the cab, "Got to find a mechanic. This ol' girl's been giving me fits all week." He went from foreman to foreman, each time following an extended finger that pointed to another foreman. Finally, he returned to the dinkey and pulled a tool box from beneath his seat in the cab. "All the mechanics are over in shaft two. I got to fix it."

Bullhead jumped down from the flatcar and motioned for Orville to join him. "You know anything about these machines, Orv?"

Orville shook his head no.

A smooth-faced young worker, white with dust, approached the men. "Maybe I can help." Coughing, he listened as the dinkey skinner again tried to re-start the engine. He picked up the tool kit and crawled under the big machine. A few minutes later he scooted out and nodded to the dinkey skinner. He coughed again, this time deeper, longer.

The dinkey skinner smiled and waved as the engine started. Bullhead and Orville climbed onto the flat car. The dinkey's wheels began the first slow turns of the trip out.

The young man began to cough so violently that he fell to the tunnel floor.

Orville leaped from the flatcar and ran to him. The dinkey stopped. Bullhead jogged to a nearby water barrel and brought a tin cup of water. Orville cradled the young man's head in his lap and put the cup to his lips. He sipped from it, then choked and coughed again. A moment later he sat up, cleared his throat, and spit out a thick white paste.

Orville and Bullhead each took one of the young man's arms, pulled him to his feet, then placed an arm over each of their shoulders. They guided him to the flat car. The three men climbed aboard.

Soon the roar of the drills and jackhammers, along with the dust, faded. The light became brighter. Lambie would enforce the law, do what's right – he had a sworn duty. And Mrs. Jimison would put pressure on from the other side. Things would get better.

Orville leaned towards the young man. "What's your name, son?"

"Shirley Jones."

"How old are you?"

"Seventeen."

He'd take Shirley to Doc Henderson's office. Doc would give him medicine, maybe tell him to take some time off.

The dinkey emerged from the tunnel into bright sunlight. Orville inhaled fresh warm air that bore the moist scent of spring. On the mountainside above the tunnel entrance a flock of yellow warblers chirped and hopped across the branches of a persimmon tree. Probably migrating. Maybe they had the right idea. He inhaled again. And again.

Second Thoughts

MID-MORNING ON WEDNESDAY Orville met Bullhead at the mess hall. They filled mugs of coffee and sat at an empty table. Orville nodded towards the coffee pot, "The army taught us to put ourselves near the supply source."

Bullhead grinned. "Taught us a lot. And we lived to tell about it." He stared out the window, then turned to Orville. "Last night, out behind the shanty camp up on the mountain," his voice dropped to a near-whisper, "they found another dead nigger. Didn't want to leave him laying in the woods all night – last time that happened some damned animal had the man's fingers for dinner. I had a couple of fellows wrap him in canvas and load him on my truck. I brought him down here." He pointed towards the far wall. "He's stretched out in the storage room." He looked out the window, "Supposed to be hot today. The cook wants him out of there before he stinks up the supplies."

Now – he could say it now, "No, it's over." He could keep his word to Mrs. Jimison.

Bullhead's voice droned like a bee lazily flying from flower to flower, "After all the excitement yesterday, this'll be a quiet day. How about after coffee we go load the body into your car? Then you take a drive over to Summersville. Nice spring day. Good day for a drive." He smiled. "Coming back, you could stop and do a little fishing."

Do a little fishing? Nice spring day – for hauling a body? Now. Say it now. An image of Mrs. Jimison stared at him, expectantly. Words hung in his throat, then pushed through. "I promised Mrs. Jimison..." then the words hit a fork in the road, took a wrong turn, and moved so fast he couldn't stop them. "I promised her I'd take care of a couple of things, move some heavy boxes. Not sure what time she wants me to do it."

Bullhead's thick eyebrows arched. "Orv, tunnel work comes first. We got a dead man out back. Cool in there now, but the temperature's rising."

"I know, I know. But I made a promise. I didn't know we had a dead man. Why don't you load him in the back of your truck and make the trip?"

"Body hauling is your job, not mine. Remember? The company pays you for it." Bullhead's eyes narrowed, "We got a problem, Orv?"

Orville glanced at his half-empty mug of coffee. Say it, he had to say it. He walked to the coffee urn and poured a re-fill. "Want some more?"

"Sure."

Orville refilled their mugs then sat down.

Bullhead laughed. "What kind of look you giving me – is the captain coming?"

"No. Just thinking about all that's happened here. In France, too."

"Yep. Lot of water's passed under the bridge."

"The water's got to stop running, Bullhead."

Bullhead's face darkened. "Don't get your drift, Orv."

"I think you know. It's been coming for a while. I already talked to you once about it. Me and the bodies…I can't keep doing it, Bullhead. I'm losing sleep every night. Without your corn liquor I wouldn't sleep at all." He squared his shoulders and looked Bullhead straight in the eye. "Just like in the army. I had to stop hauling bodies there, and I got to stop here, too. That's the long and the short of it. I'm stopping. Now."

Bullhead crossed his legs, inspected the sole of his left brogan and picked a crushed blossom off it. "You been well paid. I'd think that money would offset lots of lost sleep. The big boys upstairs are grateful for what you've done. Don't forget that. Not a week passes but one of them don't mention what they call your extry-curricular work."

"I accepted the job. I took their money. Now the job is taking me."

Bullhead leaned over the table, "I know you lost Bertie. And I'm sorry. That kind of thing does something to a man."

Orville watched for a sign, any sign, of Bullhead's reaction. Would he go along with him? He'd said maybe they'd committed crimes hauling those bodies – would Bullhead arrest him to save himself? He imagined how he looked to Bullhead at that moment, back stiff, shoulders straight, eyes wide – guilty as charged.

"Take a day to think about what you're saying, Orv, just saying, mind you. I've said lots of things I thought I'd do. Then I thought more about them and did only a few. Or none. If you go through with this, well… most likely there'll be… what's the word – repercussions? – yep, that's it. Yessir, I'd figure on repercussions." He leaned back and sipped his coffee. Then, as if a magical breeze blew over him, Bullhead smiled and spoke in a voice so friendly a listener at another table might think the two men had been planning a picnic. "Sure, I'll give that fellow out back a ride to Summersville. You take the day and think about what I said. We can talk tomorrow."

Orville's lips barely moved as he muttered, "Okay."

"And one more thing." Bullhead's smile disappeared and his voice hardened. "As your old army buddy, I'd recommend you keep this to yourself. The big boys upstairs might not be as, well, let's say they might not be as understanding as I am." Bullhead looked around the room, "In fact, they might get downright angry. Do something crazy."

Then as if speaking about anger had infected him, Bullhead stood and pointed his finger at Orville, "Do something crazy!" He jabbed the air and hissed, "You damn well better keep all this to yourself." Bullhead walked briskly to the door and whacked the screen door with the heel of his hand. Men at the tables looked up as the door slapped against its frame.

Orville stood, surprised to find his knees shaky. He gulped the remainder of his coffee. He'd told Bullhead he had to stop, and he would. But something pulled at him – fear? Or maybe Bullhead deserved a little more than his braking to a sudden stop. An inner voice asked, "You got the courage to do what you promised?"

He answered himself, "Yes. But Bullhead and me have come a long way together. Over there as well as over here."

Orville drove his Ford around the building and parked beside Bullhead's truck. He walked through the half-open door of the storage room. Wrapped in a sheet of canvas and tightly belted, a body lay among crates of supplies. Bullhead had his hands under the man's shoulders dragging him towards the door.

"I'll take his feet. Let's carry him to my Ford."

Bullhead smiled, "Now you're talking, ol' buddy."

On his return from Summersville Orville stopped along the New River and walked to the water's edge. White foam danced around boulders rising above the river's surface.

He sat on a wide flat rock. He could have held his course – stopped being a body courier for Union Carbide. Wouldn't be any easier to end it tomorrow. But he'd stood up to Germans in combat, and he'd stand up to Bullhead. And to the big boys upstairs.

Orville exhaled as if to empty himself. Then he picked up a handful of small stones and began, one by one, to throw them in alternating long, then short, arcs into the river. He studied each stone before he tossed it – its unique shape and color, this one smooth, that one etched with lines. They had identities. Like men.

THE REST OF THE WEEK PASSED without a request from Bullhead to carry a body to Summersville. Surely more workers had died. But just as surely, the company had other ways of disposing of the bodies.

On Saturday Orville drove to the Bridge View for supper, his first meal there since Chief Tackett's visit. Entering the café he breathed the pungent aroma of cooked cabbage. Armen handed him a menu and placed a glass of sweet tea in front of him. "Nice to see you, Orville." Her eyes softened and her lips formed a slight downward curve. "I'm sorry for your loss."

He managed a weak smile, "Thanks, Armen."

"Dinner's on me, okay?"

"You don't have to do that."

She placed her hand on his; her dark eyes glistened. "I know I don't. But if you lived in Gauley Bridge, I mean if you had a home here, and you lost your wife, I'd cook a hot dish and bring it to you. That's what we do. You don't have a home here. So I'll do the next best thing."

"Much obliged, Armen. How's your daddy?"

"He can't work and he keeps losing weight. Each day he walks around a little, but it's a struggle. His breathing is awfully shallow. Sometimes, when he thinks I'm not looking, he grabs his chest. But he never complains. I tell myself at least he's not worse, but I may be only wishing it." She nodded to a customer in a booth then gave Orville a wan smile. "Self-deception has always come easy to me. Want me to bring you the special?"

"That'd be nice. Thanks."

As Orville finished his meal, a middle-aged couple entered the café, followed by three young men. The men wore freshly laundered denim shirts and pants, their hair neatly combed. The woman, buxom and wide-shouldered, had salt and pepper hair pulled back in a bun. She wore a flower print dress. They seated themselves in the booth across from Orville. The boys squeezed into one side and the couple on the other, the boys laughing as they jockeyed for space. Then the two older boys bumped the youngest from the booth's outer edge right onto the floor. They laughed as he caught himself, then stood. He smiled and took a deep breath. "Okay, I'll sit here," and he sat at the counter beside Orville.

The young man began to cough, at first quick small coughs then longer and deeper. He hunched over his knees, alternately coughing and gasping for air. His face reddened.

Shirley Jones – the boy who'd had the coughing seizure in the tunnel. Orville placed one hand on his back and patted, and with the other handed him a glass of sweet tea. Shirley grabbed the glass. Tea sloshed out as he took quick swallows. The coughs slowed and spaced themselves further apart.

The couple in the booth rose and stood by Shirley, concern on their faces.

The woman put a hand to Shirley's cheek. "You okay, son?"

"I'm fine, Mom." He cleared his throat. "Just a little congestion." He nodded towards Orville, "This here's the man that helped me when I had that spell of coughing at work."

Her husband, not as tall as Orville, slight of build, sandy hair, rose and extended his hand. "I'm Shirley's Dad, Charlie Jones."

"Orville Orr." The men shook hands.

"This here's my wife, Emma."

She nodded towards Orville. "How'd do."

"Maam. Pleased to meet you."

"And these whippersnappers are my boys. You know Shirley. This is Cecil and Owen." Cecil looked like a younger version of his father, though slightly taller. Owen, stocky, dark hair and barrel-chested, favored his mother. More hand shakes.

Armen placed a glass of water and a fresh glass of sweet tea on the counter next to Shirley. He nodded thanks. She brought a chair and placed it at the end of the booth. "Here you go. Y'all sit together."

Except for Charlie, the Joneses returned to the booth. The chair remained empty for him. "Much obliged for your help with Shirley in the tunnel the other day."

"Glad to do it. Hope he can get rid of that cough."

"Just a little tunnelitis. Summer's coming, the warm air will help. Hope I can get him to soak up some sunshine. His momma wouldn't let him work in the tunnel till he turned seventeen, back in February. The very next day he signed on. Driller's helper."

"He's a pretty good mechanic too. Don't know if he told you, but right before he had that coughing spell he got a dinkey's engine running again."

"Well now, he did mention it. Shirley's got a knack for making things work. Don't know how it come to him. I been a miner forever – that is till I got laid off – all he ever learned from me was swinging a pick. But he's got a knack."

"Good mechanics are hard to come by. If he's interested in that line of work, I'm sure they'd put him to good use. I could talk to a foreman. Pays another nickel an hour."

Charlie turned to the booth. "You been listening, Shirley? Interested?"

Shirley laughed. "That's easy money, daddy." He coughed. "Mr. Orr, I'd appreciate your help. I like mechanical work."

"Call me Orville."

Charlie started to sit down, but stopped and said, "Orville, me and my boys, along with some other fellers working at the tunnel, got a baseball team, the Drillers. We got an opening at first base. You might be just the man to fill it. Maybe you'd like to join us tomorrow for a game. Over at the schoolhouse. The game's at one o'clock. We'll bring a mitt for you."

"Sounds like fun. Thanks." He hadn't played baseball since he worked for Ralph Morrison. Second base. The Ford Pistons. They'd won the Kettle summer league.

SUNDAY BROUGHT A HOT, overcast, and humid day. Orville enjoyed the game. Most of all he liked doing something away from the tunnel. The Drillers lost by one run. After the game the team stretched out on the grass of the infield and drank cold cider. They shared stories of work in the tunnel and their lives. Charlie, Owen, and Cecil talked about working in the mines"

Owen's dark eyes flashed when he talked of mining. "It was hard work, but that kind of digging seemed better, even cleaner, than tunnel drilling. Can't get my breath in there."

Cecil added. "And mine foremen didn't carry baseball bats."

Their dad spoke in a firm voice. "You boys keep this in mind, men are out of work – on breadlines – all over the country. Thank your lucky stars Union Carbide is digging this tunnel and you boys are steel nippers. We got the wages of four in our family."

Orville returned to Mrs. Jimison's house to find Bullhead's truck parked on the street. The setting summer sun rested just above the tops of the trees, its rays turning the house's tall columns into gold pillars. On the front porch Bullhead, his cap in his lap, sat on the davenport talking with Mrs. Jimison.

Mrs. Jimison stood. "Hello, Orville. I have some things to do inside. I'll leave you fellows to talk. Nice to see you again, Mr. McCloud."

Bullhead stood and raised his hand as if to tip his cap, "Maam."

"What's up?"

"Well, uh, Orv, I come to ask for your help. There's been a unfortunate… well, you know what I mean…I got a couple of dead men on my hands. One colored, one white. Need some help. I know transporting bodies is getting hard for you, but the big boys upstairs want the bodies out post haste. Would you carry them over to Mr. Sprigg? They're in shanty twenty-three – up on the mountain. Near as we can tell, they been there for at least two days, maybe three. Had the place all to their selfs." He laughed.

Orville shook his head. "Bullhead, I've been trying to tell you…"

"Oh yeah, forgot to mention," Bullhead's eyebrows raised and he spoke with the kind of enthusiasm reserved for the discovery of a mutual friend, "they told me the white man was from Kettle. Maybe you knew him – they said his name was Acey Burton."

Orville leaped from his chair. "Who?"

"Acey Burton. He a friend of yourn?"

Done

ORVILLE BOUNDED DOWN the porch steps and ran to his Ford. He revved the engine and drove down the hill. He careened at top speed along the river and up Gauley Mountain. At the camp he jogged to shanty twenty-three.

Inside, twilight eked through grimy windows. Abandoned clothes, little more than tattered rags, littered the bunks and floor. The warm days of late spring and nailed-shut windows heightened the room's stench, at once sweet and rotten. Orville gagged, stepped outside, and took a few deep breaths. He tied a bandanna over his nose and mouth, then re-entered the shanty. That smell – it rode a few feet behind him on every trip to Flanders. Each time he stopped his truck its rancid presence crawled into the front seat. Sometimes he puked, adding to the odors that assailed him.

A body lay on each of the bottom bunks along the shanty's right and left walls.

Orville turned right and struck a match. Acey Burton! His face, haggard and thin, once as dark as his brown coveralls, had become pale white. Acey's tan had been sucked out of him by the tunnel. His tattered leather ball cap lay on his chest. The stump of Acey's left arm rested next to it, as if his missing hand had grasped the cap's bill.

"Acey, why didn't you let me…" Then the futility of his thoughts hit home. He couldn't have repaired Acey's lungs. Or gotten him the hell out of here.

Like a flock of cackling starlings, images swarmed over Orville.

Christmas, 1929. Acey on the front porch, clean blue coveralls, hair combed, leather cap in his hand, and a red bandanna around his neck. "...thought I'd stop and wish you Merry Christmas."

Summer, 1930. "Orville, I...come to ask a favor...I heard some of the boys talking about hopping a freight to that tunnel where you're a working...Could I hitch a ride with you to Gauley Bridge?"

Over the past year he'd seen Acey a few times around the tunnel. "Catch up with you later, Orville. Got to make twenty-two feet."

Had all of life become twenty-two feet a day?

The match went out. He struck another. Two bodies, Bullhead had said.

He crossed the room and, hand trembling, held the match close to the face of the body on the bunk. Even in death the man's large eyes, open though now opaque, signaled his name – Frog.

"Boss man, the nipper, the boy what held my drill and brought drill bits to me...my friend, Eli." Frog's lower lip quivered. He put his upper teeth on it. "Yesterday ...he walked over to pick up his lunch poke. There was a boom ...his head rolled over to the boots of the next driller...eyes looking up... suppose Eli wondered what in hell happened? You got to go to work, Frog."

"Check your hands, Orville. Any blood there?" He knew that voice, his own. The match flickered and died.

The two men wrapped in old blankets and laid on the back seat of his Ford, Orville drove to Summersville. Even with the windows open and at speeds as fast as he dared, death's putrid odor filled the car. The bandanna tied to his face like a cattle rustler's mask did little to filter the smell. In the last rays of twilight he drove past two boys who pointed their index fingers at the car and yelled "Bam! Bam!" Twice he slammed his brakes and swerved hard to avoid tumbling into the gorge.

He stopped in front of the Sprigg Funeral Home, tossed the bandanna on the front seat and ran to the front door. Without knocking, Orville rushed into the foyer and in rose-colored light, stood on its thick carpet. Beside him a chest-high oak stand held an open guest book.

He yelled through the arch that opened into the long narrow hallway, "Mr. Sprigg? You here, Mr. Sprigg?"

A hall door opened and E.T. Sprigg, in a white shirt and necktie, a napkin in his hand, stepped out. He patted his lips with the napkin. "Why Orville, you surprised me."

"Business, Mr. Sprigg," Orville yelled, even though Mr. Sprigg stood only a few feet from him, "got some business for you."

Mr. Sprigg motioned to a chair near the door. "Please, Orville, sit down."

"No, Mr. Sprigg." He felt like a kettle of sorghum boiling over an open fire, its vapor rising into words. "There's two dead men in the car. I want them cleaned up, put in caskets. Laid to rest. Not in your momma's cornfield – in a cemetery. You understand me?"

"Of course, Orville, of course." Mr. Sprigg's voice as smooth as oil on water. "Certainly that can be arranged, though at the moment I'm here alone." He again patted his lips with the napkin. "You realize, Orville, it'll take a day or two to get the graves dug. And, ah, I have to mention there are costs for what you're asking. I assume the deceased are workers and eligible for company-paid burials. However, if we abide by your requests, your costs will be higher than our usual company rates. Though," he smiled, "I'll stretch the rules a bit and allow you our 'family friends' rate."

"God damn it E.T. – just get it done. I'm good for it."

"Yes, yes." His eyes searched Orville's face. "Are they white men?"

Orville stepped forward and thrust his face so close to Mr. Sprigg that he smelled onions on his breath. "One is white, one is Negro. What the hell does it matter?" Orville clenched his fists. He hoped it did matter.

Mr. Sprigg paled. He raised his hands, palms towards Orville. "No, no, not to me personally, it doesn't. But," he re-positioned the guest book in the center of its stand, "you must understand that arrangements and interment will have to be different for the two men. And, to your benefit," Mr. Sprigg gave Orville a weak smile, "colored fees and cemetery plots are less expensive. Still, it adds up. Are you sure you want to foot the bill?" Mr. Sprigg then looked at his napkin as if it contained the answer to his questions. "I could take them to the, well, the cemetery annex; the newly developed area where we interred the other workers." In a near whisper he added, "The place you called a cornfield," his voice became conversational and he smiled, "then I could bill the tunnel management. A lot easier on you."

Orville poked Mr. Sprigg's chest with a finger. "Where do you want the bodies?"

Mr. Sprigg fell away from Orville. "Mmmm, yes. Drive your car around back. Do you have fresh clothes for them?" In an apologetic voice he added, "Not necessary, of course. We could use the clothes they're wearing."

"I'll get some burial clothes. Be back in the morning. That okay?"

"Yes, yes, of course, Orville."

Sunday night's sleep came in short intervals. At dawn Orville got up and dressed.

Pansy lifted a pan of muffins from the oven; a rich aroma spread through the kitchen. "Why Mr. Orr, you're up early."

"Lots to do today. Can I take a couple of these muffins?"

"Take as many as you want. Plenty more coming."

"Thanks."

Under an already bright sun he drove to the mess hall and placed a sealed envelope addressed "To Bullhead" beside the coffee urn. "Some personal business to attend to this morning. Will make my rounds then see you later today – maybe tomorrow. Orville."

After his shanty rounds, Orville drove to Summersville, clean clothes in the back seat – two pairs khaki trousers, underwear and socks, two khaki shirts. They wouldn't fit well, but Acey and Frog would go to their graves in clean clothes. About a mile before the Summersville town limits he passed an apple orchard. Its pink blossoms painted the hillside. Their fragrance floated through the Ford, but didn't replace the lingering traces of last night's odors.

Folded clothes under one arm, Orville walked up the front steps of the funeral home and knocked. Mr. Sprigg, in a dark suit and tie, his face expressionless, spoke cautiously. "Hello, Orville. Feeling better this morning?"

"I am. The white man was an old friend. I knew the colored man too."

Mr. Sprigg's lips turned upwards in a brief smile, though the rest of his face remained flaccid. "Yes, yes, I understand. Death pulls our emotions, indeed what seems at the moment to be our entire being, into dark places. But, on a beautiful morning like this, we learn, once again, that life is here for us, the living." Mr. Sprigg extended his hand.

The men shook hands. Orville gave the clean clothes to Mr. Sprigg. "These are for Acey and Frog. Maybe I should say the deceased."

Mr. Sprigg squared his shoulders and smiled as he accepted the clothes.

"When can we have the burial?"

"The graves will be dug by the end of the day tomorrow. How about Wednesday noon?"

"Fine. See you then. I'll bring cash to pay your bill."

"Mmm, yes. Ah, Orville, there are a few legal matters we'll need to attend to. I'll need the full names of the deceased, their birth and death dates, and we'll need death certificates signed by a physician and specifying the cause of death."

Orville stiffened and looked Mr. Sprigg in the eye, "You bury those men, Mr. Sprigg. Got it? No signatures needed. Cause of death? Ask Union Carbide. The white man is Acey Burton. The colored man is Frog."

"Orville, please understand, the bodies we interred in the annex were one thing. But a regular cemetery plot is another. Legally, socially too, this is no simple matter."

"No, Mr. Sprigg you don't understand." Sprigg, Bullhead, the big boys upstairs – he wanted to skewer them with a giant drill-shaft. "My string has run out. You been burying men wholesale, doing it illegally. And I've been right there with you. Money has changed hands – we're in this with Union Carbide, right up to our asses. Do you have death certificates on all the men you and me deposited in the cornfield? How many were there – a hundred, two hundred. . . more? If you do, then get the same doc to sign death certificates for Acey and Frog. If you don't, then shut your mouth. Otherwise I have a story to tell the newspaper. Maybe the sheriff of Nicholas County too. My string has run out!" He lowered his voice, "You'll bury those men, Mr. Sprigg."

Mr. Sprigg's mouth fell half open. He stared at Orville and his face paled, "Mmm, well, yes, we'll work something out."

"We'll have two graveside services. Then I'll pay your bill. And no one's the wiser."

"Yes, that will be fine, Orville."

DURING HIS RETURN TRIP, light gray clouds gathered in the west over the gorge. By the time Orville arrived at the mess hall, the sky had darkened. He found Bullhead seated at a table with two dust-covered foremen.

Bullhead turned and smiled. "Missed you this morning, ol' buddy. But I got your note. Pull up a chair."

Orville joined the men.

"We was speculating on the hole-through. What date did you pick?"

Orville didn't reply.

The foremen volunteered their dates, both in July. One said, "A few weeks from now one of us could hit the jackpot. And these days, everything counts."

Bullhead added, "Watch out for September 2nd – my date." Bullhead and the foremen laughed. Orville didn't.

The men looked at Orville. "What's your hole-through date, Orville?"

Orville remained silent, his eyes on Bullhead.

"You okay, Orville?" Bullhead asked.

"I need to talk to you."

"Sure, sure." He turned to the foremen, "Orville here had a little upset last night. A white man he knew, tunnel worker, turned up dead. TB, maybe tunnelitis, I don't know. And a colored feller too, right Orville?"

Orville didn't answer.

One of the foremen stood. "Well, twenty-two feet a day don't wait for no man. Come on, let's go to work." The men walked away.

"Get your business took care of, Orville?"

"Most of it. The burials are on Wednesday."

"That's good. In France, after you got Jimmy Campbell buried, everything got back to normal. After you finish burying your friend and that colored feller, then you and me, we'll get back to normal. Everything'll be back on kilter again."

"There'll be no normal, no back on kilter, Bullhead. There was no normal in France. Jimmy went in the ground, and then another soldier went in, and another and another. And I carried them to Flanders. Eventually the fighting ended, men stopped dying, and we stopped the burying. Then soldiers, some one-legged or one-armed, others who'd lost a lung to mustard gas, went home. Men had come to serve their country, to fight. They knew the risks. Lots of 'em died, some didn't.

"Tunnel digging will end sometime this summer. No more twenty-five cents an hour jobs. Those men gave the company an honest effort for a day's pay – kept their end of the bargain. But Union Carbide didn't. Now men lucky enough to be alive are figuring it out. Folks are starting to call them the living dead. They'll shuffle around the streets of Gauley Bridge till they run out of breath and time."

Bullhead gave him a half-smile, "Come on, Orv, don't you think you're being a little preachy? I mean, tunnelitis is a risk that comes with this work. Those men've been paid a fair wage." Bullhead's voice rose, "And keep in mind, there's damn little else out there. Which do you figure is best, Orv, a man taking a wage and the risk of tunnelitis, or staying unemployed and watching his children starve to death?"

"All I know is I'm out of the business of delivering corpses to Summersville. You and the company got other means of getting rid of bodies – right? You do, don't you?" Orville slammed the palm of his hand on the table, "A straight answer, yes or no!"

"Well, if we have to, yes…"

"Then I'm done." Orville sat back in his chair. "I'll do my work each day. If that's not good enough for you and the big boys upstairs, fire me. In fact, maybe you'd do me a favor if you fired me right now."

Orville stood. He started to place his chair under the table and then, glaring at Bullhead, slammed it into place. "I'm done – hear me Bullhead? Hear me Union Carbide? Deliveries are done! Done! Done!"

In a steady rain, Orville ran to his Ford and jumped in. A moment after starting the engine, he pounded the steering wheel. Then he drove along the river to Gauley Bridge.

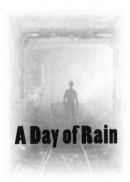

A Day of Rain

A T THE FIRST LIGHT of dawn on Wednesday morning, Orville awakened in a sweat. God damn! How could they do it? He slammed his hand against the bed. In France, enemy machine guns had cut men down. In digging the Hawks Nest tunnel men had been killed by the people they'd trusted. No, God damn it. Nooo!

The room's sluggish air, its scent his own, smelled more like a swamp's stagnant backwater than a bedroom. He reviewed the day to come – breakfast, shanty rounds, then to Summersville and Mr. Sprigg. He heard yesterday's hard words with Bullhead as if he'd just yelled them.

Orville dressed and stepped into the hallway, the house's only sound that of the grandfather clock. He walked down the stairs and out the front door.

Motionless humid air carried the sharp aroma of yesterday's mown grass. The eastern sky shone bright crimson, long horizontal stripes broken by small fluffs of purple. Red sky at morning, sailor take warning.

The Ford's engine broke the silence of the street. He'd lay Acey and Frog to rest. Then he would…he would what? He glanced in the rear-view mirror and recognized himself in sixth grade, unable to answer a teacher's question.

Orville drove down the hill to the Bridge View. He sat at the counter in the empty café and breathed the rich scent of fresh-brewed coffee. He rested his chin on his hand.

Armen walked through the kitchen's double doors, carrying clean plates. "Orville, what a nice surprise. Coffee's almost ready. Get you some soon as I stack these."

He sat up. "Surprised to see you too. Thought you worked afternoons and evenings."

Armen stacked the plates on the other side of the counter. "Usually I do. But the morning waitress had to go to Charleston. I took her place. I'll work my shift too." She smiled, "With tips, I could pick up an extra five dollars."

What's five dollars worth – an eight hour shift at the Bridge View? A body carried to Summersville? Two days of drilling and dust?

"You get enough sleep last night, Orville? You look like you need a mug of coffee."

"Didn't sleep very well"

"You want some breakfast?"

He hesitated, then said, "Sure, bacon, two eggs over easy, and toast."

She studied his face. "Coming up." She poured him a mug of hot coffee and walked to the kitchen.

Customers came into the restaurant. Tobacco smoke merged with the aromas of coffee and bacon.

Orville ate half his breakfast and pushed the plate away.

Armen laid his check on the counter; forty-five cents.

He picked it up. "You forgot to charge me for coffee."

"No I didn't. That's my contribution to putting you in a better mood."

"How could the company do it, Armen? Your daddy's sick. Lots of men have died."

"I know what my daddy tried to do about it. What he'd do now if he could get out of the house." She glanced around the café then whispered, "A better question is what are we going to do, Orville. What?" Her eyes filled with tears. "Will I see you later today?"

"I've got some business to take care of in Summersville."

"Be over there all day?"

"Could be. Well, most of it."

He walked to the cash register and handed Armen a dollar bill.

She glanced up at as she made change. "Looks like rain. Take your umbrella."

"See you at suppertime."

Her dark eyes sparkled, "I'll be here."

At the mess hall Orville placed an envelope addressed to Bullhead, its message the same as Monday's, next to the coffee urn. Then he made his rounds of the shanty camps. At camp two he walked past shanty twenty-three, silent, the door half-open. He resisted an urge to look in, moved on and banged the door of shanty twenty-four, "Time to rise and shine."

Orville drove to Summersville. How many trips, how many bodies, had there been? And what about all the bodies the company had delivered to...to... somewhere else?

At eleven o'clock he parked in front of the funeral home.

Mr. Sprigg answered the door. His black suit, white shirt with starched collar, and necktie, contrasted with Orville's khaki trousers and shirt. "Why Orville, you're early. I didn't expect you until noon."

"Sorry, I can wait in my car."

"No, come on in. Have a seat. We're almost ready." Mr. Sprigg disappeared into one of the rooms off the long hallway.

A few minutes later he called from beyond the door on Orville's right. "Orville, please come in."

The wall sconces shed a soft pink light over the windowless room. "Orville, this is the chapel for colored services." At its front, beyond a few rows of wooden chairs, a waist-high wheeled platform bearing a casket rested on the wood floor's only carpeted area. A pulpit rose from a dais behind it. Nearby hung a large framed print of the face of Jesus. An upright piano stood against the wall. A few hymnals had been distributed across each row of chairs.

Mr. Sprigg pointed to the polished wooden casket and whispered, "That's your friend, Frog." Mr. Sprigg motioned towards the chairs, "Please take a seat."

Orville sat alone in the center of the front row.

Mr. Sprigg stepped up on the dais and stood behind the pulpit. His resonant voice filled the room. "We're here to commemorate the life of

Frog. Please stand and join me in the Lord's Prayer." After "Amen," Mr. Sprigg instructed, "Please be seated." Orville looked around for other mourners but found himself alone.

Mr. Sprigg opened a Bible and began to read, "The Lord is my shepherd…" The words of the Twenty-third Psalm transported Orville to Kettle and Sunday morning services.

After the psalm's final words, "Surely goodness and mercy shall follow me all the days of my life," Mr. Sprigg said, "Would you like to say a few words, Orville?"

Orville flinched. "What?"

"This is a memorial service. Do you want to make any comments about the life of your friend, Frog?"

"Oh, uh, sure." Orville searched for words. "I didn't know Frog well, but…"

"Orville, it's customary to stand. Please rise."

"Oh, sorry." He stood. "As I was saying, I didn't know Frog well. But he came to work every day. Did his job. The foremen said he was a good worker. A man who lived in Frog's shanty told me Frog had a momma in…in Memphis I think he said. He sent part of his wages to her. He cared for his friend Eli, the boy that worked for him as a nipper. After a roof fall killed Eli, Frog took it hard. He started to walk away from his work. But he came back. Partly because of me, and maybe I was wrong. Just trying to do my job. Frog knew they needed him in his crew. The foreman said Frog was a colored man that kept his word to the company. I believe Frog was a good man." Orville started to sit down then stood. "And I'm sorry he's gone." Then he sat down.

Mr. Sprigg bowed his head. "Lord, we ask your blessings on our humble service and the soul of your departed servant, Frog." He stepped off the dais, walked to the piano, and sat on its bench. "Now for our concluding hymn. Please join me, Orville. We'll sing just the first verse. Page two-hundred and thirteen in the hymnal. Mr. Sprigg played once through the hymn "Amazing Grace," then sang, "Amazing grace, how sweet the sound…"

Orville stood and sang, "…that saved a wretch like me, I once was lost, but now am found…" He stood in silence while Mr. Sprigg sang, "…was blind, but now I see."

He stopped his lower lip's trembling by clenching it with his teeth. He stared at the floor, then closed his eyes. Like leaves in a stream's whirlpool, images of Frog's casket, the morning's red sky, and then ever faster, shanties, bodies, and trips to Summersville tumbled on top of one another.

Mr. Sprigg placed his hand on Orville's arm. "Orville, if you'll come with me."

Orville blinked as if he'd been awakened from a nap.

Mr. Sprigg nodded towards the door and whispered, "This way." In the hall he pointed to an open door. "We'll go in there for Mr. Burton's service."

Orville followed Mr. Sprigg into a larger room with ornate wall sconces and wall-to-wall flowered carpet. Instead of an upright piano, an electric organ rested against the wall. An elderly lady in a black dress, her white hair tinted rose by the soft light, sat before it playing "Nearer my God to thee."

Mr. Sprigg gestured towards the first row of chairs. Orville sat down. Mr. Sprigg mounted the dais and began Acey's service. It resembled Frog's – the Lord's Prayer, the Twenty-third Psalm, and then Mr. Sprigg's question, "Orville, would you like to say a few words about Mr. Burton?"

Orville stood. He'd expected the question but had been unable to prepare for it. He closed his eyes, "Lord, can you give me a little help?" He spoke of Acey's life in Kettle, how he'd lost a hand in his daddy's sawmill, and later his work as a mechanic at Ralph Morrison Ford. "Acey was raised a Free Will Baptist. Never went to church much, but I'm sure he loved the Lord. I'm sorry he's gone." Orville's gaze rested on the casket, "Truth is, we weren't all that close, but I'll miss you, Acey."

"Thank you, Orville. We'll now have our concluding hymn." Mr. Sprigg nodded towards the organist. "Please begin, Mother."

The Spriggs sang, "Amazing Grace, how sweet the sound, that saved a wretch like me…" Orville joined them until his knees began to shake, then he sat down.

WITH THE HELP OF TWO MEN in dark suits, Mr. Sprigg and Orville placed Frog's wooden coffin in the hearse. On either side of the Cadillac's hood, above fenders that swept in long arcs to the running boards, chrome headlights poised like powerful beacons.

"Orville, I'd recommend you not drive. Please ride with me," Mr. Sprigg said. Orville climbed into the hearse's leather front seat.

The cemetery spread across the crest of a hill. The hearse passed along the gravel road that led to its colored section. A light rain began to fall. Two Negro men in work clothes, each carrying a long-handled shovel, helped Orville and Mr. Sprigg carry the coffin; the men placed it on straps suspended above the grave.

Mr. Sprigg walked to the hearse and returned with a book. "Let us pray. Lord, we bring you the body of your servant, Frog. Please receive him into your kingdom." He opened the book and faced the coffin, "From the third chapter of the book of Wisdom, 'But the souls of the just are in the hand of God, and no torment shall touch them. They seemed, in the view of the foolish, to be dead; and their passing away was thought an affliction and their going forth from us, utter destruction. But they are at peace.' Now, Orville, please join me in the Lord's Prayer. Our Father, who art in heaven..." After an elongated "A-men," Mr. Sprigg announced, "That completes our graveside service."

He motioned for the workers to turn the handles that unrolled the straps to lower the coffin into the grave. "You boys finish up your work here. We'll meet you at the other grave site." The rain had begun to change the gravesite's dirt to mud.

"Come along Orville, we'll get Mr. Burton and take him to his final resting place."

On the return trip from the funeral home the hearse passed beneath the stone arch over the entrance to the white section of the cemetery. Stepping into the rain, Mr. Sprigg raised a black umbrella and handed it to Orville. The same two workmen met the hearse and helped Mr. Sprigg and Orville carry Acey's coffin to the gravesite.

The service resembled Frog's. After the final scripture reading and prayer, Mr. Sprigg announced, "That concludes our service." Then he instructed the workmen, "You boys can lower the coffin. Take care of things here, then go finish up Frog's grave."

Mr. Sprigg motioned for Orville to walk with him to the hearse. "That's all, Orville. We'll now go back and settle up. And if you please, I'll take that umbrella."

A Ride Home

O RVILLE PAID MR. SPRIGG and walked to his car. He gripped the steering wheel tight with both hands. His thoughts meandered over the funerals and burials then traveled to the cornfield graves. Flanders without ceremony, death without honor. Rain drops trickled down the windshield. He followed the movement of a single drop, initially slow then, as it merged with others, ever faster until it crashed and spread across the bottom of the glass. He picked a new drop and followed its course. Each drop became a worker, each crash a life ended. Armen said, "I know what my daddy has tried to do about it. What he'd do now if he could get out of bed. What are we going to do, Orville. What?"

Knuckles rapped on the passenger-side window. "Orville, are you all right?"

Startled, Orville turned to Mr. Sprigg. "I'm okay. Just wanted to sit for a minute."

"You've been here for over twenty minutes. Thought maybe you had car trouble."

"No, everything's fine. Thanks." Everything except me.

Orville started the engine and drove away.

Before he reached Gauley Bridge thunder echoed across the gorge. Soon heavy rain pounded the windshield. Then he spotted a figure running along the road's shoulder. Armen.

Orville stopped alongside her and opened the passenger door. "Hey – hop in!"

Her spicey scent filled the car. She shook her head sidewise, spraying drops of water in every direction. Orville put up one hand and laughed. "Don't know which is worse, Mother Nature's thunderstorm or yours."

"Nice to see you, too," she laughed.

"Thought you were working two shifts today. What brought you out in the rain?"

"I've been home. A neighbor came to tell me daddy slipped and fell on the front steps."

"Was he hurt?"

"He's got a bruise on his right shoulder. I gave him aspirin. But his breathing is worse. I had him swallow two of the little black pills."

"Want me to help you take him to Doc Henderson?"

"He's sleeping now. Maybe tomorrow. Thanks."

They rode in silence. Orville parked in front of the Bridge View.

"Did you finish your business in Summersville?"

"I did."

"I'd like to hear about it, if you want to tell me. Daddy says I'm a good listener."

"Sure." Tonight, he'd tell her about Frog and Acey. And about all the others; the trips to Summersville. The cornfield too. Better for her to know it now rather than later. "This rain looks like it'll last into the evening. What time do you finish work?"

"The usual, nine o'clock."

"I'll come to the Bridge View for a late supper. Then I'll give you a ride home."

"I'd appreciate the ride, Orville. I'd be pleased to talk. And listen."

Orville sat at the counter, the café's last customer. He waited while Armen gave the booths and counter a final wipe. "Bye, everyone." Women's voices, muffled by the closed kitchen doors, replied "good night."

The afternoon's downpour had drifted into a steady light rain. Orville held the car door open for Armen. A short time later he parked in front of her home.

"Come in, I'll make us some coffee." Armen motioned towards the couch, "Make yourself comfortable. I'll go check on daddy."

Orville sat on the couch and rested his head against the top of its cushions.

Armen's scream brought him to his feet. "Orville, Orville!"

He ran into the small bedroom. Armen stood beside the bed, her daddy's hand in hers. He laid motionless, his eyes open, as if gazing at the ceiling.

Her voice quavered, "He's...no, no, it can't be – Orville, make him speak to me." She burst into tears. "Make him speak to me!"

Orville gently lowered her daddy's eyelids. He put his arm around Armen.

She turned towards him, weeping, then jerked away. "I'll get the neighbors to fetch a doctor!" She bolted out the front door.

A Single Voice

ORVILLE SLUMPED ON THE COUCH. Acey and Frog. Now Al Bodigian. Emptiness spread from his stomach to his chest. It clawed at him. All those men – some now in Summersville, some carted elsewhere, others waiting for death. Why, God, why? He wanted to pound his fist into somebody's face. Union Carbide, if it had a face. O.M. Jones. The big boys upstairs. Bullhead, too.

Armen returned, her eyes downcast. She sat beside Orville and clasped her hands tightly. She sobbed profusely, rocking back and forth.

Footsteps crossed the front porch. Armen leaped up and rushed to the door. Two men in business suits stood at the door, one tall, his grey hair thinning, the other short and stout with wire-rimmed glasses. Behind them stood two middle-aged couples.

The tall man extended his hand and said, "I'm Dr. Harless. This is Mr. Bingham from the funeral home."

Armen shook his hand. "Come in."

The men entered. One of the women walked in and, her voice breaking, hugged Armen. "We're next door if you need us, honey. I'm so sorry."

Armen escorted the men to her daddy's bedroom, then rejoined Orville.

Dr. Harless came into the living room and Armen introduced him to Orville. After the men shook hands he said to Armen, much as a parent would console a child, "I'm sorry to confirm that your father has passed away. Please accept my condolences."

"Thank you, doctor."

"I noticed a bottle of pills on the bed table." Matter-of-factly, he asked, "Had your father been under a doctor's care?"

"Yes. Doctor Henderson at the tunnel."

"Did Doctor Henderson talk with you about your father's illness?"

"He told me daddy had tunnelitis. Said it happened to a lot of men working in the tunnel. He prescribed the black pills."

"I understand tunnelitis is a common diagnosis. Near as I can tell, your father died of pneumonia. Or a lung disease along with pneumonia." Dr. Harless looked away for a moment then continued, his voice less certain, "His symptoms…well, there are some indications that he'd contracted a form of pneumoconiosis. But I'll enter…"

"He'd contracted what?"

"Pneumoconiosis, a lung disease. One form of it, silicosis, is caused by inhaling silica dust. In your father's case, I'm just saying it's a possibility."

"Do you think he inhaled – what did you say, silica dust? – working in the tunnel?"

"It's possible." Dr. Harless added, "Silicosis usually takes years to develop." As if weighing his words, he paused and frowned. "I'm going to enter pneumonia on your father's death certificate."

Armen burst into tears.

Orville put his arm around her. "What about the other men that've died, Doc? Was their tunnelitis really…what did you call it, silicosis?"

"Could be, though I have no way to know." He turned to Armen. "I should be going. Mr. Bingham can do what needs to be done here. Do you have any questions?"

Armen wiped her tears. "No…well, yes. What happens next?"

"If it's all right with you, Mr. Bingham will take your father's remains to the funeral home. He can prepare him for burial, or if you prefer you can contact another funeral home. There's one over in Summersville."

"That's it?" In a near-whisper she asked, "My daddy's life ends and all I have to do is…is, choose a funeral home?"

His manner turned brusque, Dr. Harless asked, "Are there other family members?"

"No."

"Did your daddy own property, have savings and investments?"

"You must have us mixed up with someone else, Doctor Harless."

His eyes searched Armen's and his voice softened, "No maam, I know who you are. Your father's life has been straightforward and, compared to some people, relatively simple. In many ways that's a blessing. We'll enter your father's death in the county records. You can honor him with a funeral or memorial service, and then remember him as you get on with life." Dr. Harless extended his hand to Armen. She held it as he continued, "You're young and strong. You have friends and neighbors who care about you. Things will work out. Good day, young man." He nodded to Orville and left.

Mr. Bingham came into the room and after introducing himself to Orville asked, "Mr. Orr, would you give me a hand? I'd like for us to transfer Mr. Bodigian to the hearse. Then I'll carry him to the funeral home." He turned to Armen, his voice soft, "If you decide you want us to continue, we'll prepare your father for burial."

"Yes, I'd like that. Though I'll need to talk with you about the cost."

"I understand. We can have that talk tomorrow. Right now, perhaps you'd like to select some clothes for your father. I could take them with me now."

Mr. Bingham brought the gurney from the hearse, then he and Orville placed Al Bodigian's body on it and covered him with a sheet. The men took the gurney to the hearse.

When they returned to the living room Armen met them, her arms filled with neatly folded clothes, a pair of shoes, and a blue suit on a hanger. "These are what daddy called his 'Sunday-go-to-meeting clothes.'" She and Orville walked with Mr. Bingham to the hearse. Neighbors who had gathered stood in silence.

After the hearse drove away each of the neighbor women hugged Armen. "We're so sorry." "You're not alone, the Lord'll be with you." They said goodnight and walked slowly to their homes, each one a replica of the others along the dirt street.

"Orville, would you sit with me for a while?"

"Sure, as long as you want."

On the couch, Armen took Orville's hand in hers. They sat in silence. Then, her voice low, Armen said, "Daddy never liked working underground, but said it was all he knew. Then he'd say, 'It gives me a way to do something more important.'"

"More important?"

"When I was a little girl we lived in Matewan. Daddy had two jobs, mining coal and…working as an organizer for the UMW. He always regretted he was underground the day of the Matewan massacre; he said he might've made a difference. Months later he walked to the courthouse a few steps behind his friend, Sid Hatfield, when the Baldwin-Felts detectives shot Sid dead. Those hired guns murdered Sid and pleaded self-defense. The next year Daddy wore a red bandanna around his neck at the battle of Blair Mountain. The coal owners wanted to keep Daddy out of the mines. He'd get jobs for a short while, then they'd find out about his UMW ties and fire him. And we would move.

"We lived in Mabscott, over in Raleigh county, when Momma died." She stared at the empty chair across the room, her words measured and slow. "Daddy loved her so. He worried that someone who knew her family might cause problems about her passing for white. But it never happened. People in mining towns have more important things to worry about, like staying alive.

"Daddy would come home from the mine with black skin. After he took a bath, he'd let me scrub his fingers. I would scrub and scrub and never get them all white. One night I asked daddy if he was part Negro, like my grandma. He and momma laughed. It wasn't until years later that I understood.

"After Momma died, and even now, he talks about her. I hear him, alone in his bedroom, say her name then cry." Armen put her hands over her face and wept. "Oh God, I can't get it into my head that he's gone. Up in the morning, tend to him, then go to work. Come home, tend to him, then go to bed. A circle that never ended, day after day. At times I'd resent it. Now the center of the circle is gone. I'd give anything to have him back."

Armen rested her head on Orville's shoulder. The whirs of cicadas floated through the windows; a moth fluttered against a screen.

"Daddy had…he had something more important to do here, too."

"You don't have to tell me."

"Hardware Washington was his partner. Now they're both gone."

"I'm sorry."

He put his arm around her.

Armen whispered, "When I close my eyes, I feel like I'm falling into a dark cavern. Then daddy throws me a rope and I climb out. I know I've got work to do, the work he can't do any longer."

She nestled against him then dozed until Orville whispered, "You need to get to bed."

In a sleepy voice she replied, "I know…and there's so much to be done. What about you, Orville? What's in front of you?"

He put his arms around her. "We have work to do. You and me."

"You didn't get to tell me about your business in Summersville."

"We'll talk another time. I should be going. You'll…"

She wrapped her arms around him and held him tight. "See you tomorrow?"

"I'll be here after I make my morning rounds."

Over the next two days, Orville ran errands and helped Armen prepare for her daddy's funeral. At two o'clock on the third day after Al's death, he drove to the Gamoca Baptist Church, a white clapboard building with a wooden cross that towered above the front entrance. The windows along each side of the church had been fully opened. At the front of the sanctuary electric fans had been placed on either side of the pulpit; they moved air across mourners in the pews, men in shirt sleeves, a few wearing neckties, and women in gray and black cotton dresses, many waving cardboard fans.

Armen sat alone in the front pew. Orville, along with neighbors, occupied the pews immediately behind her. In the pews towards the rear of the church sat men from Al's shaft at Hawks Nest, drillers, dinkey skinners, shovel operators, and brakemen, along with a couple of foremen and supervisors.

Orville gazed alternately at Armen's dark hair and, beyond her, the casket, the upper half of its silk-lined lid open. Al lay in his Sunday-go-to-meeting clothes, his thin hair neatly combed, arms folded across his chest. A large spray of white roses perched on the lid of the casket's lower half; its perfume scented the sanctuary.

Behind Orville rose a continuous and muted sound. Human and undulating, it resembled a mixture of running water and the rustle of leaves in the wind before a storm. He looked out a rear window. The trees stood motionless.

Then he saw the source – men sat with gaping mouths and wheezed as their chests rose and fell. Not the sounds of many men breathing, but the sound of a single animal struggling for breath.

During the service Orville heard only the sound behind him. At the end of the service the preacher asked the congregation to join in a hymn. The neighbors seated near Orville sang, "What a friend we have in Jesus, all our sins and grief to bear…" In the pews behind him, some men stared at hymnals' open pages as if they'd never learned to read; the lips of others formed the hymn's words but remained silent.

After the service Orville walked towards the door. A thin man stepped into the aisle and extended his hand. He wheezed, "Howdy, Orville."

Orville shook his hand. The man looked familiar, but he couldn't remember his name. And that voice, he knew it from somewhere; had to be the tunnel.

The man wheezed then drawled, "You're not a remembering me…are you, Orville?"

"Uh, give me a minute. I know you…just can't…"

"Cletus. Cletus Pancake. Shaft one…foreman." In gaps between words, Cletus breathed in gasps, "We met way back…maybe your first day…on the job."

Shaft one with Bullhead. Cletus, pear-shaped, coated with white dust and wearing a slouch hat. His wide jowls then resembled a gourd, his mouth a narrow slit at its base. "Hey, Bullhead, what you boys up to?"

"Cletus – now I remember. Good to see you." He'd lost fifty pounds from a year ago; his eyes red-rimmed and sunken, mouth transformed from a slit to a round O.

"Al…he got there…ahead of us… He's the…dead-dead…maybe one of the lucky ones." The O became the U of a grin, "The rest…of us…" the grin disappeared. He nodded towards the men filing out of the pews, "we're the…the…walking dead."

After a brief graveside service, Orville drove to Armen's home. He found it filled with her friends and neighbors, including Charlie and Emma Jones and their three sons. The kitchen table had plates of chicken and ham, along with serving dishes filled with vegetables, a chocolate cake and an urn of coffee.

Orville filled his plate and talked with Al's friends. Many of the men worked in the tunnel. One had difficulty breathing and joined Shirley Jones on the couch. Orville and Charlie talked about the Drillers, then about Al.

Armen handed Orville a cup of coffee.

"Thanks." He nodded towards a burly man with bushy black eyebrows. "Who's that fellow? I feel like I should know him from somewhere."

"Sometimes he's in the newspapers. That's John L. Lewis."

"*The* John L. Lewis, head of the UMW?"

"Daddy worked as an organizer for him in Logan county. They were friends from way back. Come on, I'll introduce you."

"Pleased to meet you Orville." Lewis's bass voice filled the room. "Call me John. Armen told me about your helping her and Al. She said you work at the tunnel. What do you think of Union Carbide and the drilling operation?"

"I think they got a duty and they're not doing it. Engineers come in the tunnel wearing respirators. Drillers like Al have to breathe dirty air."

Lewis put his hand on Orville's shoulder. "Let's step outside and talk."

When they returned some of the guests had gone home. Orville said goodbye to John and then to Armen.

Armen asked, "Come back later?"

"You're busy – are you sure?"

"Please."

He smiled, "Then I'll see you later."

ORVILLE DROVE TO GAULEY BRIDGE. A late afternoon sun sank beneath the sky's deep blue dome. Sharp purple shadows angled across homes and yards. He parked in front of Mrs. Jimison's home. Ahead of him a long black Packard stretched along the hedges.

He walked into the foyer. Laughter came from the living room. Mrs. Jimison called, "Orville, please join us for a minute. There are some folks I'd like you to meet."

In the living room, Roy Junior, in a suit and seated in a straight-backed chair, nodded to Orville. A middle aged couple, seated on the couch, stood. He recognized the man.

"Orville, I'd like you to meet Mr. and Mrs. O.M. Jones."

He shook Mr. Jones' hand and nodded to his wife. He glanced at her pale face and the strand of pearls dangling above her ample bosom.

Had Mrs. Jimison talked to him about the tunnel's air, the illnesses and deaths?

"I've heard about the work you've done, day and night, Orville. Much appreciated by management. I hope you're enjoying Mrs. Jimison's home and Pansy's cooking."

"Yes, Mr. Jones, I am."

"Please, Orville, call me O.M."

"All right, O.M."

How much had she told him? His thoughts jumbled like leaves in a gust of wind. Day and night, he said – he means the trips to Summersville. She must've asked him to clean up the tunnel.

Smiling, Mrs. Jimison said, "The Joneses came for dinner, Orville. We were just talking about the tunnel," she emphasized her words, "and the ventilation."

Yes, she talked to him – now he'll do something.

Mrs. Jimison glanced at O.M. and placed her hand on Orville's arm, "You'll be relieved to learn that the ventilation is well engineered using the best available technology. O.M. has personally assured me of that.

"O.M., Orville and I had been concerned about talk of illness and deaths at the tunnel, possibly due to dust in the shafts. I'm pleased we can put our concerns to rest."

Put them to rest – *God!* He'd walked into a room of play-acting. His fists clenched.

"Yes, I've heard those rumors, and to be honest, some workers, mostly colored, have died. There have been three roof-falls and some heavy equipment accidents. One of those took the life of a white man."

Orville's voice quivered and rose in anger, "O.M., I have seen men, lots of men, Negro and white, sick, unable to breathe." He closed his eyes and tried to gain control. "I've found men in their bunks and in the woods," he yelled, "dead."

The room became as still as a tableau.

Mr. Jones smiled, "No doubt, Orville, no doubt you have seen that. Those darkies carouse all night, then work without sleep. And it takes its toll. Doctor Henderson tells me that under those conditions tunnelitis becomes pneumonia right fast." He turned to Mrs. Jimison, "My dear, we have a meeting later this evening at the church. Please forgive me for asking, but will we be sitting down to dinner soon?"

"I'll go check with Pansy." With a wave that said "Excuse me," Mrs. Jimison walked to the kitchen.

"Orville, I recommend you double check your facts. Always a good idea, double check your facts. This is the biggest and best-engineered tunnel in the world. I think you should take pride in being a part of it. We're making history."

Roy Junior said, "And me and sis are proud shareholders."

Mr. Jones leaned close to Orville, his face grim, "And relax. These are hard times. You've done valuable work, been well-paid. Enjoy your earnings. You've got a future at Union Carbide."

Mrs. Jimison returned, smiling. "Yes, O.M., dinner is ready. Orville, I'm glad you got to meet the Joneses. Nice to see you and have this little chat – and set things straight."

She took Mr. Jones' arm. "Bubby, if you'd please escort Mrs. Jones let's go to the dining room." Mrs. Jones took Roy Junior's arm.

Pansy stood by the table, her posture as stiff as her starched white uniform.

Orville remained alone in the living room. Then he charged into the dining room and sat down next to O.M. Jones. "You – you send engineers into the tunnel wearing respirators." The tendons in his neck strained and his face reddened, "Men are dying – in the dark of night I cart their bodies to Summersville. You know it and you don't stop it." He gripped the edge of the table then stood. "I don't know how these people sit at the same table with you." He stood and slammed his chair beneath the table. O.M. Jones' water glass tumbled over; he jumped up as water poured into his lap.

Orville walked out the front door to the street. He drove through Gauley Bridge, then along the New River. His fingers gripped the steering wheel hard. Turn down the heat, breathe deep, he told himself.

Mrs. Jimison – how could she…why would she? He parked and walked to the river's edge, then sat on a wide boulder. His anger began to cool as dusk fell. He stretched out on his back and gazed at the arc of dusk above the canopy of trees on each shore. The clouds shifted from dull orange to dark rose, then to purple. His daddy used to call this part of the evening God's time – the time between first dark, late dusk, and second dark, night. "The time of day when God checks his handiwork," he would say.

At Hawks Nest, hundreds of men had died. God's handiwork, too?

Across the river an owl hooted. Bats swooped and insects skimmed above the river, its low roar a continuous ribbon of sound. God's handiwork rested in this old river gorge and its mountains. The Garden of Eden had nothing on this place. Beechnuts, persimmons, butternuts, hickory nuts, and walnuts; paw-paws, blackberries, blueberries, and ramps…and squirrel, deer, rabbits, possum, coons; bears too…streams with bass and trout, beavers and muskrat. And oak, maple, pine, spruce, beech, hickory and walnut.

The shafts will soon hole-through Gauley Mountain. One day the gates on the dam will close and send the river through her. The riverbed below the dam will be dry for miles. "Oldest river in North America," Bullhead had written in his first letter. And now Union Carbide will change its course.

When second dark fell Orville drove to Armen's house.

Armen

ARMEN OPENED THE FRONT DOOR before he knocked. Her lips smiled but not her eyes. "Hi, Orville, come in." She'd changed from her black dress into pajamas and a robe.

He stepped into the living room. "Just wanted to make sure you're okay."

"Thanks. I'm fine. The neighbors have been kind. They'll help if I need anything."

"Armen, there are things I need to tell you. I know that now's not the time. Maybe in a week. Whenever you feel like it."

"What you started to tell me the night daddy died – about your day in Summersville?"

"Yes, but it's more than that." About his feelings for her, shame over what he'd done at Hawks Nest; about telling the whole truth.

"I've learned to read your face, Orville. Whatever it is won't come easy for you. Maybe not for me either."

Words jumped into place, ready to leap through his lips, but they'd have to wait. Soon enough he'd tell her. "When do you plan to go back to work?"

"In a couple of days."

"I'll come to the café for supper then. We can find a time to get together. Right now, promise you'll let me know if you need help."

She hugged him, her body strong yet soft.

Armen rested her forehead against his cheek. "Thanks for coming by."

THE NEXT MORNING two extra places had been set for breakfast. Shortly after Pansy served blueberry pancakes, eggs and bacon, Mrs. Jimison and Roy Junior joined the men who, except for Lloyd, stood and welcomed them.

"What a surprise – light my eyes."

Mrs. Jimison laughed, "You're quite a poet, Howard."

"Nice to see you, Mrs. J," Billy Webster said. "Is this a special occasion?" His face reddened, "What I mean is, well, it doesn't have to be special." He grinned, "I'd be pleased to have you and Roy Junior here every morning, I just meant..."

"I understand, and that's nice of you, Billy Webster."

Mrs. Jimison glanced at Orville, then smiled at the others. She and Roy Junior sat down for breakfast. She nibbled her scrambled eggs and leaned forward, "Everyone, I, well we . . . have good news to share with you."

The men put down their forks.

"I'm proud to tell you that Bubby will soon be leaving us to move to Charleston. He'll join the corporate staff of Union Carbide. And," she took a deep breath and looked at her brother, "Bubby, even you don't know this," she beamed at him, "we expect him to be elected to the company's board of directors."

"Well shuck my corn!" Howard extended his hand across the table, followed by Billy Webster. Lloyd took a sip of coffee and left the room.

"Why didn't you tell me, Sis – the board?"

"Surprises are always fun, Bubby. Isn't that right, fellows?"

"Will I have to dress in a suit every day?"

"Just listen to Mr. Jones. He'll steer you straight."

Howard and Billy Webster nodded.

Orville stood. "I've got rounds to make." He nodded to Roy Junior, "Good luck."

IN THE WEEKS that followed, when Orville had supper at the Bridge View, a ruddy-faced short, heavy-set man who always wore a black suit coat, even in hot weather, entered the café and sat alone. More than once Orville found the man's eyes on him. When that happened the man would quickly look just beyond him, as if their sight lines had accidentally collided.

One morning at the mess hall, the man sat at a table in the rear of the room. Orville nodded towards him, "Who's that fellow, Bullhead? I've seen him at the café."

With only a glance at the man, Bullhead blurted, as if impatient with Orville's question, "Somebody said he's from Charleston."

At a Sunday baseball game in late July, the man stood among the spectators.

"The man will do what he will do," Orville told himself, "there are other more important things to worry about."

During his team's turns at bat, Orville sat beside Shirley Jones. He asked, "How's your new job going?"

"I like mechanic's work. Always learning something."

"Maybe on sunny days you could stay home, soak up some sunshine and breathe the warm air. The dinkeys'll find a way to run without you."

"The hole-through's coming. Work will end. Till then I want to lay away some wages for Mom." Shirley looked towards the mountain beyond the playing field, his young face pinched with the lines of an older man. He turned to Orville and said, "A dinkey skinner, Johnny, was found dead a couple of days ago. Lived in the shanty camp up on the mountain."

At least he hadn't had to put a canvas sheet around Johnny and carry him to Summersville.

"At work Johnny had trouble breathing. Coughed a lot." Shirley picked at a blade of grass and took a deep breath, "Like me." As if there had been an explosion inside him, Shirley coughed hard. He struggled with short breaths until his breathing settled. "Do you suppose Johnny caught something up there in the camp? Or do you think the tunnel – the dust – did it to him? Is the same thing happening to me?"

Rage kicked Orville in the gut. "You're going to be okay, Shirley. A little sunshine and lots of rest will work wonders." He wished he could carry Shirley to a safe place. He wished he did not have to watch him become one of the walking dead.

A man yelled, "Orville, your turn at bat."

On a Friday evening in early August, Orville entered the café and sat at the counter. He took a drink of sweet tea then asked Armen, "Hear the news?"

She laughed, "If it weren't for bad news, I'd have no news at all. What's yours?"

Orville smiled, "The hole-through. Shafts one and two connected yesterday. They came within one inch of each other. O.M. Jones is bragging about it. "

"And you won the big money?"

"I had July 15th. My day's come and gone." He grinned, "Story of my life."

"Who won?"

"Fellow I don't know – works for Union Carbide in Charleston. Bullhead says the big boys upstairs are planning a shindig to celebrate the hole-through."

"A celebration; maybe that's why they asked me to work next Saturday. Late afternoon through the evening. Told me to make sure I wore a clean uniform."

"Bullhead said he'd got orders for us to work the big event. Make sure everything's secure, no rabble-rousers. We'll direct traffic, keep things on the up-and-up."

The next night Orville lingered over his meal while Armen kept his glass filled with sweet tea and chatted with him between serving customers. Later, the café nearly empty, she stood next to him and touched his arm. "Could you give me a ride home? If you feel up to it, we could have that talk."

His stomach jumped like a frightened grouse. "Sure, I'd like that."

"I'll go finish up a couple of things in the kitchen. Be back in a few minutes."

During the trip home, Armen leaned back in the seat and closed her eyes.

A car trailed the Ford. When Orville turned left on to Burnt Cross Road the car followed. When he stopped at Armen's home, the car drove on.

In the living room Orville took a deep breath. "Mmm, something smells good."

"I baked cinnamon rolls this morning. Want one?"

They sat on the couch; two glasses of milk and plates with cinnamon rolls on the small table before them. Armen said, "The night daddy died, you were going to tell me about your day in Summersville. Can you tell me now?"

The grouse beat its wings against the inside of his stomach. His gaze traced the perimeter of the table, then slowly made another loop. Small beads of sweat spread over his forehead. "Okay. Bear with me if I stumble." He sipped his milk then, his voice soft and cadence slow, he began to talk about the war in France, about carrying the dead to Flanders. When he described Jimmy Campbell's death, Armen touched his hand.

"One day last summer Bullhead told me we had a problem at the tunnel and he needed my help...a worker had been found dead. In the woods near one of the shanties. Bullhead said he told the big boys upstairs about my army duty at Flanders. They asked him to ask me if I'd carry the body to Summersville for burial."

"Summersville?"

"The company set up an arrangement with an undertaker there, Mr. Sprigg, to bury workers who died on the job." The grouse wings beat harder. "Bullhead said they'd pay me five dollars to deliver the body."

"And you made the trip – took the money?"

"Yes," he answered in a voice tinged with anger; at himself; at the company.

Armen shook her head and stood. She walked to the kitchen and returned with more milk and rolls. "I guess I can understand your wanting to help out." Her voice cracked, "But why didn't they ship that man home?"

"Good question. I can't answer it." He took a drink of milk. "Before long there was another death. Another trip, another five dollars." He searched her face for a clue – did she know what was coming? He gulped the rest of his milk. "During my rounds of the shanties I found more and more men laying in their bunks, sick, having a hard time breathing." He took a drink of milk and then, though he didn't intend it, he slammed his glass on the table. "I'd meet Bullhead for coffee. He'd tell me another body was in the woods, in the storehouse, or a shanty. Sometimes it'd be a man

I'd rousted the day before. After work I'd transport the body to the funeral home. Then one body after another." His voice rose, "Mr. Sprigg buried the workers in a makeshift cemetery in his mother's cornfield. Unmarked graves. Well, sometimes he tied together a little cross of cornstalks or wood slats and put it at the head of the grave."

Armen's eyes filled with tears. "I'd ask how many trips you made, but maybe it doesn't matter."

The grouse's wings beat against his stomach. "Truth is, I lost count – so many; like men shot down in France. I tried to tell myself this was a war, us against Gauley Mountain. Then I stepped back and remembered, ol' Gauley never hurt nobody. She was just there. We're the ones who invaded her, drilled and blasted a hole as big as a barn, three miles long." His voice rose and he waved his hands, "We mucked out her insides and shipped them downriver. And soon we'll send the New through her to generate electricity." He sat back. "She was just there."

He touched his fingers to the points of the star pinned to his shirt, "When I first came to work and put this on, I felt like a soldier in the company's battle against the mountain. And men who died, well, they were battle casualties. By and by I learned better."

Armen leaned back and took his hand. "And daddy...to them he was just one more casualty." Her eyes flashed, "The company went on, and nobody raised a hand. Well, daddy did, and now they're rid of him too."

He stroked her hand then dropped it. Walking into German machine gun fire seemed easy compared to this. "What the company has done – what I've done – is wrong, Armen." His words felt as hot and fluid as molten steel, "A few weeks ago a white man from Kettle, Acey, was found dead in a shanty. I'd brought him here to work. The same day another man I'd come to know, a colored driller, Frog, was found dead. I took their bodies to Summersville and paid Mr. Sprigg for proper burials. I'd been to their funerals the day your daddy died." He looked into her eyes, "That's when I told Bullhead I was through." His voice dropped. The grouse's wings beat ever faster. "He said the big boys upstairs might not understand. They might do something crazy." He leaned towards her, "Well, by God I hope they do."

Orville spoke as if searching for each word, "I'm powerful sorry for my actions, Armen." He lowered his head, "I've prayed about it. That hymn, Amazing Grace, I've said its words a thousand times. Save a wretch like me – can a wretch like me be saved? I hope you'll find it in you to forgive me. If not, well… I can't blame you."

Tears welled in her eyes. "It's not simple, Orville. Not easy to accept all you've said."

He stood. "I know. I'll leave if you want me to."

"No, please sit."

They sat in silence. Then Armen looked into his eyes and said, "I…I forgive you, Orville."

He took her hand. "Thank you."

"Months ago, that night you brought me home, we sat in your car. I liked being with you. I even wanted to hold you. But you had a wife. And there was something else – I told you then, momma was Negro, though she passed for white." She leaned back, gazed across the room. Her voice rose, "They have treated these men, Negro and white, like niggers." Her tone sharpened, "And I'm one too; that's me, Orville."

"I'm here because of you, who you are."

She clasped his hand and brought it tight against her body. "I can work for you; I can be your friend. But anything else is against the law, Orville. Against the law."

"It was against the law for your momma and daddy, too."

They sat in silence for a few minutes. Then Orville stood.

"Where are you going?"

"It's late. I've said what I wanted to tell you. I'm glad it's out of me." He took a step towards the door. "This has been a long week. For you. For me too. Tomorrow is Sunday. Maybe we can catch up on our sleep."

"Tomorrow's just another day. I go to work at two o'clock. Please, sit a little longer."

He returned to the couch. The grouse settled on its nest.

She took his hand and studied the lines across his palm. "Momma could read palms."

"Once you said you could read my face. Can you read my palm too?"

"She taught me to see lines of character. But no, I'm no palm reader."

"What can you tell about me?"

"Only that down deep you're a good man." She smiled and put her hands on either side of his face. Then she gently pulled him to her and they kissed.

Don't stop. Please, not ever.

Then Armen gently released him. She stood, turned off the light and walked to the narrow hallway's arched entrance.

Orville stood and said, "I guess it's my turn to ask – where are you going?"

"To bed. Do you plan to just stand there – or are you coming with me?"

Sunday morning Orville awakened with Armen nestled against him, her knees folded behind his and an arm over his shoulder. He began to turn to her then obeyed her whispered command, "Lie still."

Her hand slowly explored his chest, its thumb and forefinger gently pinching each nipple. Then her fingers, curved like the tines of a fork, passed down his body.

He drifted from her touch to memories of last night – in the hallway. His surprise…her lips on his, clothes dropping to the floor, whispers of "I love you," …the world fading away as he entered her. Thrusts and angles; rolling over, above and below each other; cries, then the silence of breathing.

Now Armen leaned down, stroking his feet and massaging each toe. She nudged him onto his back; her fingers slowly traced long lines up his body as she stretched over him.

Celebration

MONDAY MORNING AT THE MESS HALL Bullhead sat alone, two mugs of hot coffee in front of him. "Been waiting for you, Orv. We need to get ready for Saturday's celebration. Lots to think about." He nodded towards the second mug of coffee. "That one's yourn."

"Thanks."

"I talked to the big boys upstairs. Saturday, starting about four o'clock, the governor and company big-shots, wives too, will arrive. Special train from Charleston. Some that live around here will drive. Our job is to get cars parked. And make sure tents with tables are set up, ready for a sit-down supper. Dining tents'll be pitched along the shore. We gotta get the trenches dug – six feet deep and a hundred feet long. They'll have mutton, pork and roast ox. Carcasses on spits, juice dripping out. Can you imagine that?"

"I can imagine trenches. We spent enough time in 'em. The hard part is making my mind fill the trenches with hot coals instead of mud and soldiers."

"The war's been over for years, Orv." He squinted as if to see Orville more clearly. "I'll post notices around the shanty camps. Men can earn extra money on Saturday – set up tents, dig the pits and help with the roasting. Some will serve food. We got to make sure they don't eat more than their wages. Later they can take down the tents and clean up. Whites thirty-five cents an hour, coloreds thirty. Shouldn't have any trouble finding takers. Lloyd's going to keep track of who works and for how long.

"After supper, guests will go up the mountain to the country club. There'll be music and dancing. Hey Orv, know why Baptists are against having sex standing up?"

"What? No, I don't know."

"Afraid it'll lead to dancing." Bullhead roared a belly laugh. "Get it?" He cleared his throat. "We'll need a passel of boys to work up at the country club. Me and you'll have to keep our eyes peeled – make sure the silverware is an arm's length away from those boys. Bet not a one of the coloreds has ever been near a country club, or seen a governor, or a woman in a fancy dress. Come to think of it, the same could be said of the whites."

Orville had supper at the café and waited for Armen to finish her shift. The man in the black coat sat in a back booth and left before the café emptied.

He drove Armen home.

"Want to come in?"

He laughed, "Silly question, Sweet Lady."

Walking across the yard her face shone gold in the soft rays of early dusk. He took her hand. But she jerked it away and walked faster.

Once inside he asked, "Why'd you pull away? Can't we hold hands?"

She took his hand. "Orville, I may look like I'm white. But the truth is, I'm part colored. That makes me a Negro. And I live in Gamoca, Fayette County, West Virginia. That's where we are, Orville." She raised her voice, "I may be in love with you, but here whites and Negroes can't – don't – hold hands where they can be seen."

He wanted the two of them to run to a place where they could walk down the street holding hands, free, in love, lovers. "But no one ..."

"What if people find out about my momma?"

"Maybe they won't." He studied Armen's hand.

"Let's take it slow, Orville. Outside my house, we're just friends. Inside my house, we can do what we choose. There are lots of eyes out there. I trust my neighbors, but we need to be careful. Remember that, Orville, please." She put her arms around him.

WEDNESDAY MORNING ORVILLE READ the bulletin tacked to the front door of the mess hall. Across its top, "HOLE-THROUGH REDUCTION IN WORK FORCE," had been underlined in red ink. "Commencing with the morning shift on Thursday, August 13, 1931, the workforce in shafts 1 and 2 will be reduced, starting with drillers, muckers, pitboys, steel nippers and shovel runners. Lloyd Sykes will post the names of laid-off workers at the shaft entrances. Each man on the list is to 1) pick up his final pay from Howard McComas, 2) remove all belongings from company housing, and 3) vacate the premises. Deputy McCloud is responsible for enforcing points two and three."

Beside it a second notice had been posted. "HELP WANTED. Men needed to help with gala celebration of the hole-through. FRIDAY AUGUST 14 SITE PREPARATION, 10 AM – 6 PM. SATURDAY AUGUST 15. 12 NOON TIL 12 MIDNIGHT COOK AND SERVE. UP TO 35 CENTS PER HOUR. Saturday – daytime at the dam site and night time at the country club (near Hawks Nest overlook). Contact Lloyd Sykes at headquarters."

ON HIS FRIDAY MORNING ROUNDS of camps one and two, Orville found many shanties empty.

A worker spoke to Orville, squeezing his words in between racks of coughs. "Reckon you'll not be rousting us much longer, Deputy."

"When you boys expect to hole-through?"

The worker took a deep breath, "A few hundred feet yet to go. Still solid rock. Probably next month." He looked down, "Reckon I'll be laid off with everybody else."

"You plan to go home after the hole-through?"

"Home – where's that?" He crossed his arms tight over his chest and said in a weak voice, "Anyway, with this tunnelitis…don't know how far I'd get. I'll drift along. Maybe over to Gauley Bridge…I heard they got rooms there…maybe go down to Charleston.

"You plan to work the celebration on Saturday?"

"Don't seem right."

"What don't?"

"Them celebrating what we done…like they done it all. If there was something to celebrate, you'd think we'd be doing it." He coughed. "Getting rid of this tunnelitis, now that'd be something to celebrate." He shook his head, "I signed up with Lloyd Sykes for Saturday. I need the money."

Saturday morning Orville made his rounds, then drove to the mess hall. He and Bullhead sat at their usual table.

"Looks like a scorcher this afternoon, Orv. Here's the plan for today. You watch over the barbeque pits and the parking of cars. Make sure the boys keep the coals stoked, spits turning, and the cars tucked in straight. I'll take care of the tents and tables. Let's both meet the governor's train. Four o'clock. Then, about four-thirty, O.M. Jones will give Governor Conley and his people a ride through shafts one and two – a single smooth rail line, start to finish." Bullhead flashed a grin so wide Orville could see the line of brown stain that separated the tops of his teeth from his bright red gums.

At four o'clock Governor and Mrs. William Conley stepped down from their Pullman car into the bright sun, followed by state officials and wives who opened parasols. The visitors received greetings from a receiving line, O.M. Jones and his wife at its head, and to his left executives and wives from Union Carbide and its subsidiary, the New Kanawha Power Company, Hollis Dennis, one of the owners of Rinehart and Dennis, and near its end, beneath a pink parasol, Mrs. Jimison.

Orville and Bullhead stood behind the receiving line. Bullhead gazed wide-eyed at the governor. Orville scanned the crowd of guests and newspaper reporters; anything could happen.

He also kept his eyes on the army of men who had exchanged their dusty work clothes for white cotton jackets and trousers, most of them ill-fitting and now nearly all soaked with perspiration. Men coughed as they stoked the hot coals in the trenches and turned the slabs of meat on the large iron grills. A crew rotated the carcasses on spits.

Some of the ladies carried small valises. White-coated Negroes took their luggage and carried it to a large yellow tent, a sign over its entrance, "Guests – Ladies Only."

At six o'clock Orville and Bullhead stood near the speakers' table, just beyond the rolled up walls of the main dining tent. Continuous red, white, and blue bunting had been hung around the tents. Lloyd Sykes stood with a notebook and pencil; he glanced towards each worker and made entries in his notebook.

O.M. Jones, seated at the center of the head table, the governor to his right, stood and rhythmically tapped a teaspoon against a long-stemmed crystal glass. Bell-like pings rippled beneath the tent. Conversations subsided. Two photographers stepped forward with bulky press cameras bearing flash attachments. With each burst of light, they captured images of the white-clothed speakers' table, men in seersucker and white linen suits, women in gowns of pastel blue, pink and yellow.

When the photographers reached the rear of the large tent, O.M. Jones projected his voice over the assembly, "Governor and Mrs. Conley, ladies and gentlemen, welcome to Hawks Nest tunnel. In addition to the Conleys, we're pleased to have former Congressman and Mrs. Taylor, as well as state Senator Johnson and his lovely wife with us. And special greetings to officials from Union Carbide, the New Kanawha Power Company, and our contractor, Rinehart and Dennis." He paused as applause, led by the governor, rippled through the tent.

"This afternoon, you took a ride…"

Near the center of the tent crystal crashed and shattered – a woman's scream sliced the air as a Negro waiter fell across a table. His head and shoulders lay on the table. His arms flailed; he coughed and spit white phlegm. Men seized the waiter's upper arms and dragged him outside the tent, where they lowered him to the ground.

Orville grabbed a glass of water and knelt beside the man. "You'll be okay. Relax." The man sipped the water. He looked up at Orville, wheezed a quiet "Sorry," and then closed his eyes. Two workers raised the man to his feet, extended each of his arms over their shoulders, and led him away. When would this man be making the trip to Summersville?

Lloyd stood near Orville. "Hope that boy don't think he's going to be paid," he whined. "He done broke enough china and crystal to pay his wages for a year."

His life, Lloyd, will that be enough to cover damages?

The guests returned to their seats and waiters replaced the broken dinnerware. Mr. Jones again tapped a glass with a spoon. The guests fell quiet. "Governor and Mrs. Conley, ladies and gentlemen, I sincerely apologize for the disturbance." He paused and grinned. "Folks, just between us, I'm told the darkies working here sometimes have late night parties. Looks to me like that boy stayed a little too long at the party last night." The governor, followed by the guests, laughed.

In the center of the tent a man shouted, "Hey O.M., find out where tonight's party is at. Maybe we can all go." Everyone laughed.

The laughter ended and faces turned towards Mr. Jones. "Getting back to our dinner and the fellowship of this celebration, a little while ago you took a ride through most, though not all, of Hawks Nest tunnel. In a few weeks, when we connect the remaining shafts, well, I can hardly believe I'm saying this, except for the fact that it's true, we will have constructed the longest," he paused, "and the largest," another pause, "tunnel – in the world." Applause burst from the guests. O.M. Jones' face glowed.

The governor rose and extended his hand to Mr. Jones. When the applause ended Mr. Jones continued, "Thank you, though in all humility, I recognize your applause wasn't for me, but for the engineers, the construction managers, the C&O railroad, there are so many…"

Orville walked to the shore of the New River. The sound of its rushing water replaced the voice of O.M. Jones. He sat on a boulder. To his right the white tents and cooking pits spread along the base of the mountain – to his left rose the nearly completed dam, beside it the large open mouth of the tunnel waiting to swallow its forever-long drink of the river. Soon it would have that drink and, like an eel, send electricity out its other end.

O.M. Jones' dream come true. Orville Orr had been a cog in the giant wheel of progress. Disgust surged through him. He wished he could pour it into a pot and dump it on O.M. Jones and Bullhead; on the big boys upstairs; on Mrs. Jimison. On himself.

AT DUSK ORVILLE DROVE up the mountain to the country club, a Tudor-style building that seemed better suited to France or England than Gauley Bridge. He entered the club house. Musicians milled around the ballroom warming up by playing brief passages of tunes. Red, white and blue crepe paper had been draped in long bands across the ceiling. On the wide outdoor patio, with its commanding view of the overlook and gorge, the glow of Japanese lanterns mirrored the sky's pastel blue, pink and orange. Musicians from a second, outside, orchestra prepared for the evening.

Armen carried napkins across the patio to a serving table. Her tan face and dark hair contrasted with her starched white uniform.

"The most beautiful woman at the party."

"Thanks." She smiled, "Just remember where we are."

Orville returned to the parking lot. In an hour all the guests' cars had been parked. He seated himself in the grass on a hillside overlooking the patio and listened to the music as guests danced. Most likely many of them owned stock in Union Carbide – how many deaths did it take to boost share values?

Near midnight Armen joined him on the darkened lawn. When the band played "I Found a Million Dollar Baby in a Five and Ten Cent Store," they stretched out on the grass, their hands touching. The orchestra's music slowed. Cheek-to-cheek, couples moved around the dance floor below as the band played "I Don't Know Why I Love You Like I Do."

A few yards beyond the heavy wooden beams fencing the perimeter of the patio, men who'd dug the tunnel and tonight had served food, poured drinks, and cooked the roast ox, sat on the lawn beneath a canopy of dogwood branches. White jackets now stained and unbuttoned, the men watched the dancing couples.

The orchestra began to play a slow, almost mournful, "Good Night Sweetheart." At the same time a worker began to sing the song Hardware Washington had sung in the shanties, Joe Hill's "Preacher and the Slave," its lyrics set to the melody of the old hymn, "In the Sweet Bye and Bye." Other workers on the lawn joined him.

> *Long-haired preachers* (some men inserted "bosses") *come out every night,*
> *Try to tell you what's wrong and what's right;*
> *But when asked how 'bout something to eat*
> *They will answer in voices so sweet*

You will eat, bye and bye,
In that glorious land above the sky;
Work and pray, live on hay,
You'll get pie in the sky when you die

One by one the orchestra's musicians stopped playing and turned towards the men in the shadows. Couples on the dance floor stood motionless.

In chant and response the men sang the final chorus,

You will eat,   bye and bye,
              (you will eat),   (bye and bye),

When you've learned how to cook and how to fry;
                                        (how to fry),

Chop some wood,   'twill do you good
              (chop some wood)   (do you good),

Then you'll eat in the sweet bye and bye
                              (bye and bye).

Workers and dancers stared at one another. Coughs broke the night's silence.

Handshakes of Farewell

AT THE BASEBALL GAME on the second Sunday in September, Shirley leaned on his daddy as he walked to the grassy area behind the Drillers' bench. When the Drillers came to bat in the first inning Orville sat beside him.

"Orville, they tell me shafts three and four will hole-through pretty soon."

"That's what I hear. Could be this week."

Shirley coughed. "Then things will wind down. Hope I can work to the end."

"What makes you think you won't?"

"Momma's worried about my tunnelitis. Wants me to quit now. I keep telling her I can work okay." He took a deep breath. "They may need mechanics even after the hole-through and men get laid off. We can put my wages aside for a rainy day – there may be a lot of those. Once the drilling ends, Daddy, Cecil and Owen, too, are likely to be idle."

And with no workers there won't be a job for a shack rouster. He wondered what he'd do, where he might go; whether Armen would go with him. He had enough money put aside to get by for awhile, enough to support himself and Armen, if she'd have him, till they landed on their feet.

But he didn't know how far he had to fall before landing.

After the game players and spectators again shook hands and said their goodbyes. They reminded Orville more of troops in France who'd received orders to return home, unlikely to see each other again, than men who'd join one another for work tomorrow. He said goodbye, too.

223

Four days later, Thursday, September 13th, shafts three and four holed-through. On Friday morning when Orville arrived at the mess hall a bulletin announcing lay-offs had been tacked to the front door. He joined Bullhead at a table and nodded towards the door. "Shack rousting will soon get a lot easier."

"Tours of duty are winding down."

"How long you figure before we get laid off?"

"Well, there's a lot of work yet to do, Orv. Wrap up the dam and the sluice gates. And finish building the power house. Then install the penstocks to bring water to the turbines. Electrical systems, too. O.M. Jones has been telling people it'll take about two years. But most of the work will be done by engineers and craftsmen, not shanty workers."

"Guess that leaves us out. And unemployed."

"Well Orv, the big boys upstairs worry about labor unrest in the coal fields. To them, Matewan and Blair Mountain could've happened yesterday." Bullhead winked. "I told them a radical with a few sticks of dynamite could do some real damage around here. They'd do well to pay attention to the security of the tunnel. Power house too."

Orville cracked a sly smile. "You're always thinking about the interests of the company."

"They agreed with me." Bullhead grinned. "We got lots of work ahead of us, Orv."

On the payroll – he'd be able to keep his home in Kettle! For a moment, Orville allowed himself to imagine sharing his home with Armen.

That afternoon he went to tunnel headquarters to tell Howard he'd be staying on the job. Orville entered the old house's long hallway. Approaching Howard's office, Bullhead's raspy voice came from behind a partially open door.

"Don't know what's got into my ol' buddy – well he *used* to be my buddy. Now I'm starting to wonder if he's working for Carbide – or for the Joneses." Then after a long pause, "Or maybe for the UMW."

"You sure about all that?"

"Won't be too hard to figure out. If I'm right the big boys upstairs may want to do something about it – about him."

June, 1932: Shirley

THE BLUE-WHITE LIGHT from the gas street lamp seeped through Orville's bedroom window and gave a ghostly presence to the wallpaper's faded fleurs-de-lis. His khaki shirt, draped over the straight-back chair beside the door, stood as a diminutive sentinel. In the streetlamp's glow his deputy sheriff's star gleamed as a single watchful eye. Orville checked the luminous hands on the nightstand's brass alarm clock, its ticking the room's only sound until the call of a whip-poor-will rode in on a flower-scented breeze. Three o'clock.

"Nooooo!" he had yelled, perhaps screamed, he didn't know, a moment earlier awakening from that dream. Would it never go away? Had he awakened the men down the hall? He leaned against the bed's iron headboard, his undershirt soaked with sweat – not the hot sweat produced by a warm night in June, but the cold sweat of fear. He ran his fingers along the headboard's top rail. He'd gone to sleep in Gauley Bridge, not in a battlefield trench in France. The calendar carried the year 1932, not 1918. He pulled the sheet to his face and wiped his forehead.

Orville again lived the nightmare. Men along the trench shouted the dreaded words, "Gas! Gas! Gas!" the cry repeated a hundred times, then a hundred more, soldier to soldier, buddy to buddy, each man to himself. A light breeze turned white drifted towards him. Hunkered down in muddy trenches, men threw off helmets and put on gas masks.

He reached for his gas mask but clutched only empty hooks. Orville twisted off his knapsack and jerked it open. Empty. He searched the trench's muddy water. Waves of lethal German fog drifted towards him.

225

Orville leaped up the earthen steps and ran with the breeze, away from the trench and ahead of the gas, every fiber in his legs thrusting. The ground turned to soft mud; his feet slid. A German machine gun fired. To his right bullets pock-marked the mushy earth and came ever closer, blazing-hot points of lead searching for him. His legs churned, but he moved at little more than a crawl. Bullets thudded the earth next to him. The gas crept to just a few yards away. "Nooooo!"

"Advance! Advance!" he commanded. Men climbed out of the deep trenches and walked into machine gun fire. They fell wounded and dead. Men surprised by mustard gas choked as their lungs blistered.

Why had he been spared while men around him died? Orville rested his head on the pillow. His eyelids begged for rest, for sleep.

From the stairs beyond his room, labored breathing accompanied slow footsteps. The footsteps approached his door, then came a gentle knock. Orville opened the door.

The hallway's dim light fell on Charlie Jones, grown thin in the past nine months, his lined face now wet with perspiration, ashen and more drawn than when Orville left the Jones home yesterday evening.

"Shirley, he asked for you."

"Come in, sit down." Orville turned on the lamp and dressed.

Charlie sat on the edge of the bed and passed a red bandanna over his face. Each breath jerked his upper body. A year ago he had been a strapping center fielder on the Drillers. Now he'd become so thin his shirt borrowed from a larger man.

Orville parked in front of the Jones house, its once-white exterior now gray weathered boards turned silver by the moonlight. Similar houses lined both sides of the street. "Our rent to the company's so long overdue," Charlie had told him, "I figure we'll get an eviction notice any day."

On Orville's first visit to the Jones home, a Sunday dinner after Shirley had become a mechanic, Charlie had said with a proud smile, "Don't know where Shirley gets his smarts about mechanical things. He's only seventeen. We've never owned a car."

With the drilling ended, Charlie had told him, each day he and his sons sat on their front porch. "Hope the sun'll restore a smidgen of health.

Soak up enough of it and maybe we'll get better."

Charlie gripped Orville's forearm as they walked across the little front yard. On each of the porch's front steps they paused for Charlie to catch his breath. Cecil and Owen met them at the front door.

Mrs. Jones, her lips drawn tight, pulled a black shawl over her shoulders. She spoke in a near-whisper, "He's been waiting for you." Her voice cracked, "He wants to say goodbye." She motioned for Orville to follow her.

In the bedroom's stale warm air, yellow light from the oil lamp on the bedside table gave a trace of color to Shirley's face. His sunken cheeks and red eyelids resembled a mask, not the face of a young man. Each shallow breath would for an instant raise the quilt. Then the quilt would drop like a tunnel's rock-fall. Shirley raised his left hand a few inches and extended it to Orville. With his right hand he nudged the quilt off his chest. He pulled Orville's hand to his chest.

"Th...thump it," he whispered. His breath gave off the odor of a farm pond's decayed reeds.

"What?"

"Thump your finger," Shirley paused to inhale, "here." He pointed to his chest.

"Like this?" Orville gave Shirley's chest a light tap with his index finger.

"Harder."

Orville pressed his index finger against his thumb then released it. Its strike against Shirley's chest produced not a thump but something that sounded like a padded mallet striking a metal drum.

Shirley whispered, "I'm all hard inside... It's like my lungs're made of stone." He gasped a breath and gave a slight smile, "Or maybe...made of glass." He looked at his mother, nodded then rolled his eyes towards Orville.

"I'll tell him, Shirley," she said in a reassuring voice. Mrs. Jones turned to Orville and twisted away. Her hands covering her face, her shoulders rose and fell with her sobs.

She took a deep breath and faced Orville. "He asked me to tell you what he insisted on, a couple of weeks ago." Her voice drained of any emotion. "'Mother, after I'm dead, have them open me up and see if I didn't die from the job.'" She wiped her eyes. "'See if I didn't die from the job.' Orville, Shirley didn't believe them workers died from what Doc Henderson called tunnelitis. He said, 'The dust in the tunnel is killing us.'"

Shirley's weak smile confirmed what his mother had said. He closed his eyes.

Mrs. Jones whispered, "Let him rest."

Orville squeezed Shirley's hand, "See you in a while."

Shirley's eyes opened, "A while."

When Orville returned to the living room, Charlie rose from his chair, shuffled into the bedroom and closed the door. Orville sat with Cecil and Owen, the silence of their vigil broken only by raspy breathing.

Mrs. Jones returned, her eyes swollen. "Y'all come in."

The family and Orville stood around Shirley's bed. He labored for breath but soon the movement of his quilt slowed. His eyes flickered, the quilt became still.

Orville sat on the wooden steps of the narrow front porch and leaned his head against the banister. Along the top of the mountain behind the company houses, dawn painted the ridge pink then orange. The sun's rays trickled down the mountain into the narrow valley. The fresh colors of the morning nudged Orville towards the optimism of a new day.

Then he remembered Shirley. Jimmy Campbell. Men in France and men at the tunnel.

On Shirley's last day at work he had repaired a dinkey and come to the tunnel entrance to report its completion. He and Shirley had chatted; Shirley had waved goodbye and walked into the tunnel's fog of dust.

Orville took a deep breath and for a moment marveled in that simple act – inhale, hold the air, and then release it – an act that had become a moment-to-moment struggle for Charlie, for men in town. He imagined Gauley Bridge and the little settlements tucked into the surrounding valleys to be like an old lake with poor drainage, silting up with the sediment of men who had to gasp for breath; lungs hardening day by day, the end of their lives ever closer. Death would flush the sediment.

Cletus' words at Armen's daddy's funeral – "We're a town of the living dead."

"Safe as walking down a dusty road on a summer day," a construction manager had said to tunnel supervisors. "You boys are more likely to get hit by a train than to be done in by tunnel dust." Men laughed. One yelled, "All you need to do is…" then blew a loud honk on a blue bandana. Laughter skipped across the room.

The door to the front porch opened. Mrs. Jones stood in the doorway, shoulders slumped, arms against the door frame, tired face lit by a strand of sunlight. "Come inside, Orville. Coffee will do you good."

She held Orville's arm as they walked to the kitchen. She poured coffee for everyone and placed a plate of home-baked bread in the center of the table. "Sorry we don't have more to offer you, Orville. With nobody working we're hard pressed."

"I'm not hungry. But thanks. Coffee will do just fine."

Charlie folded his hands, rested his elbows on the table, and supported his bowed head with his hands. His voice weak, Charlie said, "Lord, bless this food to our bodies, for you know we need it if we're to do your will, and bless us to thy service." He took two deep breaths, "And we ask your special grace on Shirley, Lord. Hold him in your arms. In Heaven, once he's up and around," another pause and labored deep breath, "I know Shirley'll help out some, fix things for you. We loved him, Lord. Still do. Help us bear our grief. Amen."

No one spoke. Owen wiped his eyes. They sipped their coffee.

Mrs. Jones said, "Orville, you remember last September when Shirley took bad sick?"

"Yes. I offered to bring him home. He said, 'No, I can still walk.'"

"He came home and told me, 'Ma, I'm awful short-winded.' I said, 'Well, if you don't get to feeling better, you'll not work no more.' That was his last day at the tunnel."

Mrs. Jones walked to the kitchen stove. A year ago Charlie had pointed to the stove and said with pride, "We could afford it, with all of us working, and Emma deserved it." That seemed a lifetime ago. She carried the coffee pot to the table. "Orville, it looks to me like," her voice cracked, "it looks to me like Charlie, maybe Cecil and Owen too, have Shirley's sickness." She held the pot over Orville's cup, "More?"

Orville nodded.

She poured coffee. "I'd heard talk of how X-rays could tell what's inside a body, broken bones, tumors and such, and wondered if it would help to get Shirley's lungs X-rayed. Maybe, I thought, if we knew what we were up against we might do something about it. I asked Doc Harless if he would X-ray Shirley. He said, 'Yes, but not without the money in advance.'"

Cecil muttered, "Doc Harless won't go to his grave a poor man."

"We didn't have the money, and I didn't know how to come up with it. But I prayed and started saving from what I earned taking in wash."

"I could've helped. I have some money put away."

"You'll need your money once the tunnel is done," Mrs. Jones said. "And even though you been a friend, Orville, you're a company man. It didn't seem right to ask. Three weeks ago we finally got enough cash together. Doc Harless took our money and X-rayed Shirley's lungs. He said, 'An X-ray can't be one hundred percent certain but it looks like silicosis.' I'd never heard of silicosis. But I thought, now that we know Shirley's affliction, Doc can treat him. I was wrong. There was nothing to be done. 'Mother,' he said, 'after I'm dead, have them open me up and see if I didn't die from the job.' Without a doctor who'll cut him open and look at his lungs we still can't be sure what killed him."

The men in the shafts, the men around this table, big men, strong as stands of virgin timber, now too sick to work. Cut down in their prime. Like logs floating downstream, men drifted away, some into the hills, others on freight cars – all soon to die. Hundreds more, skin and bones, red rims around hollow eyes, the men Cletus called the living dead, shuffled along the streets of Gauley Bridge. Each sundown marked another day towards chests of glass.

The Hawks Nest war – the men of Union Carbide's army against Gauley Mountain. They had their way with the old girl. Blasted and poked their drills into her; laid down rails and carted her innards out. She did their bidding. But old Gauley fooled them. She invaded the men who ravaged her. And when men tried to counterattack, they had no weapons. Charlie, Cecil, and Owen, men walking the streets of Gauley Bridge, knew the truth. Union Carbide might declare victory, open the sluice gates and run the New to the turbines. But old Gauley had extracted her price. In lives.

He'd carried out orders; rousted men in the shacks and sent them into the tunnel. Carried out orders in France, too. Over there, over here, sending men to their deaths.

He could get in his Ford and put distance between himself and Gauley Bridge. But he still had a job. Lots of men didn't. And he had Armen.

Orville looked around the table, "Y'all going to do what Shirley asked – get a doc to cut him open and find out what killed him?"

Mrs. Jones shook her head, "We got no money to do that."

"I have a car. And some money. I could take Shirley, well, his body, to Doc Harless if he'll do the autopsy."

Shirley's voice said "Do what's right, Orville. Do what's right."

Then Cletus wheezed, "Do what's right? Hey Orville, what you think will happen if you get that autopsy done and the docs find the dust killed him? Won't be a secret for long. What if somebody points a finger at you – there's the man responsible for singling out Union Carbide and the dust, for turning things upside down. Reckon the company will thank you for shedding light on things?" The voice hooted a laugh that became a cough.

At the corn-field's make-shift burial ground, Joe Craddock's widow cried, "You done defiled the dead, deputy. And all for a few pieces of silver. Uh-huh, you and Judas, you know one another. Do what's right? My man's laughing in his grave."

His voice strained, Charlie said, "Doc just might do it, with money in advance he might." He coughed. "Lots of men is dying, Orville. And I hate to say it, but lots more," his voice fell to a near-whisper and he looked at his sons, "are on their own version of death row. If you take Shirley to Doc Harless and he finds the tunnel dust killed him, it'll point the finger of blame towards...well, towards Union Carbide."

Cecil said, "Orville, you're wearing a deputy sheriff's badge. You being a company man and all, getting involved in this is likely to put you in a hard position."

Owen gazed at Orville's gold star. "A hard position?" He turned to his brother, "Cecil, you seen what the company done to men who got crossways with it." Owen looked Orville straight in the eye, "You may be fixing for a trip to the rock crusher."

Death from the Job

S HORTLY BEFORE NINE O'CLOCK, as a thunderstorm ended, Orville parked his Ford in front of Dr. Harless' office. He and Charles sat in the car until Dr. Harless walked along the street to his office. The two men approached him.

"Doc, can we speak with you for a minute?" Charles asked.

"What can I do for you?"

"I'm Charlie Jones."

Dr. Harless nodded.

"This here's Orville Orr."

"I remember you, Orville. From the Bodigian home."

"Doc, a while back you X-rayed my boy, Shirley." Charlie looked down; his voice cracked as he continued, "A few hours ago he passed away." He looked up, "We're not sure what to do, Doc. Can you come?"

"We can take my car, Doc, it's right here."

Dr. Harless nodded and the men got in the car.

Orville parked in front of the Jones home. The three men walked across the yard, Dr. Harless and Orville well ahead of Charlie.

Mrs. Jones met them at the door. She led Dr. Harless into Shirley's bedroom.

Dr. Harless gazed at the quilt-covered form on the bed. Then he lowered the quilt. He lifted Shirley's arm, placed his fingers around his wrist, then put Shirley's hand on his chest. He briefly raised then lowered each eyelid. "What time did he pass away?"

"About three-thirty or four. Before sunrise," Mrs. Jones answered.

233

"I'm sorry," he took Mrs. Jones' hand, "though, after that chest X-ray I can't say I'm surprised. He was in a lot of pain. It's a small consolation I know, but he's at peace now. We'll need to get him to an undertaker. Do you want to use Bingham's in town?"

Charlie answered, "Bingham's would be fine, Doc, but we was thinking of another stop along the way."

"Another stop?"

"Yes sir. We'd like to, well I don't hardly know how to ask." He looked at Orville.

"Dr. Harless, the family's been discussing an autopsy."

Mrs. Jones interrupted, "Doc, before Shirley died he said 'Mother, after I'm dead, have them open me up – see if I didn't die from the job.' We want you to open him up, find out if that dust killed him."

Orville said, "I'll pay for it, Doc."

"An autopsy for a medically untended death is a legal requirement. But having already examined Shirley, I could waive it. Are you sure you want to do this?"

"It's the only way, Doc. We need to know."

On the drive to town, Shirley's quilt-draped body lay in the back seat. Dr. Harless sat beside Orville. Dr. Harless' words about the legal requirement of an autopsy for untended deaths echoed in Orville's thoughts. He heard Frog give a derisive laugh and say in his deep voice, "Well, maybe some untended deaths – that law's for white folks. Not for us."

Orville carried Shirley's quilt-draped body into Dr. Harless' office.

Dr. Harless pointed to the examining table, "Put him there, on his back, please." He removed Shirley's quilt and replaced it with a white sheet. He folded the quilt and handed it to Orville.

"Now, I'll need to get on with my work. When I've finished I'll call the funeral home and ask Mr. Bingham to come get Shirley's body, prepare him for burial."

"When will you tell us the results?"

"The typist will be here in the morning. Stop by early tomorrow afternoon."

"Thank you, Doc."

ORVILLE DROVE TO THE MESS HALL. Bullhead sat alone eating lunch. He signaled Orville to join him.

Orville put a cheese sandwich and a glass of sweet tea on a tray and walked to the table.

Bullhead looked up, his mouth full of ham sandwich, "Hey, Orv. Good to see you."

"You too."

"Missed you this morning."

"I had some personal business to take care of. Sorry."

"Now that's odd, you mentioning personal business. Just yesterday one of the big boys upstairs said, 'For a man who's got no family around Gauley Bridge, that Orville Orr sure seems to have a lot of personal business to tend to.'" Bullhead took a drink of tea then belched. "Now as far as I'm concerned, a man's private affairs is his own. It's no business of Union Carbide nor anybody else. Just thought you should know. Whatever you're doing is drawing attention."

They ate in silence until Bullhead said, the pace of his words slow, "Understand you had a late night, last night, Orv. Or maybe I should say an early, real early, morning this morning. I mean out before sunrise."

The big boys upstairs might do something crazy. Someone had been watching him.

"Shirley Jones died during the night."

"I heard." Bullhead took a large bite of sandwich. "Sorry…" He paused and probed his mouth with an index finger, then extracted a partially chewed piece of ham. "Damn, this ham's full of gristle. Wedges between my teeth. Got one that needs to be pulled." He cleared his throat. "I was saying, sorry about that Jones boy."

"Shirley asked for me."

Bullhead's eyebrows arched, "He did? Now that seems a bit odd, don't it. Shirley asking for you. His momma or daddy? I understand that. But Orville Orr? Help me, ol' buddy. Why would he ask for you?"

How much did he know about his connection to Shirley, about this morning, about Dr. Harless? Bullhead's face remained flaccid, his eyes unexpressive. A battle face. "We've been friends since last year when I got him that mechanics job; used to spend time together at the baseball games."

"Understand his daddy and brothers have took ill with tunnelitis."

"They've come down with something. Could be tunnelitis."

"Hard to say, though, ain't that right? I suppose that if a man was sick and didn't trust our own doc's diagnosis, well now, what would he do? Call Doc Harless?"

"He could."

"And then, what if the sick man in question died?"

"What're you driving at?"

Bullhead raised and lowered his glass of iced tea and stared at its moist rings on the tabletop. Then he smeared the rings with the base of the glass. "Here's my drift, Orv. Why would somebody, say the close friend of a family who'd just lost a loved one, transport the body of the man who'd died to Doc Harless' office instead of to the funeral home? Dead is dead. Ain't no coming back. Lazarus is in the Bible, not at Gauley Bridge. Doc Harless can't perform miracles, can he?"

Orville pushed his tray towards the center of the table. All night, this morning too, they had watched the Jones house, Mrs. Jimison's too. In France unknown eyes had spied upon him night after night. He'd come to fear their invisible presence. Now that fear rose up again. "Maybe you ought to go ask Doc Harless your questions. Afraid I can't help you."

"Hey, hey, easy ol' buddy. All this talk is hypo…hypo…what did the captain call it?"

"Hypothetical."

Bullhead grinned. "That's it," he snapped his fingers, "hypo-thetical."

Orville began to stand up.

"One more thing, Orv. Need to ask a favor."

Orville sat down.

"And there's a little money for you." He laughed, "Don't get that expression on your face. This don't involve no corpses. Just a packet of papers the company needs to get over to Mr. Sprigg. It'll be ready shortly after quitting time. Tacked to the front door of the construction office over at the power house. Can you deliver it?"

Did he have a reason to say no? He and Bullhead went back a long ways. They'd survived combat together, probably saved each other's lives. He'd said no to delivering more bodies, then delivered one more. He could do one more favor. "I…" he took a drink of tea "…well, I suppose so."

Bullhead handed him a ten-dollar bill. "Here you go – payment in advance." He croaked, "Thanks, ol' buddy. Knew I could count on you."

Orville stared at the bill. Two corpses delivered to Mr. Sprigg. Two days wages. One more trip.

AT FIVE O'CLOCK Orville walked into the Bridge View. A man sat at the counter drinking coffee, in a booth a couple ate lunch. He joined Armen at the end of the counter.

Her eyes flashed and she put her hand on his arm. "Hello."

"Prettiest lady in the café."

She poked him in the chest with her index finger, "You running for mayor?"

"I have something I need to do this evening. Thought you should know."

Her smile vanished. "What?"

"Bullhead asked me to take a packet of papers to Summersville. I agreed to do it."

"I thought you were through with those trips."

"He needs a favor. I've missed a lot of work in helping out with Shirley and he's covered for me. One more trip won't hurt. And once we know the results of," he looked towards the man at the counter and lowered his voice, "Doc Harless's autopsy, things are likely to change. A lot."

"Be careful. Please."

"A million Germans tried to do me in and failed. Nobody's going to harm me here in Gauley Bridge. I'll be fine."

Rock of Ages

ORVILLE DROVE TO THE JONES HOME in Gamoca. Mrs. Jones met him at the front door. "Are Owen and Cecil here?"

"Yes. Is something wrong?"

"Not sure." He told the family about Bullhead's request, and that he'd agreed to carry the packet to Summersville. "But I'm uneasy about it. Something just doesn't feel right."

"And?" Charlie asked.

Orville said to Owen and Cecil, "I'd feel a lot better if you fellows would ride along with me. Just in case."

"Just in case of what?" Mrs. Jones asked in a worried voice.

"Wish I knew. But I'd feel better if I had some friends along."

The men walked to the car. Owen said, "I think Cecil and me should sit in the back seat. Stay tucked away. Most likely nothing will happen. But if it does, anybody causing trouble will get more than they bargained for."

Orville drove along U.S. 60 to the base of Gauley Mountain, then turned onto a narrow gravel road that paralleled the New River. A mile later he parked in a clearing along the shore, still muddy from the morning's rain. Beyond it, extending into the river, rose the foundation and walls of the new powerhouse. Starting at the base of Gauley Mountain deep trenches extended from the dark mouth of the tunnel to the foundation. Next to the powerhouse stood an unpainted one-story building, a manila envelope tacked to its front door.

Over his shoulder Orville said, "There it is. I'll be back in a minute."

He walked across a muddy field to the construction office and removed the small tack that held the packet to the door. As he glanced at the handwritten note scrawled across it, "Deliver to E.T. Sprigg, Summersville," the packet slipped from his hand. He quickly bent to catch it before it fell into the mud.

A bullet wined over Orville's head and splintered the frame of the front door. He fell to the ground and rolled. He dropped the packet, jumped up and ran zig-zag along the trenches to the tunnel entrance. His feet slipped; to his left mud splattered as a bullet struck – this time he heard the crack of a rifle. He ran towards the right side of the entrance then, a second before passing through it, leaped to the left. At the moment of his leap – crack – a bullet ricocheted off the right side of the entrance and, like a hornet searching for warm flesh, sped into the tunnel's darkness.

Orville ran beyond the forward edge of the late afternoon sunlight that glinted through the entrance. In the darkness he stopped, safe for a moment, and leaned against the tunnel wall. He took deep breaths. His vision slowly adjusted to the darkness. He glanced at the entrance; whoever fired had aimed to kill him. They'd soon be after him again.

But he'd arrived first and he owned the cover of darkness – at least for now.

He walked further into the tunnel. Owen and Cecil must know what happened. He hoped they'd stayed hidden, but he wondered if whoever had shot at him might have already disabled, even killed, them. Right now, without them, he had two options, simple and straight. Run to the other end of the tunnel – over three miles – and hope that all the gates had been left open. Advantage – he'd have a head start on his hunter. Disadvantage – another hunter might be closing in from the other end. Or, he could stay and fight. Advantage – the cover of darkness until the hunter's vision adjusted. Disadvantage – his enemy had a weapon. But with darkness came the element of surprise; the hunted became the hunter.

Somewhere beyond the tunnel entrance a familiar bass voice began to slowly sing, "Rock of ages, cleft for me, let me hide myself in thee…"

Bullhead!

Orville squinted as the outside light assaulted his eyes. No, don't look there. Adjust to the darkness. Maintain night vision.

"…let the water and the blood, from thy wounded side which flowed… be of sin the double cure, save from wrath and make me pure."

The singing stopped. The silence of the tunnel felt as total as its darkness. Then Bullhead sang again, "While I draw this fleeting breath, when mine eyes shall close in death…" The tall burly silhouette of a man holding a rifle stepped into the bright arc of the entrance. "…Rock of Ages, cleft for me, let me hide myself in thee…"

Bullhead stood silent and motionless. He raised the rifle to waist level.

Orville flattened himself against the tunnel floor as the barrel flashed. The bullet hissed over him, glanced off the stone floor's rising slope, and pinged into the tunnel's recesses. His hands touched two small stones. He grasped them.

The rifle fired again. Then came the metallic clicks of new ammunition entering the rifle.

Bullhead took a step into the tunnel. Then another. In the darkness he couldn't yet see. Soon he would be able to.

Orville stood. He mirrored Bullhead's cautious gait and walked towards him – each step a careful placement of weight, heel to toe. Feet be still.

"Rock of ages…cleft for me…" Bullhead pointed the rifle in Orville's direction and fired. "let me hide myself in thee…" He fired again.

Orville's cheek burned as the bullet grazed it. He felt the sticky warmth of his blood.

"While I draw this fleeting breath, when mine eyes shall close in death…"

Now.

Orville threw the stones across the tunnel floor. Bullhead turned towards the sound and fired. Orville leaped on him. The men fell and the rifle dropped to the tunnel floor. For a moment they wrestled, each man's arms grasping for a hold on the other. Bullhead, larger and stronger, arched his back and in a burst of energy threw Orville to the side. Both men jumped to their feet and lunged for the rifle. Bullhead got there first. He picked up the rifle and aimed it at Orville, who stood motionless.

Between gasps of breath, Bullhead said, "Ain't in as good a shape as I used to be, Orv. But I got this." He thrust the barrel of the rifle towards Orville. "And I got a job to finish. After all the company done for you, hard to figure why you couldn't stay loyal." He motioned for Orville to take a step back. "You want it in the front or the back?"

Orville threw himself to the floor and rolled.

Bullhead moaned. The rifle clattered on the floor. He dropped to his knees then toppled face forward. Two steel drill-shafts rose from his back. Behind him stood Owen and Cecil.

Orville gazed at the body as if Bullhead couldn't be trusted to be dead. To stay dead. In France, how close, how often, the two of them had brushed against death. But here, tunnel deaths mounting, how they walked down separate paths. Bullhead had been a friend; at his feet laid a stranger.

"You boys saved my life."

Owen said, "You would've done the same for us. It was him or you."

"Didn't take long to figure out what we had to do," Cecil said. "But what'll we do with his body?"

"In a few days they'll drop pipe into those trenches then pour concrete. We'll bury him at the bottom of a trench. The company can finish the job for us."

After removing the drill-shafts, Cecil lifted Bullhead's feet and Owen put his arms under Bullhead's shoulders. They carried him towards the tunnel entrance, Orville walking behind them.

A familiar sound filled the tunnel, running water and the rustle of leaves before a storm – Al's funeral – lungs of glass laboring to breathe. Men covered in white dust faced Orville, they stood shoulder to shoulder, belly to back; wall to wall. Acey and Frog, and behind them Hardware Washington, Shirley Jones, and Al Bodigian. And the men he'd roused morning after morning; men who had joked with him until, as their lungs shut down, they'd struggled to walk out the shanty door; men he had wrapped in canvas and laid in the back seat of his Ford.

Shirley Jones put his hand on Orville's shoulder and whispered, "It's over."

The rustle of leaves faded, along with the men. Al waved.

Cecil found a ladder and shovels behind the construction shanty. Orville and Owen climbed into a trench and dug Bullhead's grave. When they finished, Cecil slid Bullhead's body into the trench. The men lowered him into the grave.

"Lord," Orville said, "we ask you to bless the soul of Bullhead McCloud. The preachers tell us you are forgiving, and we ask your forgiveness for Bullhead and the damage he did down here. He believed in what he did, but somewhere he lost his way. Thank you for understanding, and for hearing our prayer. Amen."

Cecil and Owen said, "Amen."

The men placed pine branches over Bullhead, then shoveled dirt into the grave. They smoothed it to look like the floor of the trench, then climbed the ladder.

Orville drove Cecil and Owen home. Then, driving to Mrs. Jimison's place, his body, feet to head, shoulders to fingertips, began to tremble. He pulled off the road and sat with a tight grip on the steering wheel until the trembling eased. He gave thanks to be alive. And wept for the friend he had lost.

Pansy stood in the foyer dusting the table. He signaled for her to remain silent. She nodded, her eyes fixed on the bloody crease across his cheek.

He bounded up the stairs and in his room tossed clothes into a suitcase. From a hiding place in the back of his closet he removed a box of cash, nearly $2,000. He put it in the suitcase, belted it shut, and walked down the stairs. In the foyer he gave Pansy a hug. "Bye, Pansy. You're a wonderful cook and a good woman."

He jogged to his car and drove downtown. On Main Street Orville turned into the alley behind the Bridge View and parked at the back door. He left the Ford's motor running and walked into the kitchen.

A woman in a stained white apron turned hamburger patties on the grill. Armen held a tray with two plates of hot food. The women turned and stared at Orville's cheek.

"Orville...what're you...."

He put a finger to his lips. "Shhh."

Armen touched the bloody crease across his cheek and whispered, "You're hurt. What happened?"

"I'll tell you later. I'm okay. Come with me."

"Now? I have customers waiting."

"I'm leaving Gauley Bridge, Armen. Now. Forget the customers." He turned to the woman at the grill and pointed to the tray. "Will you serve those people?"

"Okay."

"Armen, come with me. We have work to do."

She picked up her purse. He took her hand, nudged the back door open and looked up and down the alley. They got in the Ford and sped to Gamoca.

He described what had happened at the powerhouse then inside the tunnel. "Sooner or later the people who sent Bullhead to kill me will start searching for me. By then we'll have others with us. We'll be safe, ready to fight back."

"Who's after you?"

"I can't be sure. Probably the men Bullhead called 'the big boys upstairs,' or men who worked for them. I know too much about the bodies in Summersville – the company and the undertaker broke every law in the book. I did too. And they've been watching me – they know what I did to get Shirley's autopsy done. If the autopsy turns out the way I think it will, it'll show he died from dust in the tunnel. It's guaranteed to start legal action by men and their families. Hundreds have died; hundreds more are sick and dying. It didn't have to happen. The company is responsible and they know it. Families will soon figure it out and go after them. It could run into millions of dollars."

He parked in front of Armen's home and scanned the street for anything, anyone unfamiliar. They went inside.

"Pack your suitcase and let's go."

"Where?"

"After your daddy's funeral, John L. Lewis asked me lots of questions about what had been happening at the tunnel. I told him about the dust, the deaths, and trips to Summerville. He said he'd talk to his people at

UMW headquarters in Indianapolis. And he gave me the name of a contact in Clifton Forge, Virginia. Insisted that I go to him when I was ready. He told me about your daddy's work as an organizer. How the two of them stood shoulder to shoulder against armed deputies. He asked me – us – to carry on your daddy's work."

Armen pulled a suitcase from the closet and put some clothes in it. "We can get the rest of my things some other time."

Dusk had fallen when they stepped out onto the front porch. As Armen locked the door Orville put his arms around her. "I love you, Sweet Lady. This is forever."

"Forever."

They embraced.

ORVILLE AND ARMEN drove all night across the mountains. Away from the death and dying of Hawks Nest; away from Bertie, Hack, and Ralph Morrison. Towards a second chance.

At dawn the Ford glided down the eastern face of the Blue Ridge Mountains into Clifton Forge. Armen pointed out the address John L. Lewis had given them. Orville parked in front of a modest white frame home, now pink with the light of a bright sunrise.

"Now, we can do it now," Orville said. He took Armen's hand. They smiled at each other and, holding hands, they walked up to the front door.

Epilogue: The Dark at the End of the Tunnel

The Scope of the Disaster

THE FOREWORD TO EPIDEMIOLOGIST Martin Cherniack's 1980s investigation of the impact of the Hawks Nest tunnel on the health of workers concluded, "The disaster at Gauley Bridge, West Virginia, killed a hitherto unimagined number of workers. Most of these men died of acute silicosis and a few in falls and cave-ins. The Gauley Bridge disaster remains today the greatest American industrial tragedy; indeed, more people died during the drilling of the Hawks Nest Tunnel than in the Triangle Shirt Waist fire, the Sunshine Mine disaster, and the Farmington Mine disaster combined. Yet Gauley Bridge is almost forgotten."[1]

Within five years of completion, Cherniack estimated Hawks Nest Tunnel claimed the lives of 764 workers, about 67% of them black. Further, he wrote, this estimate "...may well be too small. It is clear that many deaths occurring in Fayette County went unreported...The death toll of the disaster at Gauley Bridge was immense when compared with any other outbreak of industrial disease in modern history."

Cherniack's interest in Hawks Nest began in 1981. He then worked at the National Institute of Occupational Safety and Health in Cincinnati, Ohio, and took a raft trip on the Gauley River. On the trip he had an opportunity to visit the dam, power station and surge tank at the tunnel. Months later NIOSH assigned him to investigate an elevated number

---

1   *The Hawk's Nest Incident: America's Worst Industrial Disaster*, Martin Cherniack, MD, MPH. 1986, New Haven: Yale University Press.

of deaths at the Elkem metals plant in Alloy, West Virginia, near Gauley Bridge. Elkem, a large electrometallurgical operation, had been owned by Union Carbide. His inquiries brought him into contact with stories of silicosis and deaths related to the construction of Hawks Nest tunnel, including allegations that the Negro workers had brought illness and death upon themselves; that people had blown tragedy out of proportion.

Along with colleague Michael Bader, Cherniack examined records of the tunnel's construction donated by Union Carbide to West Virginia University. "Oddly, there was not a single document related to work on the tunnel, allegations of silicosis, or the hundreds of legal actions that were brought on behalf of former workers."

Cherniack applied epidemiological methods in a retrospective analysis of illness and deaths among tunnel workers. He reviewed public records, conducted personal interviews, and assessed tunnel illnesses and deaths by reconstructing data from state and county records, particularly Fayette County. He also examined physician reports and did comparative assessments of community mortality rates.

Cherniack's work stands today as the definitive inquiry into the texture and scope of the human tragedy at Hawks Nest tunnel – a full account of the tunnel's construction, its engineering near-perfect, but for the tragic neglect of workers' health and lives.

Circuit Court Justice

HAWKS NEST TUNNEL may have been a dream-come-true for the project's designer and chief engineer, O.M. Jones. But for the more than 2,400 men who worked underground, the tunnel became a darker dream.

By the end of 1932, attorneys representing tunnel workers had filed over 80 silicosis claims with the West Virginia Workmen's Compensation Commission. Simultaneously they filed silicosis lawsuits in the Fayette County Circuit Court against the tunnel's contractor, Rinehart and Dennis.

The widow of Cecil Jones, a tunnel employee who died of silicosis at age 23, filed the first case in the Fayette County Circuit Court. Attorneys for defendant Rinehart and Dennis asked for a demurral. Silicosis claims, they argued, should be managed under the state's workmen's compensation laws. On appeal the question went to the West Virginia Supreme Court. On February 14, 1933, the court ruled that the state's workmen's compensation laws did not include silicosis as a compensable form of workplace injury or death. Therefore silicosis claims would have to be settled in circuit courts. Within a few weeks 111 silicosis cases had been filed in Fayette County; by August 336.

On March 22, 1933, the first case came to trial. The plaintiff, Raymond Johnson, age 38 and suffering from silicosis, sued Rinehart & Dennis for $25,000. He had worked for a year as a driller in Shaft 1. The plaintiffs called as witnesses a long list of men who had worked in the tunnel. They testified that: often so much dust filled the tunnel's air a worker five to eight feet away could not be seen; men had been ordered back to the tunnel head immediately after dynamite shots; dinkeys operated without lights; air hoses blew dust from the drill holes; the two-feet-in-diameter hose bringing air to the tunnel face had frequent punctures by rock particles and the fans did not work. Thirteen local citizens testified that men left work covered with white dust. The minister who had given the invocation at the ground-breaking ceremony said that harm had come to men who worked there. A worker described how company engineers wore respirators when they entered the tunnel while workers had none.

Raymond Johnson testified that his weight had dropped from 175 to 143 pounds. He stripped off his shirt to show the court his skeletal upper body. Dr. Leroy Harless testified that Johnson suffered from second or early third-stage silicosis and had only a year to live. Outside medical experts confirmed his findings.

The defendants testified that workers had never complained of the dust; that the tunnel's ventilation exceeded the requirements of mining regulations. R. M. Lambie, former director of the West Virginia Department of Mines, by then a consultant to the mining industry, testified that he had written a memo to tunnel officials requiring that respirators be worn in the tunnel. But, he told the court, the requirement had been later verbally removed after conferences with the contractor; men could be seen from 500 to 700 feet away. Representatives of three large tunnel construction firms testified they had never heard of silicosis. Mine inspectors stated that drillers used wet drilling. Medical experts from outside the state testified that Johnson suffered from tuberculosis.

At no time in the trial did plaintiffs or defendants present any measurement of silica dust in the tunnel's air.

On April 20th, after twenty hours of deliberation, the jury reported itself standing seven to five in favor of Johnson, but hopelessly deadlocked. After forty-one days and 169 witnesses, Judge J. W. Eary dismissed of the jury. One of the five jury members voting for the defendant later received a contempt citation from Judge Eary because he had been chauffeured to and from the trial by employees of Rinehart and Dennis.

On June 5th the case of Cecil Jones came to trial. Attorneys for his widow hoped that unambiguous autopsy evidence showing that 50% silica in the ash of Jones' lungs (compared to 3 – 10% in healthy lungs) would convince the jury of his having died of silicosis. Judge Eary suspended the trial when attorneys announced an out-of-court agreement to settle the $4,000,000 claims in all pending cases. The plaintiffs received $130,000; half to them and half to attorneys. Later disclosure revealed an additional $20,000 payment to plaintiffs' attorneys in exchange for agreement not to pursue further lawsuits, and the surrender of all case records to the defense.

Judge Eary suggested the following schedule of payments for workers: $400 for an unmarried black man, $600 for a married black man; $800 for an unmarried white man, $1,000 for a married white man. Families of white men should receive an additional $600. Eventual payments took into account the severity of silicosis and ranged from $30 to $1,600.

Final Settlement

ATTORNEYS CONCERNED ABOUT JURY TAMPERING in the Johnson case solicited new silicosis claims. By the end of January, 1934 thirty cases had been filed; by June over fifty.

In June the case of Donald Shay, a foreman in Shaft 1, came to trial. Shay brought suit against Rinehart and Dennis for $50,000. The plaintiffs presented X-rays, reports and evidence paralleling that of the Johnson trial. They produced medical reports that confirmed silicosis among workers, including an affidavit from Dr. Leroy Harless that he had examined 300 former tunnel workers and 60% of them suffered from silicosis. As in the Johnson trial, the defendants presented expert testimony and engineering designs supporting well-ventilated shafts. The associate editor of *The Engineering News Record* testified to the tunnel's safe working conditions and warned of silicosis racketeering against responsible contractors. The trial ended with a hung jury, the vote 10 – 2 in favor of Shay. Later Judge Ben Moore, then a plaintiff's attorney, wrote that the two dissenters withdrew early from jury discussions, sat alone and refused to talk with other jury members.

In October, 1934 Judge Eary transferred all of his court's outstanding cases to the Kanawha County Circuit Court in Charleston. In November the state Supreme Court voted to transfer an additional 60 cases to Kanawha County and to bar 200 additional suits because they had either become subject to the prior settlement agreement or had exceeded the statute of limitations.

The 1935 session of the West Virginia legislature passed legislation amending the state's workman's compensation laws to include silicosis as a compensable illness. The changes had widespread support among industry, but not labor, leaders because of restrictive eligibility provisions. Under the new law no Hawks Nest tunnel workers would have qualified for worker's compensation payments.

In view of the obstacles facing former tunnel workers, plaintiffs' attorneys negotiated a final settlement of $70,000 for the remaining claims, over $5,000,000. Again, as a condition of settlement the attorneys agreed to turn over all legal papers to the defense, permanently removing from future investigations all evidence supporting the claims of tunnel workers.

The law firm waived all client legal fees.

The Press and Congress

IN 1935 THE LITERARY JOURNAL, *New Masses*, published a story that described a conversation with a hitchhiker, a man who had worked in the Hawks Nest tunnel and would soon die of silicosis. A thousand men would die, the hitchhiker said. [2]

New Masses then published a two-part series, "Two Thousand Dying on the Job" by Bernard Allen, the pen name of Philippa Allen.[3] [4] The articles described the high silica content of the tunnel's rock, the shanty camps for workers, silicosis among workers, and the Raymond Johnson trial. The publicity generated by those articles, as well as stories in *Time*[5] [6] and *Newsweek*[7], captured congressional attention.

On January 16, 1936, the Subcommittee on Labor of the U. S. House of Representatives met to consider House Joint Resolution 446, "To authorize the Secretary of Labor to appoint a board of inquiry to ascertain the facts relating to health conditions of workers employed in the construction and maintenance of public utilities." (Union Carbide had received West Virginia Public Service Commission approval of the Hawks Nest tunnel as a public works project to produce electric power for the region.)

The committee called author Philippa Allen as its first witness. Over two days of testimony she described the dust-filled working conditions in the tunnel, and the crowded and dirty living conditions of the work camp shanties.

On January 17, Mrs. Emma Jones appeared before the committee. Her testimony held the undivided attention of the committee and the press.

---

2   Maltz, A. 1936. Man on a road. *New Masses*, January 8, 19-21.

3   Allen, B. 1935a. Two thousand dying on a job. *New Masses*, January 15, 18-19.

4   _____. 1935b. Two thousand dying on a job: 2. How the tunnel workers lived. *New Masses*, January 22, 19-21.

5   *Time*. 1936a, untitled article, January 6.

6   *Time*, 1936b, untitled article, February 3.

7   *Newsweek*. 1936. Tunneling through an atmosphere of deadly dust. January 25.

Here are selected excerpts.[8]

> Mrs. Jones: I lost my three sons, and my husband is in very bad condition as the result of working at the Hawks Nest tunnel. One son was 23 years of age, the other son was 21 years of age, and the other son was 18 years of age. My husband is not able to work. He has not been able to work for quite some time. He has silicosis, according to the doctor. We have been having a very hard time making a living since this trouble came to us.
>
> Mr. Dunn of Pennsylvania: Your three sons died within 2 years?
>
> Mrs. Jones: They died within 13 months.
>
> Mr. Dunn of Pennsylvania: How old was the youngest son?
>
> Mrs. Jones: He was 18.
>
> Mr. Dunn of Pennsylvania: How old was the next son?
>
> Mrs. Jones: He was 21 years old.
>
> Mr. Dunn of Pennsylvania: And the next?
>
> Mrs. Jones: 23.
>
> Mr. Marcantonio: Did you talk to many of the men who came there to work in the tunnel, who worked in and out of the tunnel?
>
> Mrs. Jones: Yes, sir. The foreman told me that this was not dangerous work. I asked one of them about the boys' health and he said I was too fearful for them. The boys kept getting shorter and shorter breath, and I didn't know what else could be wrong with them. The foreman told me that he had worked in tunnels for 30 years and it hadn't hurt him… His brother too was a foreman and he is dead.

On February 5, 1936, the subcommittee submitted its report to the chairman of the House of Representatives' Committee on Labor. They concluded, "The committee, therefore, recommends that a resolution be presented to the House asking for sufficient funds and authority to require the attendance of witnesses and to do all things necessary to procure a full and complete investigation.

---

8   *Report of the U. S. House Representatives Subcommittee on Labor, Investigation Relating to Health Conditions of Workers Employed in the Construction and Maintenance of Public Utilities*, Feb 5, 1936.

256   *Dwight Harshbarger*

"Your committee can do no more. Congress should do no less than to see that these citizens from many States who have paid the price for the electricity to be developed from the tunnel are vindicated. If by their suffering and death they will have made life safer in future for the men who go beneath the earth to work, if they will have been able to establish a new and greater regard for human life in industry, their suffering may not have been in vain."

The House took no action on the committee's recommendation. Neither did it authorize any further inquiries into the construction of Hawks Nest tunnel.

POET MURIEL RUKEYSER attended the hearings. Emma Jones' testimony moved her to write a widely read narrative poem on Hawks Nest tunnel, *U.S. 1, The Book of the Dead.*[9]

DURING THE CONGRESSIONAL HEARINGS newsreels by Fox, Hearst Metro-Tone, Paramount, Pathé, and Universal Studios featuring Hawks Nest tunnel and Gauley Bridge, "the town of the walking dead," appeared in theatres across the country. Mrs. Emma Jones appeared on-camera. "I have lost three sons working in Hawks Nest Tunnel – died with the silicosis. And I have a husband that is not expected to live very long."

Charles Jones died of complications from silicosis.

---

9   Ibid, Muriel Rukeyser. 1938, New York: Covici Friede.

Footprints in the Dust

IN 1932 HOMER A. HOLT, a member of the Fayetteville law firm that served as counsel for Union Carbide contractor Rinehart and Dennis in the Hawks Nest lawsuits, successfully ran for the post of West Virginia Attorney General. During his term in office the federal government claimed jurisdiction over the New River as a non-navigable waterway. Attorney General Holt opposed the action in a case before the U. S. Supreme Court and won when the high court dismissed the case on a technicality. Had the federal government gained control of the New River, it could have regulated, possibly removed, the dam diverting the New River into Hawks Nest tunnel.

Touting his Supreme Court victory, Holt ran for governor and won. He took office in 1937. While serving as governor, the federal Works Progress Administration employed writers to prepare a history of each state. The West Virginia Superintendent of Education, an elected official, initially supervised the project. Governor Holt successfully fought to have its control transferred to his office.

When the writers submitted their completed history of West Virginia, the governor rejected it until portions describing the state's turbulent labor history, the coal mine wars, and Hawks Nest tunnel had been removed or heavily edited.

In 1944 Homer Holt became a member of the board of directors of Union Carbide and Carbon Corporation. In 1947 he became the corporation's general counsel.

Hubert Skidmore and Hawks Nest

IN 1941 DOUBLEDAY DORAN published the novel *Hawks Nest,* by West Virginia native Hubert Skidmore. [10] The novel described working conditions in the tunnel and the sad consequences for workers and their families. *Hawks Nest* received a review in *The New York Times.*

Within one year Doubleday Doran had removed all copies of *Hawks Nest* from circulation.

Skidmore returned from WW II suffering from combat fatigue. He lived alone on a farm near Dauberville, Pennsylvania, while undergoing treatment at the Martinsburg, West Virginia, Veterans' Administration Hospital. On February 6, 1946, after dinner with a friend he returned home and died in a late-night house fire. After an inconclusive investigation of the fire's origin, there remained among people who knew Skidmore a suspicion of foul-play.

In the early 1980s West Virginia publisher Jim Comstock contacted Doubleday and inquired about publication rights to *Hawks Nest.* He found that all the Skidmore – *Hawks Nest* files had been removed.

---

10   *Hawks Nest,* Hubert Skidmore. 1941, New York: Doubleday, Doran and Company, Inc. Reprinted by the University of Tennessee Press, 2004.

Union Carbide

IMMEDIATELY AFTER the December 3, 1984, Bhopal disaster, Indian police arrested Union Carbide CEO Warren Anderson. On December 7th they released him. Less than a week later he addressed the US Congress, emphasizing the company's commitment to safety.

Soon the GAF Corporation announced a bid to take over Union Carbide. The takeover bid ended when Union Carbide responded with plans for major divestitures. The company then sold businesses in films packaging, metals, battery products, specialty polymers and composites, home and automotive as well as agricultural products.

In 1985 the Indian Government passed the Bhopal Gas Leak Act, allowing the Government of India to act as legal representative for disaster victims. In March, 1986 Union Carbide proposed a settlement of $350 million, later raised to $470 million, 15% of the original $3 billion claimed by plaintiffs. By the end of October 2003, according to the Bhopal Gas Tragedy Relief and Rehabilitation Department, compensation had been awarded to 554,895 people for injuries received and 15,310 survivors of those killed. The average amount to families of the dead was $2,200.

Warren Anderson retired in 1986. In 1991 Bhopal authorities charged him with manslaughter; if convicted he faced a maximum of 10 years in prison. He avoided an international arrest warrant and a US court summons. On February 1, 1992, the Chief Judicial Magistrate of Bhopal declared Anderson a fugitive from justice. Greenpeace later found him to be living comfortably in the Hamptons.

On February 6, 2001, Union Carbide Corporation became a wholly owned subsidiary of The Dow Chemical Company.

About the Author

Dwight Harshbarger, a native of Milton, West Virginia, served a seven-year tenure as the Executive Director of the Cambridge Center for Behavioral Studies (Massachusetts). Previously he headed human resources in two corporations—as a senior vice president for Reebok International, Ltd., and vice president of Sealy, Inc.

He earned both an AB and an MA in psychology at West Virginia University. He continued his education at the University of California-Berkley and went on to complete a Ph.D. in psychology at the University of North Dakota. He then did post-graduate study at Harvard University before returning to his home state to join the faculty of West Virginia University. He is currently Adjunct Professor of Community Medicine, West Virginia University Health Sciences Center, and Senior Fellow, Cambridge Center for Behavioral Studies.

Harshbarger published his first work of fiction, *In the Heart of the Hills: A Novel in Stories*, in 2005. After his retirement from the Cambridge Center in 2008, he settled in Morgantown, West Virginia, to make a transition from a psychologist who is also a writer, to a writer who is also a psychologist.